Adèle Dubois
A Story of the Miramichi Valley

Adèle Dubois

A Story of the Miramichi Valley

by

Mrs. William T. Savage

Introduced and edited by

Tony Tremblay

CHAPEL STREET EDITIONS

Appreciation of Place

Chapel Street Editions exists within the unceded and unsurrendered territories of the Wolastoqiyik, Mi'kmaq, and Peskotomuhkati people. The work we do is born from the stories carried by this land and its inhabitants. The animals, plants, soil, water, and air make this place home for the Indigenous people who belong to this land, for the descendants of those who took this land and made it a belonging, and for those who have since come from away. Chapel Street Editions holds a deep appreciation for our place within this land and the stories it tells. We honour the land's Indigenous caretakers and are grateful for their wisdom and guidance.

Text adapted from the 1868 edition found in the Early Canadiana Collection.
https://www.canadiana.ca/view/oocihm.48310/79

Published by
Chapel Street Editions
150 Chapel Street
Woodstock, NB E7M 1H4
chapelstreeteditions@gmail.com
www.chapelstreeteditions.com

ISBN 978-1-988299-60-0

Library and Archives Canada Cataloguing in Publication

Title: Adèle Dubois : a story of the Miramichi Valley / by Mrs. William T. Savage ; introduced and edited by Tony Tremblay.
Other titles: Miramichi
Names: Savage, Mary Langdon Bradbury, 1817-1872, author. | Tremblay, M. Anthony (Michael Anthony), editor, writer of introduction
Description: First published in 1865 under the title Miramichi. | The main text is a reprint of the 1868 edition, originally published under the title Adèle Dubois: a story of the lovely Miramichi Valley in New Brunswick. | Includes bibliographical references.
Identifiers: Canadiana 20250268965 | ISBN 9781988299600 (softcover)
Subjects: LCGFT: Novels.
Classification: LCC PS2779.S58 M5 2025 | DDC 813/.3—dc23

Book design by Brendan Helmuth

Contents

ADÈLE DUBOIS:

A Story

OF THE

LOVELY MIRAMICHI VALLEY,

IN

NEW BRUNSWICK.

————◆————

LORING, Publisher,

319 WASHINGTON STREET,
BOSTON.

Figure 1. Original Title Page of 1868 Edition

Introduction
to the Reprint of
Adèle Dubois: A Story
of the Miramichi Valley

Published in Boston under the single-word title *Miramichi* in 1865, the novel at hand was re-issued by the same publisher under different titles for the next three years, eventually ceasing publication as *Adèle Dubois: A Story of the Lovely Miramichi Valley, in New Brunswick.*[1] (See Figure 1, 1868 title page.) Though all editions were published anonymously, the author was known to be Mrs. William T. Savage, the married name of Mary Langdon Bradbury.[2] Despite its rapid re-issues and the fact that the novel appeared in Loring's widely circulated Railway Library series, *Adèle Dubois* received little critical or popular attention in its day, going out of print soon after release and falling into the maw of silence for over a century. Mary Savage suffered the same fate. Her legacy became that of a writer who would be remembered, if at all, as "contribut[ing] more or less of poetry to the public press."[3] Archival sleuthing and the digitization revolution have brought her novel back to our attention.

The first question the novel raises, then, is an obvious one: why reprint a work that seems to have been judged as much by the indifference of early readers as by its fall into the abyss of time? There are a couple of answers to the question. The academic answer is that in the continuing absence of comprehensive social and political histories of New Brunswick, a rediscovered novel like *Adèle Dubois* is key to our understanding of the beliefs, tensions, and biases that contributed to our provincial formation—and continue to inform our sense of who we are. That we address such things is vital to reversing the still-pervasive belief that much in our past was second-rate, thus not warranting a closer look. *Adèle Dubois* counters that easy stereotype, revealing rich and surprising details about a New Brunswick on the eve of Confederation, about the mix of religions and ethnicities of early settlers, about the porous Maine/New Brunswick border, and about how the province is viewed from inside and outside its territory.

The other answer to the question of the wisdom of a reprint is that the novel is such fun to read. It opens as a mystery; it is rife with local colour, dialect, character nuance, and gothic flashes typical of the time; it is full to the brim with crime, adventure, romance, sport, judgment, and redemption; and it is unusually advanced in what we would today term its modernist techniques. Its heroine possesses a kind of self-assurance that reminds us that female agency wasn't an invention of the 1970s, and its author is so playful that she occasionally breaks the spell of her fiction to upend her timeline and address us as readers. "Look at him a moment," she directs us at one point, "occupied with the memories of the past," that invitation not only collapsing the distance between author and reader, but also reminding us of our complicity in her artifice.[4]

The novel is thus a looking glass in which we see ourselves and watch others looking at us. It doesn't contest history and identity as much as lay them bare. Required reading, then, in our ongoing effort to understand our provincial selves as a mix of origins, grievances, stories, and other inheritances.

What follows is a full-text reprint of the 1868 edition of *Adèle Dubois* as well as a detailed critical apparatus that provides context for what the novel sought to address in its time and how we might read it purposefully today.

Endnotes to Introduction

1   I will be referring to the novel in this introduction as *Adèle Dubois*. Aside from slight differences in early page arrangement and presentation, *Miramichi* and *Adèle Dubois*, as well as all other re-issues of the novel, derive from the first press.

2   Deciding on how to address a married woman of the nineteenth century requires careful thought. I have chosen to refer to the author as Mary Savage rather than Mrs. William T. Savage, the name she wrote under. If I am referring to Mary Savage before marriage, I use her birth name, Mary Bradbury.

3   Lapham, *Bradbury Memorial*, 114.

4   *Adèle Dubois*, 170.

Notes on the Text and Title

For ease of reading, spellings have been normalized slightly, for example "mean time" to meantime, "any one" to anyone, etc. The phonetically rendered idioms and phrasings of the different classes and ethnicities that populate the fictional Miramichi have been left intact.

Punctuation has also been altered slightly for contemporary readers. Mostly, however, it has been left as author and printer intended, resulting in what we would now consider overuse of the comma.

Typesetting errors and inconsistencies that were in the original copy text are corrected, with the corrected word or phrase indicated in square brackets. For instance, "a Being infinitely higher that earthly friends" is corrected as "a Being infinitely higher [than] earthly friends."

Finally, the title has been shortened slightly from its early iterations to the cleaner but still-descriptive *Adèle Dubois: A Story of the Miramichi Valley.*

CHAPTER I

THE DUBOIS HOUSE

"Well, verily, I didn't expect to find anything like this, in such a wild region," said Mr. Norton, as he settled himself comfortably in a curiously carved, old-fashioned arm-chair, before the fire that blazed cheerily on the broad hearth of the Dubois [house]. "'Tis not a Yankee family either," added he, mentally. "Everything agreeable and tidy, but it looks unlike home. It is an Elim in the desert! Goodly palm trees and abundant water! O! why," he exclaimed aloud, in an impatient tone, as if chiding himself, "should I ever distrust the goodness of the Lord?"

The firelight, playing over his honest face, revealed eyes moistened with the gratitude welling up in his heart. He sat a few minutes gazing at the glowing logs, and then his eyelids closed in the blessed calm of sleep. Weary traveller! He has well-earned repose.

There will not be time, during his brief nap, to tell who and what he was, and why he had come to sojourn far away from home and friends. But let the curtain be drawn back for a moment, to reveal a glimpse of that strange, questionable country over which he has been wandering for the last few months, doing hard service.

Miramichi (pron. *Mir'imisheé*), a name unfamiliar, perhaps, to those who may chance to read these pages, is the designation of a fertile, though partially cultivated portion of the important province of New Brunswick, belonging to the British Crown. The name, by no means uneuphonious, is yet suggestive of associations far from attractive. The Miramichi River, which gives title to this region, has its rise near the centre of the province, and flowing eastward empties into the Gulf of St. Lawrence, with Chatham, a town of considerable importance, located at its mouth.

The land had originally been settled by English, Scotch, and Irish, whose business consisted mostly of fishing and lumbering. These occupations, pursued in a wayward and lawless manner, had not exerted on them an elevating or refining influence, and the character of the people had degenerated from year to year. From the remoteness and obscurity of the country, it had become a convenient hiding-place for the outlaw and the criminal, and its surface was sprinkled over with the refuse and offscouring of the New England States and the [province]. With a few rare exceptions, it was a realm of almost heathenish darkness and vice. Such Mr. Norton found it, when, with heart full of compassion and benevolence, thirty-five years ago, he came to bear the message of heavenly love and forgiveness to these dwellers in death shade.

The Dubois [house], where Mr. Norton had found shelter for the night, was situated on the northern bank of the river, about sixty miles west from Chatham. It was a respectable looking, two story building, with large barns adjacent. Standing on a graceful bend of the broad stream, it commanded river views, several miles in extent, in two directions, with a nearer prospect around, consisting of reaches of tall forest, interspersed with occasional openings, made by the rude settlers.

Being the only dwelling in the neighborhood sufficiently commodious for the purpose, its occupants, making a virtue of necessity, were in the habit of entertaining occasional travellers who happened to visit the region.

But, softly—Mr. Norton has wakened. He was just beginning to dream of home and its dear delights, when a door-latch was lifted, and a young girl entering, began to make preparations for supper. She moved quickly towards the fire, and with a pair of iron tongs, deftly raided the ponderous cover of the Dutch oven, hanging over the blaze. The wheaten rolls it contained were nearly baked, and emitted a fragrant and appetizing odor.

She refitted the cover, and then opening a closet, took from it a lacquered Chinese tea-caddy and a silver urn, and proceeded to arrange the tea-table.

Mr. Norton, observing her attentively with his keen, gray eyes, asked, "How long has your father lived in this place, my child?"

The maiden paused in her employment, and glancing at the broad, stalwart form and shrewd yet honest face of the questioner, replied, "Nearly twenty years, sir."

Mr. Norton's quick ear immediately detected in her words a delicate, foreign accent, quite unfamiliar to him. After a moment's silence he spoke again.

"Dubois—that is your name, is it not? A French name?"

"Yes, sir, my parents are natives of France."

"Ah! indeed!" responded Mr. Norton, and the family in which he found himself was immediately invested with new interest in his eyes.

"Where is your father at the present time, my dear child?"

"He is away at Fredericton. He has gone to obtain family supplies. I hope he is not obliged to be out this stormy night, but I fear he is."

She made the sign of the cross on her breast and glanced upward.

Mr. Norton observed the movement, and at the same time saw what had before escaped his notice, a string of glittering, black beads upon her neck, with a black cross, half hidden by the folds in the waist of her dress. It was an instant revelation to [him] of the faith in which she had been trained. He fell into a fit of musing.

In the meantime, Adèle Dubois completed her preparations for the tea-table—not one of her accustomed duties, but one which she sometimes took a fancy to perform.

She was sixteen years old—tall already, and rapidly growing taller, with a figure neither large, nor slender. Her complexion was pure white, scarcely tinged with rose; her eyes were large and brown, now shooting out a bright, joyous light, then veiled in dreamy shadows. A rich mass of dark hair was divided into braids, gracefully looped up around her head. Her dress was composed of a plain red material of wool. Her only ornaments were the rosary and cross on her neck.

A mulatto girl now appeared from the adjoining kitchen and placed upon the table a dish of cold, sliced chicken, boiled eggs and pickles, together with the steaming wheaten rolls from the Dutch oven.

Adèle having put some tea in the urn, poured boiling water upon it and left the room.

Returning in a few minutes, accompanied by her mother and Mrs. McNab, they soon drew up around the tea-table.

When seated, Mrs. Dubois and Adèle made the sign of the cross and closed their eyes. Mrs. McNab, glancing at them deprecatingly for a moment, at length fixed her gaze on Mr. Norton. He also closed his eyes and asked a mute blessing upon the food.

Mrs. Dubois was endowed with delicate features, a soft, Madonna-like expression of countenance, elegance of movement and a quiet, yet gracious manner. Attentive to those around the board, she said but little. Occasionally, she listened in abstracted mood to the beating storm without.

Mrs. McNab, a middle-aged Scotch woman, with a short, square, ample form, filled up a large portion of the side of the table she occupied. Her coarse-featured, heavy face, surrounded by a broad, muslin cap frill that nearly covered her harsh yellow hair, was lighted up by a pair of small gray eyes, expressing a mixture of cunning and curiosity. Her rubicund visage, gaudy-colored chintz dress, and yellow bandanna handkerchief, produced a sort of glaring sun-flower effect, not mitigated by the contrast afforded by the other members of the group.

"Madam," said Mr. Norton to Mrs. Dubois, on seeing her glance anxiously at the windows, as the wild, equinoctial gale caused them to clatter violently, "do you fear that your husband is exposed to any particular danger at this time?"

"No special danger. But it is a lawless country. The night is dark and the storm is loud. I wish he were safely at home," replied the lady.

"Your solicitude is not strange. But you may trust him with the Lord. Under His protection, not a hair of his head can be touched."

Before Mrs. Dubois had time to reply, Mrs. McNab, looking rather fiercely at Mr. Norton, said, "Yer dinna suppose, sir, if the Lord had decreed from all eternity that Mr. Doobyce should be drowned, or rabbed, or murdered to-night, that our prayin' an' trustin' wad cause Him to revoorse His foreordained purpose? Adely," she continued, "I dinna mind if I take anither egg an' a trifle more o' chicken an' some pickle."

By no means taken aback by this pointed inquiry, Mr. Norton replied very gently, "I believe, ma'am, in the power of prayer to move the Almighty throne, when it comes from a sincere and humble heart, and that He will bestow His blessing in return."

"Weel," said Mrs. McNab, "I was brought up in the church o' Scotland, and dinna believe anything anent this new-light doctrine o' God's bein' turned roun' an' givin' up his decrees an' a'that. I think it's the ward o' Satan," and she passed her cup to be again refilled with tea.

Adèle, who had noticed that Mrs. McNab's observations had suggested new solicitudes to her mother's mind, remarked, "What you said just now, Aunt Patty, is not very consoling. Whoever thought that my father would meet with anything worse than perhaps being drenched by the storm, and half eaten up with vermin in the dirty inns where he will have to lodge? I do not doubt he will be home in good time."

"Yes, Miss Adely, yes. I ken it," said Aunt Patty, as she saw a firm, defiant expression gathering in the young girl's countenance. "I'd a dream anent him last night that makes me think he's comin."

"Hark!" said Adèle, starting and speaking in a clear, ringing tone, "he has come. I hear his voice on the lawn."

Murmuring a word or two of excuse, she rose instantly from the table, requested Bess, the servant, to hand her a lantern, and arrayed herself quickly in hood and cloak.

As she opened the door, her father was standing on the step in the driving rain, supporting in his arms the form of a gentleman, who seemed to be almost in a state of insensibility.

"Make way! make way, Adèle. Here's a sick man. Throw some blankets on the floor, and come, all hands, and rub him. My dear, order something warm for him to drink."

Mrs. Dubois caught a pile of bedding from a neighboring closet and arranged it upon the floor, near the fire. Mr. Dubois laid the stranger down upon it. Mr. Norton immediately rose from the tea-table, drew off the boots of the fainting man, and began to chafe his feet with his warm, broad hand.

"Put a dash of cold water on his face, child," said he to Adèle, "and he'll come to, in a minute." Adèle obeyed.

The stranger opened his eyes suddenly and looked around in astonishment upon the group.

"Ah! yes. I see," he said, "I have been faint, or something of the kind. I believe I am not quite well."

He attempted to rise, but sank back, powerless. He turned his head slowly towards Mr. Dubois, and said, "Friend Dubois, I think I am going to be ill, and must trust myself to your compassion," when immediately his eyes closed and his countenance assumed the paleness of death.

"Don't be down-hearted, Mr. Brown," said Mr. Dubois. "You are not used to this Miramichi staging. You'll be better by and by. My dear, give me the cordial—he needs stimulating."

He took a cup of French brandy, mixed with sugar and boiling water, from the hand of Mrs. Dubois, and administered it slowly to the exhausted man. It seemed to have a quieting effect, and after a while Mr. Brown sank into a disturbed slumber.

Observing this, and finding that his limbs, which had been cold and benumbed, were now thoroughly warmed, Mr. Dubois rose from his kneeling position and turning to his daughter, said, "Now then, Adèle, take the lantern and go with me to the stables. I must see for myself that the horses are properly cared for. They are both tired and famished."

Adèle caught up the lantern, but Mr. Norton interposed. "Allow me, sir, to assist you," he said, rising quickly. "It will expose the young lady to go out in the storm. Let me go, sir."

He approached Adèle to take the lantern from her hand, but she drew back and held it fast.

"I don't mind weather, sir," she said, with a little sniff of contempt at the thought. "And my father usually prefers my attendance. I thank you. Will you please stay with the sick gentleman?"

Mr. Norton bowed, smiled, and reseated himself near the invalid.

In the meantime, Mr. Dubois and his daughter went through the rain to the stables; his wife replenished the tea-urn and began to rearrange the table.

Mrs. McNab, during the scene that had thus unexpectedly occurred, had been waddling from one part of the room to the other, exclaiming, "The Lord be gude to us!" Her presence, however, seemed for the time to be ignored.

When she heard the gentle movements made by Mrs. Dubois among the dishes, her dream seemed suddenly to fade out of view. Seating herself again at the table, she diligently pursued the task of finishing her supper, yet ever and anon examining the prostrate form upon the floor.

"Peradventure he's a mon fra' the States. His claithes look pretty nice. As a gen'al thing them people fra' the States hae plenty o' plack in their pockets. What do you think, sir?"

"He is undoubtedly a gentleman from New England," said Mr. Norton.

CHAPTER II

Mrs. M'Nab

Mrs. McNab was a native of Dumfries, Scotland, and had made her advent in the Miramichi country about five years previous to the occurrences just mentioned.

Having buried her husband, mother, and two children—hoping that change of scene might lighten the weight upon her spirits—she had concluded to emigrate with some intimate acquaintances to the Province of New Brunswick.

On first reaching the settlement, she had spent several weeks at the Dubois [house], where she set immediately at work to prove her accomplishments by assisting in making up dresses for Mrs. Dubois and Adèle.

She entertained them with accounts of her former life in Scotland—talking largely about her acquaintance with the family of Lord Lindsay, in which she had served in the capacity of nurse. She described the castle in which they resided, the furniture, the servants, and the grand company; and, more than all, she knew or pretended to know the traditions, legends, and ghost stories connected, for many generations past, with the Lindsay race.

She talked untiringly of these matters to the neighbors, exciting their interest and wonder by the new phases of life presented, and furnishing food for the superstitious tendencies always rife in new and ignorant settlements. In short, by these means, she won her way gradually in the community, until she came to be the general factotum.

It was noticed, indeed, that in the annual round of her visits from house to house, Mrs. McNab had a peculiar faculty of securing to herself the various material comforts available, having an excellent appetite and a genius for appropriating the warmest seat at the fireplace and any other little luxury a-going. These things were, however, overlooked, especially by the women of the region, on account of her social qualities, she being an invaluable companion during the long days and evenings when their husbands and sons were away, engaged in lumbering or fishing. When the family with which she happened to be sojourning were engaged in domestic occupations, Mrs. McNab, established in some [cosy] corner, told her old wife stories and whiled away the long and dismal wintry hours.

Of all the people among whom she moved, Adèle Dubois least exercised the grace of patience toward her.

On the return of Mr. Dubois and his daughter to the house, after having seen the horses safely stowed away, he refreshed himself at the tea-table and left the room to attend to necessary business. Mrs. Dubois and Mrs. McNab went to fit up an apartment for the stranger.

In the meantime Mr. Norton and [Adèle] were left with the invalid.

Mr. Brown's face had lost its pallid hue and was now overspread with the fiery glow of fever. He grew more and more restless in his sleep, until at length he opened his eyes wide and began to talk deliriously. At the first sound of his voice, Adèle started from her seat, expecting to hear some request from his lips.

Gazing at her wildly for a moment, he exclaimed, "What, *you* here, Agnes! you, travelling in this horrible wilderness! Where's your husband? Where's John, the brave boy? Don't bring them here to taunt me. Go away! Don't look at me!"

With an expression of terror on his countenance, he sank back upon the pillow and closed his eyes. Mr. Norton knelt down by the couch and made slow, soothing motions with his hand upon the hot and fevered head until the sick man sank again into slumber. Seeing this, Adèle, who had been standing in mute bewilderment, came softly near and whispered, "He has been doing something wrong, has he not, sir?"

"I hope not," said the good man, "He is not himself now, and is not aware what he is saying. His fever causes his mind to wander."

"Yes, sir. But I think he is unhappy beside[s] being sick. That sigh was *so* sorrowful!"

"It was sad enough," said Mr. Norton. After a pause, he continued, "I will stay by his bed and take care of him to-night."

"Ah! will you, sir?" said Adèle. "That is kind, but Aunt Patty, I know, will insist on taking charge of him. She thinks it her right to take care of all the sick people. But I don't wish her to stay with this gentleman to-night. If he talks again as he did just now, she will tell it all over the neighborhood."

At that moment the door opened, and Mrs. McNab came waddling in, followed by Mr. and Mrs. Dubois.

"Now, Mr. Doobyce," said she, "if you and this pusson will just carry the patient upstairs, and place him on the bed, that's a' ye need do. I'll tak' care o' him."

"Permit me the privilege of watching by the gentleman's bed to-night," said Mr. Norton, turning to Mr. Dubois.

"By no means, sir," said his host; "you have had a long ride through the forest today and must be tired. Aunt Patty here prefers to take charge of him."

"Sir," said Mr. Norton, "I observed a while ago that his mind was quite wandering. He is greatly excited by fever, but I succeeded in quieting him once and perhaps may be able to do so again."

Here Mrs. McNab interposed in tones somewhat loud and irate.

"That's the way pussons fra' your country always talk. They think they can do everything better'n anybody else. What can a mon do at nussin', I wad ken?"

"Mr. Norton will nurse him well, I know. Let him take care of the gentleman, father," said Adèle.

"Hush, my dear," said Mr. Dubois, decidedly, "it is proper that Mrs. McNab take charge of Mr. Brown to-night."

Adèle made no reply, and only showed her vexation by casting a defiant look on the redoubtable [Aunt] Patty, whose face was overspread with a grin of satisfaction at having carried her point.

Mr. Norton, of course, did not press his proposal farther, but consoled himself with the thought that some future opportunity might occur, enabling him to fulfil his benevolent intentions.

A quieting powder was administered and Mrs. McNab established herself beside the fire that had been kindled in Mr. Brown's apartment.

After having indicated to Mr. Norton the bedroom he was to occupy for the night, the family retired, leaving him the only inmate of the room.

As he sat and watched the dying embers, he fell into a reverie concerning the events of the evening. His musings were of a somewhat perplexed nature. He was at a loss to account for the appearance of a gentleman, bearing unmistakable marks of refinement and wealth, as did Mr. Brown, under such circumstances, and in such a region as Miramichi. The words he had uttered in his delirium added to the mystery. He was also puzzled about the family of Dubois. How came people of such culture and superiority in this dark portion of the earth? How strange that they had lived here so many years without assimilating to the common herd around them.

Thus his mind, excited by what had recently occurred, wandered on, until at length his thoughts fell into their accustomed channel — dwelling on his own mission to this benighted land, and framing various schemes by which he might accomplish the object so dear to his heart.

In the meantime, having turned his face partially aside from the fire, he was watching unconsciously the fitful gleaming of a light cast on the opposite wall by the occasional flaring up of a tongue of flame from the dying embers.

Suddenly he heard a deep, whirring sound as if the springs of some complicated machinery had just then been set in motion.

Looking around to find whence the noise proceeded, he was rather startled on observing in the wall, in one corner, just under the ceiling, a tiny door fly open, and emerging thence a grotesque, miniature man, holding, uplifted in his hand, a hammer of size proportionate to his own figure. Mr. Norton sat motionless while this small specimen proceeded, with a jerky gait and many bobbing grimaces, across a wire stretched to the opposite corner of the room, where stood a tall, ebony clock. When within a short distance of the clock another tiny door in its side flew open; the little man entered and struck deliberately with the hammer the hour of midnight. Near the top of the dial-plate was seen from without the regular uplifting of the little arm, applying its stroke to the bell within. Having performed his duty, this personage jerked out of the clock, the tiny door closing behind him, bobbed and jerked along the wire as before, and disappeared at the door in the wall, which also immediately closed after his exit.

Having witnessed the whole manœuvre with comic wonder and curiosity, Mr. Norton burst into a loud and hearty peal of laughter that was still resounding in the room when he became suddenly aware of the presence of Mrs. McNab. There she stood in the centre of the apartment, her firm, square figure apparently rooted to the floor, her head enveloped in innumerable folds of white cotton, a tower of strength and defiance.

Her unexpected appearance changed in a moment the mood of the good man, and he inquired anxiously, "Is the gentleman more ill? Can I assist you?"

"He's just this minnut closed his eyes to sleep, and naw I expect he's wide awake again, with the dreadfu' racket you were just a makin' O! my! wadna you hae made a good nuss?"

Mr. Norton truly grieved at his inadvertency in disturbing the household at this late hour of the night, begged pardon, and told Mrs. McNab he would not be guilty of a like offence.

"How has the gentleman been during the evening?" he asked.

"O! he's been ravin' crazy a'maist, and obstacled everything I've done for him. He's a very sick pusson naw. I cam' down to get a bottle of muddeson," and Mrs. McNab went to a closet and took from it the identical bottle of brandy from which Mrs. Dubois had poured when preparing the stimulating dose for the invalid. Mr. Norton observed this performance with a twinkle of the eye, but making no comment, the worthy woman retired from the room.

That night Mr. Norton slept indifferently, being disturbed by exciting and bewildering dreams. In his slumbers he saw an immense cathedral, lighted only by what seemed some great conflagration without, which, glaring in, with horrid, crimson hue upon the pictured walls, gave the place the strange, lurid aspect of Pandemonium. The effect was heightened by the appearance of thousands of small, grotesque beings, all bearing more or less resemblance to the little man of the clock, who were flying and bobbing, jerking and grinning through the air, beneath the great vault, as if madly revelling in the scene. Yet the good man all the while had a vague sense of some awful, impending calamity, which increased as he wandered around in great perplexity, exploring the countenances of the various groups scattered over the place.

Once he stumbled over a dead body and found it the corpse of the invalid in the room above. He seemed to himself to be lifting it carefully when a lady, fair and stately, in rich, sweeping garments, took the burden from his arms, and, sinking with it on the floor, kissed it tenderly and then bent over it with a look of intense sorrow.

Farther on he saw Mr. and Mrs. Dubois, with Adèle, kneeling imploringly, with terror-stricken faces, before a representation of the Virgin Mary and her divine boy. Then the glare of light in the building increased. Rushing to the entrance to look for the cause of it, he there met Mrs. McNab coming towards him with a wild, disordered countenance — her white cotton headgear floating out like a banner to the breeze — shaking a brandy bottle in the faces of all she met. He gained the door and found himself enwrapped in a sheet of flame.

Suddenly the whole scene passed. He woke. A glorious September sun was irradiating the walls of his bedroom. He heard the movements of the family below, and rose hastily.

A few moments of thought and prayer sufficed to clear his healthy brain of the fantastic forms and scenes which had invaded it, and he was himself again, ready and panting for service.

CHAPTER III

Mr. Norton

In order to bring Mr. Norton more distinctly before the reader, it is necessary to give a few particulars of his previous life.

He was the son of a New England farmer. His father had given him a good moral and religious training and the usual common school education, but, being poor and having a large family to provide for, he had turned him adrift upon the sea of life to shape his own course and win his own fortunes. These, in some respects, he was well calculated to do.

He possessed a frame hardened by labor, and, to a native shrewdness and self-reliance, added traits which threw light and warmth into his character. His sympathies were easily roused by suffering and want. He spurned everything mean and ungenerous—was genial in disposition, indeed brimming with mirthfulness, and, in every situation, attracted to himself numerous friends. He was, moreover, an excellent blacksmith.

After leaving his father's roof, for a half score of years, he was led into scenes of temptation and danger. But, having passed through various fortunes, the whispers of the internal monitor, and the voice of a loving wife, drew him into better and safer paths. He betook himself unremittingly to the duties of his occupation.

By the influence of early parental training, and the teachings of the Heavenly Spirit, he was led into a religious life. He dedicated himself unreservedly to Christ. This introduced him into a new sphere of effort, one in which his naturally expansive nature found free scope. He became an active, devoted, joyous follower of the Great Master, and, thenceforward, desired nothing so much as to labor in his service.

About a year after this important change, a circumstance occurred which altered the course of his outward life.

It happened that a stranger came to pass a night at his house. During the conversation of a long winter evening, his curiosity became greatly excited, in an account, given by his guest, of the Miramichi region. He was astonished at the moral darkness reigning there. The place was distant, and, at that time, almost inaccessible to any, save the strong and hardy. But the light of life ought to be thrown into that darkness. Who should go as a torch-bearer? The inquiry had scarcely risen in his breast before he thought he heard the words spoken almost audibly, *Thou must go.*

Here, a peculiarity of the good blacksmith must be explained. Possessed of great practical wisdom and sagacity, he was yet easily affected by preternatural influences. He was subject to very strong "impressions of mind," as he called them, by which he was urged to pursue one course of conduct instead of another; to follow out one plan of business in preference to another, even when there seemed to be no apparent reason why the one course was better than its alternative. He had sometimes obeyed these impressions, sometimes had not. But he thought he had found, in the end, that he should have invariably followed them.

A particular instance confirmed him in this belief. One day, being in New York, he was extremely anxious to complete his business in order to take passage home in a sloop, announced to leave port at a certain hour in the afternoon. Resolving to be on board the vessel at the time appointed, he hurried from place to place, from street to street, in the accomplishment of his plan. But he was strangely hindered in his arrangements and haunted by an impression of trouble connected with the vessel. Having, however, left his wife ill at home, and being still determined to go, he pressed on. It happened that he arrived at the wharf just as the sloop had got beyond the possibility of reaching her, and he turned away bitterly disappointed. The night that followed was one of darkness and horror; the sloop caught fire and all on board perished.

He had now received an impression that it was his duty to go, as an ambassador of Christ, to Miramichi.

Having for some time previous "exercised his gift" with acceptance at various social religious meetings, he applied to the authorities of his religious denomination for license to preach.

After passing a creditable examination on points deemed essential in the case, he obtained a commission and a cordial God speed from his brethren. They augured well for his success.

To be sure, the deficiencies of his early education sometimes made themselves manifest, notwithstanding the diligent efforts he had put forth, of late years, to remedy the lack. But on the other hand, he had knowledge of human nature, sagacity in adapting means to ends, a wide tolerance of those unfortunate ones, involved by whatever ways in guilt, deep and earnest piety, and a remarkable natural eloquence, both winning and forcible.

So he had started on his long journey through the wilderness, and here, at last, he is found, on the banks of the Miramichi, cheerful and active, engaged in his great work.

The reader was informed, at the close of the last chapter, that after the perplexing visions of the night, by the use of charms of which he well knew the power, Mr. Norton had cleared his brain of the unpleasant phantoms that had invaded it during his slumbers. Being quick and forgetive in his mental operations, even while completing his toilet, he had formed a plan for an attack upon the kingdom of darkness lying around him.

As he entered the room, the scene of his last night's adventure, his face beaming with cheerfulness and courage, Adèle, who was just then laying the table, thought his appearance there like another sunrise.

After the morning salutations were over, he looked around the apartment, observing it, in its daylight aspect, with a somewhat puzzled air. In some respects, it was entirely unlike what he had seen before. The broad stone hearth, with its large blazing fire, the Dutch oven, the air of neatness and thrift, were like those of a New England kitchen, but here the resemblance ceased.

A paper-hanging, whose originally rich hues had become in a measure dimmed, covered the walls; and curious old pictures hung around; the chairs and tables were of heavy dark wood, elaborately and grotesquely carved, as was also the ebony clock in the corner, whose wonderful mechanism had so astonished him on the previous evening. A low lounge, covered with a crimson material, occupied a remote corner of the room, with a Turkish mat spread on the floor before it. At the head of the couch was a case, curiously carved, filled with books, and beneath, in a little niche in the wall, a yellow ivory crucifix.

It did not occur to the good man to make any comparison between this room, with its peculiar adornings, and the Puritan kitchen with its stiff, stark furniture. One of the latter description was found in his own home, and the place where his loved ones lived and moved, was to him invested with a beauty altogether independent of outward form and show. But, as he looked around with an air of satisfaction, this room evidently pleased his eye, and he paid an involuntary tribute to its historic suggestiveness by falling into a reverie concerning the life and times of the good Roman Catholic [Fénelon], whose memoir and writings he had read.

Soon Adèle called him to the breakfast-table.

Mrs. McNab not having made her appearance, he inquired if any tidings had been heard from the sick-room. Mrs. Dubois replied that she had listened at the door and hearing no sound, concluded Mr. Brown was quiet under the influence of the sleeping powder, and consequently, she did not run the risk of disturbing him by going in.

"Should Aunt Patty happen to begin snoring in her chair, as she often does," said Adèle, "Mr. Brown would be obliged to wake up. I defy anyone to sleep when she gets into one of those fits."

"Adèle," said her father, while a smile played round his mouth and twinkled in his usually grave eyes, "can't you let Mrs. McNab have any peace?"

"Is Mr. Brown a friend of yours?" inquired Mr. Norton of his host.

"I met him for the first time at Fredericton. He was at the hotel when I arrived there. We accidentally fell into conversation one evening. He made, then and subsequently, many inquiries about this region, and when I was ready to start for home, said that, with my permission, he would travel with me. I fancy," Mr. Dubois added, "he was somewhat ill when we left, but he did not speak of it. We had a rough journey and I think the exposure to which he was subjected has increased his sickness. If he proves to be no better today, I shall send Micah for Dr. Wright," said he, turning to his wife. "I hope you will, father," said Adèle, speaking very decidedly. "I should be sorry to have him consigned over wholly to the tender mercies of Mrs. McNab."

"Mr. Dubois," said the missionary, laying down his knife and fork, suddenly, "I must confess, I am perfectly surprised to find such a family as yours in this place. From previous report, and indeed from my own observation in reaching here, I had received the idea that the inhabitants were not only a wicked, but a very rude and uncouth set of people."

"Whatever may be your opinion of ourselves, sir," replied his host, "you are not far amiss in regard to the character of the people. They are, in general, a rough set."

"Well, sir," said Mr. Norton, "as an honest man, I must inform you, that I came here with a purpose in view. I have a message to this people — a message of love and mercy; and I trust it will not be displeasing to you if I promulgate it in this neighborhood."

"I do not understand your meaning," said Mr. Dubois.

"I wish, sir, to teach these people some of the truths of morality and religion such as are found in the Bible. I have ventured to guess that you and your family are of the Roman Catholic faith."

"We belong to the communion of that church, sir."

"That being the case, and thinking you may have some interest in this matter, I would say, that I wish to make an attempt to teach the knowledge of divine things to this people, hoping thereby to raise them from their present state to something better and holier."

"A worthy object, sir, but altogether a hopeless one. You have no idea of the condition of the settlers here. You cannot get a hearing. They scoff at such things utterly," said Mr. Dubois.

"Is there any objection in your own mind against an endeavor to enlist their interest?" asked Mr. Norton.

"Not the least," said Mr. Dubois.

"Then I will try to collect the people together and tell them my views and wishes. Is there any man here having influence with this class, who would be willing to aid me in this movement?"

Mr. Dubois meditated.

"I do not know of one, sir," he said. "They all drink, swear, gamble, and profane holy things, and seem to have no respect for either

God or man."

"It is too true," remarked Mrs. Dubois.

"Now, father," said Adèle, assuming an air of wisdom that sat rather comically on her youthful brow, "*I* think Micah Mummychog would be just the person to help this gentleman."

"Micah Mummychog!" exclaimed Mr. Norton, throwing himself back in his chair and shaking out of his lungs a huge, involuntary haw, haw, "where does the person you speak of hail from to own such a name as *that*, my dear child?"

"I rather think he came from Yankee land — from your part of the country, sir," said Adèle, mischievously.

"Ah, well," said Mr. Norton, with another peal of laughter, "we *do* have some curious names in our parts."

"Micah Mummychog!" exclaimed Mr. Dubois, "what are you thinking of, Adèle? Why, the fellow drinks and swears as hard as the rest of them."

"Not quite," persisted the child, "and besides, he has some good about him, I know."

"What have you seen good about him, pray?" said her father.

"Why, you remember that when I discovered the little girl floating down the river, Micah took his boat and went out to bring her ashore. He took the body, dripping, in his arms, carried it to his house, and laid it down as tenderly as if it had been his own sister. He asked me to please go and get Mrs. McNab to come and prepare it for burial. The little thing, he said, was entirely dead and gone. 3I started to go, as he wished, but happened to think I would just step back and look at the sweet face once more. When I opened the door, Micah was bending over it, with his eyes full of tears. When I asked, what is the matter, Micah? he said he was thinking of a little sister of his that was drowned just so in the Kennebec River, many years ago."

"That showed some feeling, certainly," said Mrs. Dubois.

"Then, too, I know," continued Adèle, "that the people here like him. If anyone can get them together, Micah can."

"Well!" said Mr. Dubois looking at his child with a fond pride, yet as if doubting whether she were not already half spoiled, "it seems you are the wiseacre of the family. I know Micah has always been a favorite of yours. Perhaps the gentleman will give your views some consideration."

"Father," replied Adèle, "I have only said what I think about it."

"I'll try what I can do with Micah Mummychog," said Mr. Norton decidedly, and the conversation ended.

CHAPTER IV

MICAH MUMMYCHOG

About ten years before the period when this narrative begins, Micah Mummychog had come to this country from the Kennebec River, in the State of Maine.

He soon purchased a dozen acres of land, partially cleared them, and built a large-sized, comfortable log house. It was situated not far from the Dubois house, at a short distance from the bank of the river, and on the edge of a grove of forest trees.

Micah inhabited his house usually only a few months during the year, as he was a cordial lover of the unbroken wilderness, and was as migratory in his habits as the native Indian. On the morning after the events related in the last chapter, he happened to be at home. While Adèle was guiding the missionary to his cottage, he was sitting in his kitchen, which also served for a general reception room, burnishing up an old Dutch fowling-piece.

The apartment was furnished with cooking utensils, and coarse wooden furniture; the walls hung around with fishing tackle, moose-horns, skins of wild animals and a variety of firearms.

Micah was no common, stupid, bumpkin-looking person. Belonging to the genus Yankee, he had yet a few peculiar traits of his own. He had a smallish, bullet-shaped head, set, with dignified poise, on a pair of wide, flat shoulders. His chest was broad and swelling, his limbs straight, muscular, and strong. His eyes were large, round, and blue. When his mind was in a state of repose and his countenance at rest, they had a solemn, owl-like expression. But when in an excited, observant mood, they were keen and searching; and human orbs surely never expressed more rollicking fun than did his, in his hours of recreation. He had a habit of darting them around a wide circle of objects, without turning his head a hairsbreadth.

This, together with another peculiarity of turning his head, occasionally, at a sharp angle, with the quick and sudden motion of a cat, probably was acquired in his hunting life.

Micah had never taken to himself a helpmate, and as far as mere housekeeping was concerned, one would judge, on looking around the decent, tidy apartment in which he sat and of which he had the sole care, that he did not particularly need one. He washed, scoured, baked, brewed, swept and dusted as deftly as any woman, and did it all as a matter of course. These were, however, only his minor accomplishments. He commanded the highest wages in the lumber camp, was the best fisherman to be found in the region, and had the good luck of always bringing down any game he had set his heart upon.

Micah had faults, but let these pass for the present. There was one achievement of his, worthy of all praise.

It was remarked that the loggery was situated on the edge of a grove. This grove, when Micah came, was "a piece of woods," of the densest and most tangled sort. By his strong arm, it had been transformed into a scene of exceeding beauty. He had cut away the undergrowth and smaller trees, leaving the taller sons of the forest still rising loftily and waving their banners toward heaven. It formed a magnificent natural temple, and as the sun struck in through the long, broad aisles, soft and rich were the lights and shadows that flickered over the green floor. The lofty arches, formed by the meeting and interlaced branches above, were often resonant with music. During the spring and summer months, matin worship was constantly performed by a multitudinous choir, and praises were chanted by tiny-throated warblers, raising their notes upon the deep, organ base, rolled into the harmony by the grand old pines.

It is true, that hardly a human soul worshipped here, but when the "Te Deum" rose toward heaven, thousands of blue, pink, and white blossoms turned their eyes upward wet with dewy moisture, the hoary mosses waved their tresses, the larches shook their tassels gayly, the birches quivered and thrilled with joy in every leaf, and the rivulets gurgled forth a silvery sound of gladness. On this particular September morning Micah's [Grove] was radiant with beauty. The wild equinoctial storm, which had so fiercely assailed it the day before, had brightened it into fresh verdure and now it glittered in the sunbeams as if bejewelled with emerald.

Mr. Norton and Adèle reached the cottage door, on which she tapped softly.

"Come in," Micah almost shouted, without moving from his seat or looking up from his occupation.

The maiden opened the door, and said, "Good morning, Micah."

At the sound of her voice he rose instantly and handing a chair into the middle of the floor, said, "O! come in, Miss Ady; I didn't know ez it was yeou."

"I cannot stop now, Micah, but here is a gentleman who has a little business with you. I came to show him the way. This is Mr. Norton."

And away Adèle sped, without [further] ceremony.

Micah looked after her for a moment, with a half-smile on his weather-beaten face, then turned and motioning Mr. Norton to a chair, reseated himself on a wooden chest, with his gun, upon which he again commenced operations, his countenance setting into its usual owl-like solemnity.

He was not courtly in his reception of strangers. The missionary, however, had dealt with several varieties of the human animal before, and was by no means disturbed at this nonchalance.

"I believe you are from the States, as well as myself, Mr. Mummychog," said he, after a short silence.

"I'm from the Kennebec River," said Micah, laconically.

"I am quite extensively acquainted in that region, but do not remember to have heard your name before. It is rather an uncommon one."

"I guess ye won't find many folks in them parts, ez is called Mummychog," said Micah, with a twinkle of the eye and something like a grin on his sombre visage.

"You've a snug place here, Mr. Micah," said Mr. Norton, who, having found some difficulty in restraining a smile when repeating Mr. Mummychog's surname, concluded to drop it altogether, "but what could have induced you to leave the pleasant Kennebec and come to this distant spot?"

"Well, I cam' to git a chance and be somewhere, where I could jest be let alone."

"A chance for what, Mr. Micah?"

"Why, hang it, a chance to live an' dew abeout what I want tew. The moose an' wolves an' wildcats hev all ben hunted eout o' that kentry. Thar wa'nt no kind ev a chance there. So I cam' here."

"You have a wife, I suppose, Mr. Micah?"

"Wife! no. Do ye spose I want to hev a woman kep' skeered a most to death abeout me, all the time? I'm a fishin' an' huntin [a] good part o' the year. Wild beasts and sech, is what I like."

"Don't you feel lonely here, sometimes, Mr. Micah?"

"Lunsum! no. There's plenty o' fellers reound here, all the time. They're a heowlin' set tew, ez ever I see."

"You have a good gun there," suggested the missionary.

"Well, tolable," said Micah, looking up for the first time since Mr. Norton had entered the house, and scanning him from head to foot with his keen, penetrating glance. "I spose you aint much used to firearms?"

"I have some acquaintance with them; but my present vocation don't require their use."

Here Mr. Mummychog rose, and laying his gun on the table, scratched his head, turned toward Mr. Norton and said, "Hev yeou any pertikilar business with me?"

"Yes sir, I have. I came to Miramichi to accomplish an important object, and I don't know of another person who can help me about it so well as you can."

"Well, I dunno. What upon arth is it?"

"To be plain upon the point," said the missionary, looking serious and earnest, "I have come here to preach the gospel of Christ."

"Whew! religin, is it? I can tell ye right off, [it's] no go en these ere parts."

"Don't you think a little religion is needed here, Mr. Micah?"

"Well, I dunno. Taint *wanted*. Folks ez lives here, can't abide sermans and prayers en that doleful stuff."

"You say you came here for a chance, Mr. Micah. I suppose your friends came for the same purpose. Now, I have come to show them, not a *chance*, but a glorious certainty for happiness in this world and in the eternity beyond."

"Well, they don't want tew know anything abeout it. They just want tew be let alone," said Micah.

"I suppose they do wish to be let alone," said Mr. Norton. "But I cannot permit them to go down to wretchedness and sorrow unwarned. You have influence with your friends here, Mr. Micah. If you will collect the men, women, and children of this neighborhood together, some afternoon, in your beautiful grove, I will promise to give them not a long sermon, but something that will do them good to hear."

"I can't dew it no heow. There's ben preachers along here afore, an' a few 'ud go eout o' curiosity, an' some to make a disturbance an' sech, an' it never 'meounts to anything, no heow. Then sposin we haint dun jest as we'd oughter, who'se gin *yeou* the right tew twit us on it?"

"I certainly have no right, on my own responsibility, to reproach you, or your friends for sin, for I am a sinful man myself and have daily need of repentance. But I trust I have found out a way of redemption from guilt, and I wish to communicate it to my fellow-beings that they also may have knowledge of it, and fly to Christ, their only safety and happiness in this world."

Micah made no reply.

There was a pause of several minutes, and then the missionary rose and said, "Well, Mr. Micah, if you can't help me, you can't. The little maiden that came with me told me you could render me aid, if any one could, and from what she said, I entertained a hope of your assistance. The Lord will remove the obstacles to proclaiming this salvation in some way, I know."

"Miss Ady didn't say I could help ye neow, did she?" said Micah, scratching his head.

"Certainly. Why did she bring me here?"

"Well, ef that aint tarnal queer," said Micah, falling into a deep reverie.

In a few moments, Mr. Norton shook his new acquaintance heartily by the hand and bade him good morning. Was the good man discouraged in his efforts? By no means.

He had placed in the mind of Micah Mummychog a small fusee, so to speak, which he foresaw would fire a whole train of discarded ideas and cast-off thoughts, and he expected to hear from it.

He filled up the day with a round of calls upon the various families of the neighborhood, and came home to his lodgings at Mr. Dubois's with his heart overwhelmed by the ignorance and debasement he had witnessed.

Yet his courage and hopes were strong.

CHAPTER V

MRS. LANSDOWNE

P -- is a city by the sea. Built upon an elevated peninsula, surrounded by a country of manifold resources of beauty and fertility, with a fine, broad harbor, it sits queenlike in conscious power, facing with serene aspect the ever-restless waves that wash continually its feet. The place might be called ancient, if that term could properly be applied to any of the works of man on New England shores. There are parts of it where the architecture of whole streets looks quaint and time-worn; here and there a few antique churches appear, but modern structures predominate, and the place is full of vigorous life and industry.

It was sunset. The sky was suffused with the richest carmine. The waters lay quivering beneath the palpitating, rosy light. The spires and domes of the town caught the ethereal hues and the emerald hills were bathed in the glowing atmosphere.

In a large apartment, in the second story of a tall, brick mansion on -- Street, sat Mrs. Lansdowne. Susceptible though she was to the attractions of the scene before her, they did not now occupy her attention. Her brow was contracted with painful thought, her lip quivered with deep emotion. The greatest sorrow she had known had fallen upon her through the error of one whom she fondly loved.

Though enwrapped in a cloud of grief, one could see that she possessed beauty of a rich and rare type. She had the delicate, aquiline nose, the dark, lustrous eyes and hair, the finely arched eyebrows of the Hebrew woman. But she was no Jewess.

Mrs. Lansdowne could number in her ancestry men who had been notable leaders in the Revolutionary war with England, and, later in our history, others, who were remarkable for patriotism, nobility of character, intellectual ability, and high moral and religious culture.

Early in life, she had been united to Mr. Lansdowne, a gentleman moving in the same rank of society with herself. His health obliged him to give up the professional life he anticipated, and he had become a prosperous and enterprising merchant in his native city. They had an only child, a son eighteen years old, who in the progress of his collegiate course had just entered the senior year.

Edward Somers was Mrs. Lansdowne's only brother, her mother having died a week after his birth. She was eleven years of age at the time, and from that early period had watched over and loved him tenderly. He had grown up handsome and accomplished, fascinating in manners and most affectionate toward herself. She had learned that he had been engaged in what appeared, upon the face of it, a dishonorable affair, and her sensitive nature had been greatly shocked.

Two years before, Mr. Lansdowne had taken him as a junior partner in his business. He had since been a member of his sister's family.

A young foreigner had come to reside in the city, professing himself a member of a noble Italian family. Giuseppe Rossini was poet, orator, and musician. As poet and orator he was pleasing and graceful; as a musician he excelled. He was a brilliant and not obtrusive conversationalist. His enthusiastic expressions of admiration for our free institutions won him favor with all classes. In the fashionable circle he soon became a pet.

Mrs. Lansdowne had from the first distrusted him. There was no tangible foundation for her suspicions, but she had not been able to overcome a certain instinct that warned her from his presence. She watched, with misgivings of heart, her brother's growing familiarity with the Italian. A facility of temper, his characteristic from boyhood, made her fear that he might not be able to withstand the soft, insinuating voice that veils guilty designs by winning sophistries and appeals to sympathy and friendship. And so it proved.

One day, in extreme agitation, Rossini came to Mr. Somers, requesting the loan of a considerable sum of money to meet demands made upon him. Remittances daily expected from Europe had failed to reach him. Mr. Somers was unable to command so large a sum as he required. His senior partner was absent from home. But the wily Rossini so won upon his sympathies, that he went to the private safe of his brother-in-law, and took from thence the money necessary to free his friend from embarrassment. He never saw the Italian again.

When the treachery of which he had been the victim burst upon him, together with his own weakness and guilt, he was filled with shame and remorse. Mr. Lansdowne was a man of stern integrity and uncompromising justice. He dared not meet his eye on his return, and he dreaded to communicate the unworthy transaction to his sister, who had so gently yet so faithfully warned him.

He made desperate efforts to get traces of the villain who had deceived him. Unsuccessful—maddened with sorrow and shame—he wrote a brief note of farewell to Mrs. Lansdowne, in which he confessed the wrong he had committed against her husband, which Mr. Lansdowne would reveal to her. He begged her to think as kindly of him as possible, averring that an hour before the deed was done, he could not have believed himself capable of it. Then he forsook the city.

When these occurrences were communicated to Mr. Lansdowne, he was filled with surprise and indignation—not at the pecuniary loss, which, with his ample wealth, was of little moment to him, but on account of such imprudence and folly, where he least expected it.

A few hours, however, greatly modified his view of the case. He had found, in the safe, a note from Mr. Somers, stating the circumstances under which he had taken the money and also the disappearance of Rossini. This, together with his wife's distress, softened his feelings to such a degree that he consented to recall his brother and reinstate him in his former place in business.

But whither had the fugitive gone? Mrs. Lansdowne found no clue to his intended destination.

During the morning of the day on which she is first introduced to the attention of the reader, she had visited his apartment to make a more thorough exploration. Looking around the room she saw lying in the fireplace a bit of paper, half buried in the ashes. She drew it out, and after examining carefully found written upon it a few words that kindled a new hope in her heart. Taking it to her husband, a consultation was held upon its contents and an expedition planned, of which an account will be given in the next chapter.

She was now the prey of conflicting emotions. The expedition, which had that day been arranged, involved a sacrifice of feeling on her part, greater she feared than she would be able to make.

But in order to recover her brother to home, honor, and happiness, it seemed necessary to be made. Voices from the dead were pleading at her heart incessantly, urging her, at whatever cost, to seek and save him, who, with herself, constituted the only remnant of their family left on earth. Her own affection for him also pressed its eloquent suit, and at last the decision was confirmed. She resolved to venture her son in the quest.

In the meantime, the sunset hues had faded from the sky and evening had approached. The golden full moon had risen and was now shining in at the broad window, bringing into beautiful relief the delicate tracery on the high cornices, the rich carvings of the mahogany furniture, and striking out a soft sheen from Mrs. Lansdowne's black satin dress, as she moved slowly to and fro, through the light.

She seated herself once more at the window and gazed upon the lovely orb of night. A portion of its serenity entered and tranquillized her soul. The cloud of care and anxiety passed from her brow, leaving it smooth and pure as that of an angel.

CHAPTER VI

"John, Dear"

On the evening that Mrs. Lansdowne was thus occupied, John, her son, who had been out on the bay all the afternoon, rushed past the drawing-room door, bounded up the long staircase, entered his room, situated on the same floor, not far from his mother's, and rang the bell violently.

In a few minutes, Aunt Esther, an ancient black woman, who had long been in the service of the family, made her appearance at the door, and inquired what "Massa John" wanted.

"I want some fire here, Aunt Esther. I've been out on the bay, fishing. Our smack got run down, and I've had a ducking; I feel decidedly chilly."

"Law sakes!" said she, in great trepidation, "yer orter get warm right away," and hastened down stairs.

A stout, hale man soon entered the room, with a basket of wood and a pan of coals, followed immediately by Aunt Esther, who began to arrange them on the hearth.

Aunt Esther's complexion was of a pure shining black, her features of the size and cut usually accompanying that hue, and lighted up by a contented, sunshiny expression, which truly indicated the normal state of her mind. A brilliant, yellow turban sat well upon her woolly locks and a blue and red chintz dress, striped perpendicularly, somewhat elongated the effect of her stout dumpy figure. She had taken care of John during his babyhood and early boyhood, and he remained to this day her especial pet and pride.

"Aunt Esther," said that young man, throwing himself into an easy-chair, and assuming as lackadaisical an expression as his frank and roguish face would allow, "I have just lost a friend."

"Yer have?" said his old nurse, looking round compassionately.

"When did yer lose him?"

"About an hour ago."

"What did he die of, Massa John?"

"Of a painful nervous disease," said he.

"How old was he?"

"A few years younger than I am."

"Did he die hard?"

"Very hard, Aunt Esther," said John, looking solemn.

"Had yer known him long?"

"Yes, a long time."

Aunt Esther gave a deep sigh. "Does yer know weder he was pious?"

"Well, here he is. Perhaps you can tell by looking at him," said he, handing her a tooth, he had just had extracted, and bursting into a boyish laugh.

"O! yer go along, Massa John. I might hev knowed it was one of yer deceitful tricks," said Aunt Esther, trying to conceal her amusement, by putting on an injured look. "There, the fire burns now. Yer jest put on them dry clothes as quick as ever yer can, or mebbe ye'll lose another friend before long."

"It shall be done as you say, beloved Aunt Esther," said he, rising and bowing profoundly, as she left the room.

Having obeyed the worthy woman's injunction, he drew the easy-chair to the fire, leaned his head back and spent the next half hour hovering between consciousness and dreamland.

From this state, he was roused by a gentle tap on his door, followed by his mother's voice, saying, "John, dear?"

John rose instantly, threw the door wide open and ushered in the lady, saying, "Come in, little queen mother, come in," and bowing over her hand with a pompous, yet courtly grace.

Mrs. Lansdowne, when seen a short time since walking in her solitude, seemed quite lofty in stature, but now, standing for a moment beside the regal height of her son, one could fully justify him in bestowing upon her the title with which he had greeted her.

John Lansdowne was fast developing, physically as well as mentally into a noble manhood, and it was no wonder that his mother's heart swelled with pride and joy when she looked upon him. Straight, muscular, and vigorous in form, his features and expression were precisely her own, enlarged and intensified. Open and generous in disposition, his character had a certain quality of firmness, quite in contrast with that of his uncle Edward, and this she had carefully sought to strengthen. In the pursuit of his studies, he had thus far been earnest and successful.

During the last half year, however, he had chafed under the confinements of student life, and having now become quite restive in the harness, he had asked his father for a few months of freedom from books. He wished to explore a wilderness, to go on a foreign voyage, to wander away, away, anywhere beyond the sight of college walls.

"John," said Mrs. Lansdowne, "I have been conversing with your father on the subject, and he has consented to an expedition for you."

"O! glorious! mother where am I to go? to the Barcan desert, or to the Arctic Ocean?"

"You are to make a journey to the Miramichi River?"

"Miramichi!" said John, after a brief pause, "I thought I had a slight acquaintance with geography, but where in the wide world is Miramichi?"

"It is in the province of New Brunswick. You will have seventy-five miles of almost unbroken wilderness to pass through."

"Seventy-five miles of wilderness! magnificent! where's my rifle, mother? I haven't seen it for an age."

"Don't be so impetuous, John. This journey through the wilderness will be anything but magnificent. You will meet many dangers by the way and will encounter many hardships."

"But, mother, what care I for the perils of the way. Look at that powerful member," stretching out his large, muscular arm.

"Don't trust too much in that, John. Your strong arm is a good weapon, but you may meet something yet that is more than a match for it."

"Possibly," said John, with a sceptical air, "but when am I to start, mother?"

"Tomorrow."

"Tomorrow! that is fine. Well! I must bestir myself," said he, rising.

"Not to-night, my dear. You've nothing to do at present. Arrangements are made. Be quiet, John. We may not sit thus together again for a long while."

"True, mother," said he, reseating himself. "But how did you happen to think of Miramichi?" he asked, after a pause.

"That is what I must explain to you. Your uncle Edward has committed an act of imprudence which he fancies your father will not forgive him. He has left us without giving any information of his destination. We hope you will find him in New Brunswick, and this is your errand. You must seek him and bring him back to us."

John had been absent at the time of Mr. Somers's departure, and, without making definite inquiries, supposed him to be away on ordinary business.

After his first surprise at his mother's announcement, he was quite silent for a few moments.

Then he said, firmly, "If he is there, I will find him."

Mrs. Lansdowne did not explain to him the nature of her brother's offence, but simply communicated her earnest desire for his return. Then going together to the library they consulted the map of Maine and New Brunswick. Mr. Lansdowne joined them — the route was fully discussed, and John retired to dream of the delights of a life untrammelled by college, or city walls.

CHAPTER VII

A Journey Through the Wilderness

Two days after the arrival of Mr. Norton at the Dubois [house], on the banks of the Miramichi, John Lansdowne, on a brilliant September morning, started on his memorable journey to that region.

He was up betimes, and made his appearance at the stables just as James, the stout little coachman, was completing Cæsar's elaborate toilet.

Cæsar was a noble-looking, black animal, whose strength and capacity for endurance had been well tested. This morning he was in high spirits and looked good for months of rough-and-tumble service.

"Here's yer rifle, Mister John. I put it in trim for ye yesterday. I s'pose ye'll be a squintin' reound sharp for bears and wolves and other livin' wild beasts when ye git inter the woods."

"Certainly, James. I expect to set the savage old monsters scattering in every direction."

"Well, but lookeout, Mister John and keep number one eout o' fire and water and sech."

"Trust me for doing that, James."

After many affectionate counsels and adieus from his parents, John, mounted on the gallant Cæsar, with his rifle and portmanteau, posted on at a rapid rate, soon leaving the city far behind.

The position of one who sits confidently upon the back of a brave and spirited horse is surely enviable. The mastery of a creature of such strength and capacity—whose neck is clothed with thunder—the glory of whose nostrils is terrible, gives to the rider a sense of freedom and power not often felt amidst the common conditions of life. No wonder that the Bedouin of the desert, crafty, cringing, abject in cities, when he mounts his Arab steed and is off to the burning sands, becomes dignified and courteous. Liberty and power are his. They elevate him for the time in the scale of existence.

John was a superb rider. From his first trial, he had sat on horseback, firm and kingly.

He and Cæsar apparently indulged in common emotions on this morning of their departure from home. They did not it is true "smell the battle afar off, the thunder of the captains and the shouting," but they smelt the wilderness, the wild, the fresh, the free, and they said ha! ha! And so they sped on their long journey.

The young man made a partial acquaintance with lumbering operations at Bangor; had his sublime ideas of the nobility of the aborigines of the country somewhat discomposed by the experience of a day spent in the Indian settlement at Oldtown; found a decent shelter at Mattawamkeag Point; and, at last, with an exultant bound of heart, struck into the forest.

The only road through this solitary domain was the rough path made by lumbermen in hauling supplies to the various camps, scattered at intervals through the dense wilderness, extending seventy-five miles, from Mattawamkeag Point to the British boundary.

Here Nature was found in magnificent wildness and disarray, her hair quite unkempt. Great pines, shooting up immense distances in the sky skirted the path and flung their green-gray, trailing mosses abroad on the breeze; crowds of fir, spruce, hemlock, and cedar trees stood waving aloft their rich, dark banners; clusters of tall, white birches, scattered here and there, relieved and brightened the sombre evergreen depths, and the maple with its affluent foliage crowned each swell of the densely covered land. Here and there, a scarlet tree or bush shot out its sanguine hue, betokening the maturity of the season and the near approach of autumn's latest splendor. Big boulders of granite, overlaid with lichens, were profusely ornamented with crimson creepers. Everything appeared in splendid and wasteful confusion. There were huge trees with branches partially torn away; others, with split trunks leaning in slow death against their fellows; others, prostrate on the ground; and around and among all grew brakes and ferns and parasitic vines; and nodded purple, red, and golden berries.

The brown squirrels ran up and down the trees and over the tangled rubbish, chirping merrily; a few late lingering birds sang little jerky notes of music, and the woodpecker made loud tapping sounds which echoed like the strokes of the woodman's axe. The air was rich and balmy—spiced with cedar, pine, and hemlock, and a thousand unknown odors.

The path through this wild of forest was rude and difficult, but the travellers held on their way unflinchingly—the horse with unfaltering courage and patience, and his rider with unceasing wonder and delight.

At noon they came to a halt, just where the sun looked down golden and cheery on a little dancing rivulet that babbled by the wayside. Here Cæsar received his oats, for which his master had made room in his portmanteau, at the expense, somewhat, of his own convenience. The young man partook of a hearty lunch and resigned himself to dreams of life under the greenwood tree.

After an hour's rest, again in the saddle and on—on, through recurring scenes of wildness, waste, and beauty. Just as the stars began to glint forth and the traveller and horse felt willing perhaps to confess to a little weariness, they saw the light of the expected cabin fire in the distance. Cæsar gave a low whinny of approval and hastened on.

Two or three red-shirted, long-bearded men gave them a rude welcome. They blanketed and fed Cæsar, and picketed him under a low shed built of logs.

John, as hungry as a famished bear, drank a deep draught of a black concoction called tea, which his friends here presented to him, ate a powerful piece of dark bread, interlarded with fried pork, drew up with the others around the fire, and, in reply to their curious questionings, gave them the latest news from the outside world.

For this information he was rewarded by the strange and stirring adventures of wilderness life they related during the quickly flitting evening hours.

They told of the scores who went into the forest in the early part of winter, not to return until late in the spring; of snow-storms and packs of wolves; of herds of deer and moose; they related thrilling stories of men crushed by falling trees, or jammed between logs in the streams, together with incidents of the long winter evenings, usually spent by them in storytelling and card playing. Thus he became acquainted with the routine of camp life.

Wearied at last with the unaccustomed fatigues of the day, he wrapped himself in his cloak, placed his portmanteau under his head for a pillow and floated off to dreamland, under the impression that this gypsying sort of life was just the one of all others he should most like to live.

The following morning, the path of our traveller struck through a broad reach of the melancholy, weird desolation, called a burnt district. He rode out, suddenly, from the dewy greenness and balm-breathing atmosphere of the unblighted forest, into sunshine that poured down in torrents from the sky, falling on charred, shining shafts and stumps of trees, and a brilliant carpet of fireweed.

It is nearly impossible to give one who has not seen something of the kind an adequate impression of the peculiar appearance of such a region. The strange, grotesque-looking stems, of every imaginable shape, left standing like a company of black dwarfs and giants scattered over the land, some of them surmounted with ebony crowns; some, with heads covered like olden warriors, with jetty helmets; some with brawny, long arms stretched over the pathway as if to seize the passer by, and all with feet planted, seemingly in deep and flaming fire. How quickly nature goes about repairing her desolations! So great in this case is her haste to cover up the black, unseemly surface of the earth, that, from the strange resemblance of the weed with which she clothes it to the fiery elements, it would seem as if she had not yet been able to thrust the raging glow out of her fancy, and so its type has crept again over the blighted spot.

John rode on over the glowing ground, the black monsters grimacing and scowling at him as he passed. What a nice eerie place this would be thought he for witches, wizards, and all Satan's gentry, of every shape and hue, to hold their high revels in. And he actually began to shout the witches song —

"Black spirits and white, Red spirits and gray."

At which adjuration, Cæsar, doubtless knowing who were called upon, pricked up his ears and started on a full run, probably not wishing to find himself in such company just at that time.

An establishment similar to the one that had sheltered him the night previous proffered its entertainment at the close of our adventurer's second day. The third day in the wilderness was signalized by an incident, which excited such triumphant emotions as to cause it to be long remembered. About an hour subsequent to his noon halt, as he and Cæsar were proceeding along at a moderate pace, he heard a rustling, crackling noise on the right side of the path and suddenly a deer, frightened and panting, flew across the road, turned for a moment an almost human, despairing look toward him, plunged into the tangled undergrowth on the left and was gone from sight. John drew his reins instantly, bringing his horse to a dead stand, loosened his rifle from his shoulder and after examining it closely, remained quiet. His patience was not taxed by long waiting. Within the space of two minutes there was another sharp crunching and crackling of dry boughs, when a wolf, large, gray, and fierce, sprang into the path from the same opening, following on the trail of the deer. He had nearly crossed the narrow road in hot pursuit and was about springing into the thicket beyond, when an accidental turn of his head brought our hero suddenly to his attention. He stopped, as if struck by a spell of enchantment.

Whiz! the ball flew. The very instant it struck, the bloodthirsty monster fell dead. When John reached the spot, there was scarcely the quiver of a limb, so well had the work of death been accomplished. Yet the wolfish face grinned still a savage, horrible defiance.

"Here, Cæsar," he exclaimed, in a boastful tone, "do you know that this old fellow lying here, won't get the drink out of the veins of that dainty creature he was so thirsty for? No! nor ever cheat any sweet little Red Riding Hood into thinking him her grandmother? This is the last of him. Didn't I do the neat thing, Cæsar?"

Cæsar threw his head on one side, with an air of admiration and gave a low whinny that betokened a state of intense satisfaction at the whole transaction.

It may appear frivolous to those who have read with unwavering credulity the olden tales of the prowess and achievements of knights errant in the days of chivalry, that one should stop to relate such a commonplace incident as the shooting of a wolf, and above all, that the hero of this narrative should betray, even to his horse, such a decided emotion of self-admiration for having performed the feat. Such a trifle would not indeed be worth mentioning in company with the marvellous deeds and mysterious sorceries of the old romaunt, but this being a true story, the hero young, and this the first game of the kind he has yet brought down, it must be excused.

After a critical examination of his victim, our traveller mounted his horse and proceeded on his journey, much gratified at his afternoon's work, and inwardly resolving how he would make the eyes of James and Aunt Esther stand out, while listening to the account of it he should give them, on his return home.

In about seventeen days after his departure from P --, John safely accomplished his journey. Amidst the subsequent hardships, rough fare and toils of that journey, which, in truth, thirty-five years ago, were things not to be laughed at, he had a constant satisfaction in the recollection of having, with one keen shot, killed a large, fierce, gray wolf.

CHAPTER VIII

A FUNERAL

The day following the call made by Mr. Norton on Micah Mummychog, the last-named personage came to Mr. Dubois's house and Adèle happening to open the outside door, just as he hove in sight, he called out, "Miss Ady, do ye know where that individooal that ye brought to my heouse yisterday, is?"

"You mean the missionary?" said Adèle.

"Well, yis, I spose so; where is he?"

"He is engaged with a sick gentleman we have here. He has taken the place of Aunt Patty, who is tired out and has gone to rest."

"Well, that piece of flesh, what's called McNab, has the greatest fakkilty of gittin' tired eout when there's any work reound that ever I see. Any heow, she's got to stir herself this time. But I want to see the minister, neow."

"Yes, I will speak to him. But I shall not call Aunt Patty. She *is* tired now. I can take care of the sick gentleman. But what has happened, Micah?"

"Well, there's goin' to be a funeral. I can't jestly tell ye abeout it neow. Ye can ax yer sir, when he comes in," said Micah, reluctant to go into particulars which he knew would shock Adèle.

"Well, Captin," said Micah, when Mr. Norton made his appearance at the door, "here's a reg'lar wind-fall for ye. Here's an Irishman over here, as is dead as a door nail. He's goin' to be buried to-night, 'beout sunset, and I dunno but what I can git a chance for ye to hold forth a spell in the grove, jest afore they put him under greound."

"Dead! the poor man dead! indeed!" exclaimed Mr. Norton.

"Yis. He was shot right through his heart, and I hope a swingin' cuss 'ill come on him that put the ball threough, tew."

"Why, how was it, Mr. Micah?" said Mr. Norton earnestly.

"Well, yeou jest tell me fust wether yeou'll say prayers, or somethin' or 'nother over the poor chap's reeliks."

"Certainly, I will, Mr. Micah."

"Well, ye see, Pat McGrath lived back here, half a mile or so, an' he's got lots o' cousins an' friends 'ut live all along on this 'ere river, more or less, till ye git to Chartham, *that's* sitooated to the mouth. Well, these fellers has been in the habit o' gittin' together and goin' deown river and hirin' once in a spell, some sort of old, cranky craft and goin' skylarking reound to Eastport and Portland. Arter a while they'd cum back and smuggle in a cargo o' somethin' or 'nother from the States, and sheirk the dooties. Well, 'beout a week ago, there was a confounded old critter 'ut lives halfway from here to Chartham that informed on 'em. So they jes' collected together—'beout twenty fellers—and mobbed him. And the old cuss fired into 'em and killed this 'ere man. So neow they've brought his body hum, and his wife's a poor shiftless thing, and she's been a hollerin' and screechin' ever sence she heerd of it."

"Poor woman!" said Mr. Norton, greatly shocked.

"Well, I might as well tell yer the whole on 't," said Micah, scratching his head. "Yer see, he was one o' these Catholics, this Pat was, and the fellers went to the priest (he lives deown river, little better'n ten mile from here) in course to git him to dew what's to be done to the funeral, and the tarnal old heathen wouldn't dew it. He sed Pat had gone agin the law o' the kentry, and he wouldn't hev anything to do 'beout it. So the fellers brought the body along, and I swear, Pat McGrath shall hev a decent funeral, anyway."

"Where is the funeral to be?" asked Mr. Norton, after listening attentively to the account Micah had given him.

"O! deown here 'n the grove. The body's to my heouse, and Maggie his wife's there a screechin'. The graveyard's close here, and so they didn't carry him hum."

"I'll go down and see this poor Maggie," said Mr. Norton.

"Don't, for the Lord's sake. I'm eenermost crazy neow. The heouse is jammed full o' folks, and there ain't nothin ready. You jes' wait here, till I git things in shape and I'll cum arter ye."

Micah then departed to complete his arrangements, and Mr.

Norton returned to his post in the sick-room.

It was nearly five o'clock in the afternoon before a messenger came to inform him that the hour of burial had arrived.

A strange scene presented itself to his view as he approached the grove. A motley company, composed of the settlers of every grade and condition for miles around, had collected there. Men, women, and children in various costume—the scarlet and crimson shirt, or tunic, carrying it high above all other fashions—were standing, or walking among the trees, conversing upon the event that had brought them together.

As the missionary approached, the loud indignant voices subsided into a low murmur, and the people made way for him to reach the centre of the group.

Here he found the coffin, placed upon a pile of boards, entirely uncovered to the light of day and to the inspection of the people, who had, each in turn, gazed with curious eyes upon the lifeless clay it enclosed.

In the absence of Mrs. McNab, who was still sleeping away the effects of her late fatigues at the house of Mr. Dubois, the women of the neighborhood had arrayed Patrick McGrath, very properly, in a clean shirt of his accustomed wearing apparel, so arranging it that the folds of the red tunic could be lifted in order to expose to those who came to look upon him the wound he had received. There he lay, the rude smuggler, turned gently upon his side, one cheek pressing the pillow. Death had effaced from his countenance every trace of the stormy passions which raged in his breast when the fatal bullet struck him, and had sealed it with even a pleasant serenity.

Not so with the compeers of his race, who encircled the coffin. *They* scowled a fierce fury from beneath their bushy brows and muttered vows of vengeance. The rays of the sun, now rapidly declining, shot into their angry faces, the evening breeze shook out their matted locks of hair. A peculiar glow was cast over their wild, Erin features, now gleaming with unholy passion.

Mr. Norton bent for a few minutes over the coffin, while an expression of sorrow and deep commiseration overspread his countenance. Then he stepped upon a slight knoll of ground nearby, raised himself to his full height and began to speak in a voice that rose above the crowd, clear, melodious, full and penetrating as the notes of a bugle. It thrilled on every ear and drew instant attention.

"Friends, brethren, fellow-sinners, one of our number has been suddenly struck down by the relentless hand of death, and we are here to pay the last honors to his mortal remains—each and all to learn a solemn lesson while standing at the mouth of the grave. Brethren, we are to learn anew from this occasion that death often comes to man with the suddenness of the lightning flash. One moment before your comrade was struck by the fatal bullet, his eye glowed as keenly and his right arm was as powerful as yours. The next moment he was prostrate on the ground, with no power to move a single limb of his body, or utter a single sigh, or breathe a single prayer. He was dead."

"I am ignorant whether he was prepared to make such a sudden transit from this world to that scene of judgment to which he has been summoned. *You* know, who were his friends and comrades, what his former course has been, and whether he was prepared to meet the Judge of all the earth. I know nothing of all this, but I fervently hope that at the last erring, awful moment, when he had just committed an act of transgression against the laws of his country, he had in his heart, and did, offer up this prayer, 'God be merciful to me, a sinner.' We must leave him in the hands of the Almighty, who is both merciful and just. We cannot change his lot, but we have it in our power to profit by the circumstances of his death. Beholding how suddenly he has been cut off, in the prime and strength of his days, we may learn that we too may be called at some unexpected moment, and that it behooves us to be found ever in the right path, so living, so acting, that we shall be ready, when death comes, to meet our Judge without fear and with the assurance that when we depart this life, through the righteousness of Christ, we shall be introduced into a better and nobler country. I beg of you earnestly, my dear brethren, in order to secure this happy result, to turn immediately from your sins, repenting of them without delay, and apply to Christ whose blood can alone wash them away. Take the Bible, this precious gift from Heaven, for your counsellor and guide, follow its instructions, and you will be safe and happy, whether in life or in death."

"My brethren, I will say but one word more; that word I earnestly implore you to listen to. This book from God says, vengeance is mine; I will repay. I fear it is in your hearts to seek revenge upon him who is the author of your comrade's death. I beseech you not to do it. God knows where the wrong is, in this case, and He, the great Avenger, will not suffer it to go unpunished. Sooner or later He brings every wicked and wrong-doer to a just reward. Leave all in His righteous hands, and stain not your souls with blood and violence. Let us seek the divine blessing."

Mr. Norton then offered a short and simple prayer, imploring the forgiveness of sins, and blessings upon Patrick's wife, his companions, and the community.

Maggie, who had wailed herself into perfect exhaustion and almost stupor, sat gazing fixedly in his face; the rest seemed hushed as by a spell, and did not begin to move until some moments after his voice ceased.

Then the tongues were loosened, and amid the ebbs and flows of murmuring sound the coffin was covered, placed upon a bier and borne to the grave, followed by the crowd.

"And shure," said a poor Irishwoman to her crony as they trudged along behind, "the praste's voice sounded all the while like a great blessed angel, a blowin' through a silver trumpet. Shure, he's a saint, he is."

CHAPTER IX

Adèle Dubois

The Dubois family, though widely separated by social rank and worldly possessions from the population around them, had yet, to a certain degree, mingled freely with the people. Originating in France, they possessed the peculiar national faculty of readily adapting themselves to the manners and customs of races foreign to their own.

It is impossible to forget in the early history of the North American colonies what facility the French displayed, in contrast with the English, in attaining communication with the children of the forest, in acquiring and retaining their confidence, in taking on their rude and uncultivated modes of life, and in shaping even their superstitions to their own selfish purposes.

Of all the foreigners who have attempted to demonstrate to the world the social and political problems of America, who has investigated with such insight, and developed so truly our manners and customs and the spirit and genius of our government as Tocqueville?

Mr. Dubois, though possessing a conservative power that prevented him from descending to the low type of character and the lax principles of the country, yet never made any other than the most quiet assertion of superiority. It was impossible indeed for him to hold business connections with the rough settlers without mingling freely with them. But he never assumed the air of a master. He frequently engaged with them in bold, adventurous exploits, the accomplishment of which did not involve an infringement of law; sometimes he put hand and shoulder to the hard labors they endured, and he was ever ready with his sympathy and aid in redressing their grievances. Though often shocked at their lawless and profane customs, he yet recognized in many of them traits of generosity and nobleness.

Without a particle of aggressiveness in his disposition, he had never undertaken actively the work of reform, yet his example of uprightness and integrity had made an impression upon the community. The people treated him with unvarying respect and confidence, partly from a sense of his real superiority, and partly, perhaps, from the very lack of self-assertion on his side. Consequently without having made the least effort to do so, he exercised an autocratic power among them.

Mrs. Dubois visited the women of the place frequently, particularly when the men were absent in their lumbering or fishing operations, conversing with them freely, bearing patiently their superstitions and ignorance, aiding them liberally in temporal things, and sometimes mingling kindly words of counsel with her gifts.

Adèle's intercourse with the settlers was in an altogether different style. Her manner from earliest childhood, when she first began to run about from one cottage to another, had been free, frank, and imperious. Whether it was that having sniffed from babyhood the fresh forest air of the new world, its breath had inspired her with a careless independence not shared by her parents, or, whether the haughty blood that had flowed far back in the veins of ancestors, after coursing quietly along the generations, had in her become stimulated into new activity, certain it is, she had always the bearing of one having authority and the art of governing seemed natural to her. It was strange, therefore, that she should have been such a universal favorite in the neighborhood. But so it was. Those who habitually set public law at defiance came readily under the control of her youthful sway.

Possessing a full share of the irrepressible activity of childhood, she enacted the part of lady of the Manor, assuming prerogatives that even her mother did not think of exercising.

When about eleven summers old, she opened one afternoon the door of an Irish cabin and received at once a cordial, noisy welcome from its inmates. She did not, however, make an immediate response, for she had begun taking a minute survey of the not over-nice premises. At length she deigned to speak.

"Bridget Malone, are you not ashamed to have such a disorderly house as this? Why don't you sweep the floor and put things in place?"

"Och! hinny, and how can I swape the floor without a brum?" said Bridget, looking up in some dismay.

"Didn't my father order James to give you a broom whenever you want one? Here Pat," said she, to a ragged urchin about her own age, who was tumbling about over the floor with a little dirty-faced baby, "here, take this jack-knife and go down to the river by Mrs. Campbell's new house and cut some hemlock boughs. Be quick, and bring them back as fast as you can." Pat started at once.

Adèle then deliberately took off her bonnet and shawl, rolled them up into as small a package as she could make, and placed them on the nearest approximation to a clean spot that could be found. Then she stooped down, took the baby from the floor and handed him to his mother.

"Here, Bridget, take Johnny, wash his face and put him [in] a clean dress. I know he has another dress and it ought to be clean."

"Yes. He's got one you gave him, Miss Ady, but it aint clane at all. Shure it's time to wash I'm wanting, it is."

"Now, don't tell me, Bridget, that you have not time to wash your children's clothes and keep them decent. You need not spend so many hours smoking your pipe over the ashes."

"You wouldn't deprive a poor cratur of all the comfort she has in the world, would ye, hinny?"

"You ought to take comfort in keeping your house and children clean, Bridget."

In the meanwhile, Bridget had washed Johnny's face, and there being no clean dress ready for the little fellow, Adèle said, "Come, Bridget, put on a kettle of water, pick up your clothes, and do your washing."

"Shure, and I will, if ye say so, Miss Ady."

The poor shiftless thing, having placed the baby on the floor again, began to stir about and make ready.

Adèle sat poking and turning over the chubby little Johnny with her foot.

At last, Pat appeared with a moderate quantity of hemlock

boughs, which Adèle told him to throw upon the floor—then to hand her the knife and sit down by her side and learn to make a broom. She selected, clipped, and laid together the boughs until she had made quite a pile; sent Pat for a strong piece of twine and an old broom handle and then secured the boughs firmly upon it.

"Now Pat," she said, "here is a nice, new jack-knife. If you will promise me that you will cut boughs and make your mother two new brooms, just like this, every week, the knife shall be yours."

Pat, with eyes that stood out an unmentionable distance, and mouth stretched from ear to ear, promised, and Adèle proceeded vigorously to sweep the apartment. In the course of half an hour, the room wore a wholly different aspect.

"And who tould the like of ye, how to make a brum like that, hinny?" said Bridget, looking on in admiration of her skill.

"Nobody told me. I saw Aunt Patty McNab do it once. You see it is easy to do. Now, Bridget, remember. Have your house clean after this, or I will not come to see you."

"Yes, shure, I'll have them blessed brums as long's there's a tree grows."

And true it was, that Adèle's threat not to visit her cabin proved such a salutary terror to poor Bridget, that there was a perceptible improvement in her domestic arrangements ever after.

As Adèle grew older, the ascendency she had obtained in her obscure empire daily increased. At twelve, she was sent to a convent at Halifax, where she remained three years. At the end of that period, she returned to Miramichi, and resumed at once her regal sceptre. The sway she held over the people was really one of love, grounded on a recognition of her superiority. Circulating among them freely, she became thoroughly acquainted with their habits and modes of living, and she was ever ready to aid them, under their outward wants and their deeper heart troubles. A community must have someone to look up to, whether conscious of the want or not. Hero-worship is natural to the human soul, and the miscellaneous group of women and children scattered over the settlement found in Adèle a strong, joyous, self-relying spirit, able to help them out of their difficulties, who could cheer them when down-hearted, and spur them up when getting discouraged or inefficient.

But, added to this were the charms of her youthful beauty, which even the humblest felt, without perhaps knowing it, and an air of authority that swept away all opposition, and held, at times, even Aunt Patty McNab at arms' length. Yes, it must be confessed that the young lady was in the habit of queening it over the people; but they were perfectly willing to have it so, and both loved and were proud of their little despot.

In the meantime, the Dubois family were living a life within a life, to the *locale* of which the reader must now be introduced.

It has been said that the outward aspect of their dwelling was respectable, and in that regard was not greatly at variance, except in size, with the surrounding habitations. Within, however, there were apartments furnished and adorned in such a manner as to betoken the character and tastes of the inmates.

In the second story, directly over the spacious [dining-room] already described, there was a long apartment with two windows reaching nearly to the floor. It was carpeted with crimson and black Brussels, contained two sofas of French workmanship, made in a heavy, though rich style, covered with cloth also of crimson and black; with chairs fashioned and carved to match the couches, and finished in the same material. A quaint-looking piano stood in one corner of the room. In the centre was a Chinese lacquered table on which stood a lamp in bronze, the bowl of which was supported by various broadly-smiling, grotesque creatures, belonging to a genus known only in the domain of fable.

On the evening following the burial of poor Pat McGrath, Mrs. Dubois sat in this apartment, engaged in embroidering a fancy piece of dress for Adèle. That young lady was reclining upon a sofa, and was looking earnestly at a painting of the Madonna, a copy from some old master, hanging nearly opposite to her. It was now bathed in the yellow moonlight, which heightened the wonderfully saintly expression in the countenances of the holy mother and child.

"See! *ma bonne mère*, the blessed Marie looks down on us with a sweet smile to-night."

"She always looks kindly upon us, *chère*, when we try to do right," said Mrs. Dubois, smiling. "Doubtless you have tried to be good today and she approves your effort."

"Now, just tell me, *ma chère mère*, how she would regard me to-night if I had committed one wicked deed today."

"This same Marie looks sad and wistful sometimes, my Adèle."

"True. But not particularly at *such* times. It depends on which side the light strikes the picture, whether she looks sad or smiling. Just that, and nothing more. Now the moonlight gives her a smiling expression. And please listen, *chère mère*. I have heard that there is, somewhere, a Madonna, into whose countenance the old painter endeavored to throw an air of profoundest repose. He succeeded. I have heard that that picture has a strange power to soothe. Gazing upon it the spirit grows calm and the voice unconsciously sinks into a whisper. Our priests would tell the common people that it is a miraculous influence exerted upon them by the Virgin herself, whereas it is only the effect produced by the exquisite skill of the artist. *Eh, bien!* our church is full of superstitions."

"We will talk no more of it, *ma fille*. You do not love the holy *Marie* as you ought, I fear."

"Love her! indeed I do. She is the most blest and honored among women — the mother of the Saviour. But why should we pray to her when Jesus is the only intercessor for our sins with the Father? Why, *ma chère mère*?"

"*[Hélas]! ma fille*. You learned to slight the intercession of the holy saints while you were at the convent. It is strange. I thought I could trust you there."

"Do not think it the fault of the sisters, *chère mère*. They did their duty. This way of thinking *came* to me. I did not seek it, indeed."

"How did it come to you, *ma pauvre fille*?"

"I will tell you. The first time I went into the convent parlor, Sister Adrienne, thinking to amuse me, took me around the room and showed me its curiosities. But I was filled with an infinite disgust. I did not distinctly know then why I was so sickened, but I understand it all now."

"What did you see, Adèle?"

"Eh! those horrid relics of saints — those teeth, those bones, those locks of hair in the cabinet. Then that awful skeleton of sister Agnes, who founded the convent and was the first Abbess, covered with wax and preserved in a crystal case! I thought I was in some charnel-house. I could hardly breathe. Do you like such parlor ornaments as those, *ma chère mère?*"

"Not quite."

"What do we want of the dry bones of the saints when we have memoirs of their precious lives? They would themselves spurn the superstition that consecrates mere earthly dust. It nauseates me to think of it."

"*[Procédez], ma fille.*"

"My friend from the States, Mabel Barton, came to the convent the day I arrived. As our studies were the same, and as, at first, we were both homesick, the sisters permitted us to be together much of the time. *Eh! bien!* I read her books, her Bible, and so light dawned. She used to pray to the Father, through the Redeemer. I liked that way best. But *ma mère*, our cathedral service is sublime. There is nothing like *that*. Now you will forgive me. The arches, the altar, the incense, the glorious surging waves of music—these raised me and Mabel, likewise, up to the lofty third heaven. How high, how holy we felt, when we worshipped there. Because I like the cathedral, you will forgive me for all I said before—will you not, *ma chère mère?*"

Turning her head suddenly towards her mother, Adèle saw her eyes filled with tears.

"*Eh! ma chère mère, pardonnez moi.* I have pained you." And she rose and flung her arms, passionately, around her mother's neck.

"*Pauvre fille!*" said the mother, returning her embrace mournfully, "you will wander away from the church—our [Holy Church]. It would not have been thus had we remained in sunny Picardy. *Eh! oublier je ne puis.*"

"What is it, *chère mère*," said Adèle, "that you cannot forget? There is something I have long wished to know. What was there, before you came here to live? Why do you sometimes sit and look so thoughtful, so sad and wishful? Tell me;—tell me, that I may comfort you."

"I will tell you all, Adèle, yes—all. It is time for you to know, but—not to-night—not to-night."

"Tomorrow then, *ma mère?*"

"Yes. Yes—tomorrow."

CHAPTER X

PICARDY

"Weep ye not for the dead, neither bemoan him: but, weep sore for him that goeth away: for he shall return no more, nor see his native country." The prophet, who wrote these words, well knew the exile's grief. He was himself an exile. He thought of Jerusalem, the city of his home, his love, and his heart was near to breaking. He hung his harp upon the willow; he sat down by the streams of Babylon and wept.

The terrible malady of homesickness — it has eaten out the vigor and beauty of many a life. The soul, alien to all around, forlorn amid the most enchanting scenes, filled with ceaseless longing for a renewal of past delights, can never find a remedy until it is transplanted back to its native clime.

Nor was the prophet singular in his experience of the woes of exile. We have heard of the lofty-spirited Dante, wandering from city to city, carrying with him, in banishment, irrepressible and unsatisfied yearnings for his beloved Florence; we have seen the Greek Islander, borne a captive from home, sighing, in vain, for the dash and roar of his familiar seas; we have seen the Switzer, transplanted to milder climes and more radiant sides, yet longing for the stern mountain forms, the breezes and echoes of his native land. Ah! who does not remember, with a shudder, the despairing thoughts, choking tears, and days of silent misery that clouded his own boyhood, and perhaps even some days of his early manhood?

Oublier je ne puis. Poor lady! she had been homesick twenty years.

On the afternoon following the conversation recorded in the last chapter, Mrs. Dubois was ready to unfold to Adèle the story of her past life. They were sitting in the parlor. The golden glory of the September sun gave an intense hue to the crimson furniture, lighted up the face of the Madonna with a new radiance, and touched the ivory keys of the piano with a fresh polish. Adèle's eyes were fixed with eager expectation upon her mother.

"You know, *ma chère*," Mrs. Dubois began, "we once lived in France. But you cannot know, I trust you never may, what it cost us to leave our beautiful Picardy—what we have suffered in remaining here, exiled in this rude country. Yet then it seemed our best course. Indeed, we thought there was no other path for us so good as this. We were young, and did not enough consider, perhaps, what such a change in our life involved. I must tell you, my Adèle, how it came about.

"In the province of Picardy not many miles from the city of Amiens, there was a fine, but not large estate, bordering on the River Somme. A long avenue of poplars led from the main road up a gentle slope until it opened upon a broad, green plateau of grass, studded with giant trees, the growth of centuries. Here and there were trim little flower-beds, laid out in a variety of fantastic shapes, with stiff, glossy, green, closely-clipped borders of box. And, what was my childish admiration and delight, there was a fountain that poured itself out in oozing, dripping drops from the flowing hair and finger tips of a marble Venus, just rising in the immense basin and wringing out her locks. Then the park—there was none more beautiful, more stately, extending far back to the banks of the Somme, where birds sat on every bough and the nightingale seemed to pour its very heart away, singing so thrillingly and so long. I hear the liquid notes now, my Adèle, so tender, so sweet! At the end of the avenue of poplars of which I spoke stood the chateau, with the trim flower-beds in front. It was built of brown stone, not much ornamented externally, with four round towers, one in each corner. Though not as old as some of those castles, it had been reared several centuries before, by a Count de Rossillon, who owned the estate and lived on it.

"In that chateau, I first saw the light of day, and there I spent my happy childhood and youth.

"The estate of Rossillon had been bequeathed by the will of my grandfather, to his two sons. The elder, the present Count de Rossillon, inherited the larger portion; my father, the younger son, the smaller share.

"My father was a Bonapartist, and at the time of his marriage held a high rank in the army. During his absence from the country, my mother resided at the chateau with her brother-in-law, the Count.

"One day in June, news arrived of the sudden death of my father. It was communicated to my mother, by the messenger who brought it, without precaution. That night, one hour after, I was ushered into an orphaned existence and my mother took her departure from the world. Think of me, Adèle, thus thrown a waif upon the shore of life. Yet, though born in the shadow of a great sorrow, sunlight struck across my path.

"The faithful *bonne*, who had taken care of my mother in her infancy and had never left her, now took charge of me. She watched over me faithfully and filled up my childhood with affectionate attention and innocent pastime. My uncle, the Count, who had never been married, loved, petted, and indulged me in every wish. When I grew old enough, he secured a governess well qualified to teach and discipline me. Under her care, with the aid of masters in Latin, music, and drawing, from Amiens, I went through the course of instruction considered necessary for young ladies at that time.

"I was at your age my Adèle when I first met your father. He was not the bronzed and careworn man you see him now. Ah! no. He was young and gay, with a falcon glance and black wreathing locks hanging over his white, smooth brow. His father was of noble blood, and sympathized warmly with the dethroned Bourbons. He was no lover of the great Consul. The political troubles in France had operated in ways greatly to impoverish his house.

"He owned and occupied only the remnant of what had been a large estate, adjoining that of the Count de Rossillon.

"While acquiring his education, your father, except at occasional intervals, was six years from home, and it so happened that I never met him in my childhood. Indeed, the families were not on terms of intimacy. On his return from the University, I first saw him. *Eh! bien!* It is the same old story that you have heard and read of in your books, my Adèle. We became acquainted, I will not stop now, to tell you how, and soon learned to love each other. Time passed on, and at last your father sought the consent of my uncle to our marriage. But he put aside the proposition with anger and scorn. He thought that Claude Dubois was neither distinguished nor rich enough to match his niece. In his heart, he had reserved me for some conspicuous position in the great circle at Paris, while I had given myself to an obscure youth in Picardy.

"Your father was too honorable to ask me to marry him without the consent of the Count, and too proud to take me in his poverty. So one day, after his stormy interview with my uncle, he came to me and said he was going away to endeavor to get fame, or wealth, to bestow upon me and make himself more worthy in the eyes of the Count de Rossillon. Yet he wished to release me from any feeling of obligation to him, as, he said, I was too young and had too little acquaintance with life and society to know fully my own heart. It would not be right, he thought, to bind me to himself by any promise. I told him my affection for him would never change, but acquiesced in his arrangements with a sad and foreboding heart. In a few weeks, he embarked for India.

"Then my uncle roused himself from the inertia of his quiet habits and made arrangements for a journey through France and Italy, which he said I was to take with him.

"I received the announcement with indifference, being wholly occupied with grief at the bitter separation from your father. The change, however, proved salutary, and, in a week after our departure, I felt hope once more dawning in my heart.

"The country through which we travelled was sunny and beautiful, veined with sparkling streams, shadowed by forests, studded with the olive and mulberry, and with vines bearing the luscious grape for the vintage. The constant change of scene and the daily renewal of objects of interest and novelty, combined with the elasticity of youth, brought back some degree of my former buoyancy and gayety. My uncle was so evidently delighted with the return of my old cheerfulness, and exerted himself so much to heighten it in every way, that I knew he sincerely loved me, and was doing what he really thought would in the end contribute to my happiness. He judged that my affection for your father was a transient, youthful dream, and would soon be forgotten; he fancied, no doubt, I was even then beginning to wake up from it. He wished to prevent me from forming an early and what he considered an imprudent marriage, which I might one day regret, unavailingly.

"And it proved to be all right, my Adèle. Your father and I were both young, and the course the Count de Rossillon took with us was a good though severe test of our affection. In the meanwhile, I was secretly sustained by the hope that your father's efforts would be crowned with success, and that, after a few years, he would return and my uncle, having found that nothing could draw me from my attachment to him, would out of his own love for me and consideration for my happiness, at last consent to our union.

"We crossed the Alps and went into Italy. Here a new world was opened to me — a world of beauty and art. It bestowed upon me many hours of exquisite enjoyment. The Count travelled with his own carriage and servants, and we lingered wherever I felt a desire to prolong my observations. He purchased a collection of pictures, statues, and other gems and curiosities of art. Among the rest, the Madonna there, my Adèle, which he presented to me, because I so much liked it. But I must not linger now. On our return to France, we spent a month at Paris, and there, though too young to be introduced into society, I met in private many distinguished and fashionable people who were friends of the Count.

"We were absent from the chateau one year. It was pleasant to get back to the dear old place, where I had spent such a happy childhood, the scene too of so many precious interviews with your beloved father. We returned again to our former life of quiet ease, enlivened at frequent intervals by the visits of guests from abroad and by those of friends and acquaintances among the neighboring nobility. Though I received no tidings from your father, a secret hope still sustained me. A few times only, during the first three years of his absence, did I lose my cheerfulness. Those were when some lover pressed his suit and I knew that in repelling it I was upsetting some cherished scheme of my uncle. But I will do him the justice to say that he bore it patiently, and, only at long intervals, gave vent to his vexation and disappointment.

"It was when my hope concerning your father's return began to fail, and anxiety respecting his fate began to be indulged in its stead, that my spirits gave way. At the close of the fourth year of his absence, my peace was wholly gone and my days were spent in the restless agony of suspense. My health was rapidly failing, and my uncle who knew the cause of my prostration, instead of consulting a physician, in the kindness of his heart, took me to Paris. But the gayeties to which I was there introduced were distasteful to me. I grew every moment more sad. Just when my uncle was in despair, I was introduced accidentally to the Countess de Morny, a lovely lady, who had lost her husband and three children, and had passed through much sorrow.

"Gradually, she drew me to her heart and I told her all my grief. She dealt very tenderly with me, my Adèle. She did not seek to cheer me by inspiring fresh hopes of your father's return. No. She told me I might never be Claude Dubois's happy bride, but that I might be the blessed bride of Jesus. In short, she led me gently into the consolations of our Holy Church. Under her influence and guidance I came into a state of sweet resignation to the divine will — a peaceful rest, indeed, after the terrible alternations of suspense and despair I had suffered. But, my Adèle, it was only by constant prayers to the blessed *Marie* that my soul was kept from lapsing into its former state of dreadful unrest. *Ma chère* Adèle, you know not what you do when you speak slightingly of our Holy Church. I should then have died had I not found rest in my prayers to the blessed mother. Now, you are young and gay, but the world is full of sorrow. It may overtake you as it did me. Then you will need a hope, a consolation, a refuge. There is no peace like that found at the foot of the cross, imploring the intercession of the compassionate, loving *Marie*. Do not wander away from the sweet eyes of the mother of Christ, *ma fille*."

Here Mrs. Dubois ceased speaking, and turned a tearful, affectionate gaze upon her daughter. Adèle's eyes, that had been fixed upon her mother with earnest, absorbed attention, filled with tears, instantly.

"*Ma chère mère*, I would not make you unhappy. I will try not to give you pain. Please go on and tell me all."

"*Eh! bien! ma chère*, my uncle was pleased to see me becoming more peaceful. Finding I was not attracted by the pleasures of the gay city, he proposed our return to the chateau and begged the

Countess de Morny to accompany us. At my urgent request, she consented.

"On the day of our arrival, the Countess weary with the journey, having gone to her own apartments, I went to stroll in the beautiful, beloved park. It was June—that month so full of leaves, flowers, birds, and balmy summer winds. I sat at the foot of an old beech-tree, leaning my head against its huge trunk, listening to the flow of the river, indulging in dangerous reverie—dangerous certainly to my peace of mind. Suddenly, I was startled by the sound of footsteps. Before I could collect my scattered senses, your father stood before me. *'Marie,'* he said, *'Marie.'*

"For one moment, I met his earnest, questioning gaze, and then rushed into his open arms. In short, he had come back from India, not a rich man, but with a competence, and when he found I had not forgotten him, but had clung to him still, through those weary years of absence, he resolved to see the Count de Rossillon and renew the request he had made four years previous.

"My uncle, though much surprised at his sudden appearance, received him politely, if not cordially. When your father had laid before him a simple statement of our case, he replied frankly.

"'I am convinced,' he said, 'by what I have observed during your absence, M. Dubois, that the arrangement you propose is the only one which will secure Marie's happiness. I will say, however, honestly, that it is far enough from what I designed for her. But the manliness and honorable feeling you have manifested in the affair make me more willing to resign her to you than I should otherwise have been, as I cannot but hope that, although deprived of the advantages of wealth and station, she will yet have the faithful affection of a true and noble heart.'

"This was enough for us both and more than we expected.

"But a new difficulty arose. Upon observing the troubled and uncertain state of affairs in France, your father became convinced that his chances to secure the ends he had in view would be greater in the new world. After a brief period of deliberation, he fixed upon a plan of going to British America, and purchasing there a large tract of land, thus founding an estate, the value of which he anticipated would increase with the growth of the country.

"To this arrangement, the Count was strenuously opposed. There was a pretty embowered residence, a short distance from the chateau, on the portion of the estate I had inherited from my father. There he wished us to live. In short, he wished to retain us near himself. But your father, with the enterprise and enthusiasm of youth, persisted in his purpose. At last, my uncle gave a reluctant consent and purchased my share of the estate of Rossillon.

"Not to my surprise, but to my great gratification, soon after this, the gentle Countess de Morny consented to become the Countess de Rossillon.

"Surrounded by a joyous group of friends, one bright September morning, in the chapel of [Ste.] *Marie*, they were married, and then the priest united me to your father. The sweet mother looked down from above the altar and seemed to give us a smiling blessing. We were very happy, my Adèle.

"In a few days we set sail for New Brunswick. We arrived at St. John in October and there spent the following winter. In the spring, your father explored this region and made a large purchase of land here. At that time it seemed a desirable investment. But you see how it is, my Adèle. All has resulted strangely different from what we anticipated. And somehow it has always been difficult to change our home. From time to time, we have thought of it—obstacles have arisen and—we are still here."

"But where is the Count de Rossillon, mother? It is twenty years, is it not, since you left France? Does he yet live?"

"*Ah! ma chère*, we know not. After our departure from France we received frequent letters from him and the dear Countess until five years since, when the letters ceased. They constantly urged our return to Rossillon. You remember well the thousand pretty toys and gifts they showered upon your childhood?"

"Ah! yes, mother, I remember. And you have not heard a word from them for five years!"

"Not a word."

"Do you wish to go back to France, mother?"

"It is the only wish of my heart that is unsatisfied. I am full of ceaseless yearnings for the beautiful home of my youth. Would that we could return there. But it may not be. France is in a state of turmoil. I know not what fate has befallen either my uncle, or his estate. He may be dead. Or, if living, he may no longer be the proprietor of beautiful Rossillon. We cannot learn how it is."

"Cannot my father go to France and ascertain what has happened there? Perhaps, mother, he might find a home for you once more in your dear Picardy."

"He is thinking of it even now, *ma fille*."

"Is he, mother? Then be comforted. You will see that sweet home once more, I feel assured."

She rose and flung her arms around Mrs. Dubois, exclaiming, "Dear, beautiful mother!"

An hour later, Adèle might have been seen wandering about in Micah's [Grove], her mind and heart overflowing with new, strange thoughts and emotions. She had just received the first full revelation of the early life of her parents. Her knowledge of it before had been merely vague and confused. Now a new world was opened for her active fancy to revel in, and fresh fountains of sympathy to pour forth, for those whom she so fondly loved. She sighed as she recalled that yearning, wistful look upon her mother's face, in those hours when her thoughts seemed far away from the present scene, and grieved that her gentle spirit should so long have suffered the exile's woe.

For weeks after, she continually fell into reverie. In her day dreams she wandered through the saloons and corridors of the old chateau, where her mother had spent so many years, chequered with sunshine and shade. She rambled over the park and cooled her fevered head and hands in the water that dripped from the tresses of the marble Aphrodite. Fancy took her over the route of foreign travel her mother had pursued with the Count de Rossillon. She longed herself to visit those regions of classic and romantic interest. During the long, golden, September afternoons, she spent hours in the Madonna room, questioning her mother anew respecting the scenes and events of her past life, and listening eagerly to her replies. The young examine distant objects as through a prism. Adèle's imagination invested these scenes and events with rainbow splendors and revelled in the wealth and beauty she had herself partially created. The new world thus opened to her was infinitely superior to the one in which she held her commonplace, humdrum existence. She never wearied of her mother's reminiscences of the past. Each fresh description, each recalled item of that history, added to the extent and the charms of her new world.

Mrs. Dubois herself felt a degree of pleasure in thus living over again her former life with one who entered artlessly and enthusiastically into its joys and sorrows. She also experienced an infinite relief in pouring out to her sympathizing child the regrets and longings which had, for so long a period, been closely pent in her own breast. Mother and daughter were drawn nearer to each other day by day, and those hours of sweet communion were among the purest, the happiest of their lives.

CHAPTER XI

Mr. Brown

Nearly two weeks had elapsed since the night when Mr. Dubois had brought Mr. Brown, in a sick and fainting condition, into his house. That gentleman had lain very ill ever since. The disease was typhoid fever; the patient was in a critical state, and nothing now but the utmost care and quiet could save his life.

"What directions have you left for today, Dr. Wright?" said Adèle to the physician, as he came one morning from the sick-room.

"Mrs. McNab has the programme," he replied.

"Will you please repeat it to me, sir? Mrs. McNab has been called elsewhere, and will not have charge of the gentleman today."

Mrs. Dubois looked at Adèle with some surprise. She made no remark, however, as Dr. Wright immediately began to give the directions for his patient to that young lady.

When he had taken leave and closed the door, Adèle turned to her mother and said, "I have suspected for several days that things were not going on properly in that sick-room. Last night, I became convinced of it. I cannot stop to tell you about it now, mamma, as there is no time to lose with our invalid. But Mrs. McNab must decamp. I have it all arranged, and I promise you I will not offend Aunt Patty, but will dismiss her peaceably. Do trust her to me once, mamma. Please go now and tell her there is a message waiting for her in the dining-room. Stay with Mr. Brown just one half hour, and you shall have no more trouble today."

"But, *ma chère*, you have no patience with Aunt Patty. I am afraid you will be too abrupt with her."

"Don't fear, mamma, I promise you I will not outrage Aunt Patty. Please go."

"Ah! well! I will go," said Mrs. Dubois.

Mrs. McNab soon made her appearance in the dining-room, and, with some degree of trepidation, inquired who wanted her there.

"Micah was here an hour ago," replied [Adèle], "and said Mrs. Campbell sent him here to ask you to come and help her. Four of her children are sick with the measles and she is nearly down herself, in consequence of fatigue and watching. I did not speak to you then, as I supposed you were sleeping. I told Micah I had no doubt you would come, as there are enough here to take care of the sick gentleman, and Mrs. Campbell needs you so much."

"Weel, Miss Ady," said Mrs. McNab, twitching violently a stray lock of her flaming hair and tucking it beneath her cap, "I dinna ken how you could tak' upon yourself to send such a ward as that, when Mr. Brown is just on the creesis of his fever and not one of ye as knows how-to tak' care o' him more than a nussin' babe."

"Ah! indeed! Aunt Patty," said Adèle, pretending to be offended, "do you say that my mother knows nothing about sickness when you are aware she has carried my father through two dangerous fevers and me through all the diseases of babyhood and childhood?"

"That mon 'ull never get weel if I leave him noo when I've the run of the muddesons and directions. A strange hand 'ull put everything wrang and he'll dee, that's a'."

"And if he does die," said Adèle, "you will not be responsible. You have done what you could for him and now you are called away. I am sure you will not permit Mrs. Campbell to suffer when she gave you a comfortable home in her house all last winter."

"Weel, Mrs. Cawmmells' a gude woman enough and I'm sorry the bairns are sick. But what's the measles to a fever like this, and the mon nigh dead noo?" Aunt Patty's face flushed scarlet.

"Aunt Patty," said Adèle, very slowly and decidedly, "Mr. Brown is my father's guest. We are accountable for his treatment, and not you. My mother and I are going to take charge of him now. I sent word to Mrs. Campbell that there was nothing to prevent you from coming to assist her. You have had your share of the fatigue and watching with our invalid. Now we are going to relieve you." There was something in Adèle's determined air that convinced Mrs. McNab the time for her to yield had at length come, and that it was of no use for her to contest the field longer. Feeling sure of this, there were various reasons, occurring to her on the instant, that restrained her from a further expression of her vexation. After a few moments of sullen silence, she rose and said—

"Weel! I'll go and put my things tegither, that's in Mr. Brown's room, and tell Mrs. Doobyce aboot the muddesons and so on."

"That is not necessary," said Adèle; "The [doctor] has given me directions about the medicines. Here is breakfast all ready for you, Aunt Patty. Sit down and eat it, while it is hot. I will go to the gentleman's room and gather up what you have left there. Come, sit down now."

Adèle placed a pot of hot coffee and a plate of warm rolls upon the table.

Mrs. McNab stood for a moment, much perplexed between her impulse to go back to Mr. Brown's room and unburden her mind to Mrs. Dubois, and the desire to partake immediately of the tempting array upon the breakfast-table. Finally, her material wants gained the ascendency and she sat down very composedly to a discussion of the refreshments, while Adèle, anticipating that result, hastened upstairs to collect the remaining insignia of that worthy woman's departing greatness.

Mrs. Dubois, on going to Mr. Brown's room, had found the atmosphere close and suffocating, and that gentleman, tossing restlessly on the bed from side to side, talking to himself in a wild delirium. She left the door ajar and began bathing his fevered head in cool water. This seemed to soothe him greatly and he sank back almost immediately into a deathlike slumber, in which he lay when Adèle entered the chamber.

Cautioned by her mother's uplifted finger, she moved about noiselessly until she had made up a large and miscellaneous package of articles; then descended quietly, inwardly resolving that the "Nuss," as she called herself, should not for several weeks, at least, revisit the scene of her late operations.

Mrs. McNab was still pursuing her breakfast, and Adèle sat down, with what patience she could command, to wait for the close.

"You'll be wanting some ain to watch to-night, Miss Ady," said Aunt Patty.

"Yes, Mr. Norton will do that. He has offered many times to

watch. He will be very kind and attentive to the invalid, I know."

"I s'pose he'll do as weel as he knows hoo, but I havena much faith in a mon that sings profane sangs and ca's 'em relegious heems, to a people that need the bread o' life broken to 'em."

"Have you heard him sing, Aunt Patty? I did not know you had attended his meetings at the grove."

"I havena, surely. But when the windows were up, I heard him singin' them jigs and reels, and I expectin' every minut to see the men, women, and bairns a dancin'.'"

"They sit perfectly still while he is singing," said Adèle, "and listen as intently as if they heard an angel. His voice is sometimes like a flute, sometimes like a trumpet. Did you hear the words he sang?"

"The wards! yes! them's the warst of a!" said Mrs. McNab, expanding her nostrils with a snort of contempt. "They bear na resemblance whatever to the Psalms o' David. I should as soon think o' singing the' sangs o' Robby Burns at a relegious service as them blasphemous things."

"Oh! Aunt Patty, you are wrong. He sings beautiful hymns, and he tells these people just what they need. I hope they will listen to him and reform."

"Weel he's a very light way o' carryin himself for a minister o' the gospel, I must say."

"He is cheerful, to be sure, and sympathizes with the people, and helps them in their daily labor sometimes, if that is what you refer to. I am sure that is right, and I like him for it," said Adèle.

"Weel! I see he's a' in a' with you, noo," said Mrs. McNab, at last rising from the table. "I'll go up noo and tak' leave o' the patient."

"No, no," said Adèle. "He is sleeping. He must not be disturbed on any account. His life may depend upon this slumber remaining unbroken."

She rose involuntarily and placed herself against the door leading to the stairs.

Mrs. McNab grew red with anger at being thus foiled. Turning aside to hide her vexation, she waddled across the room, took her bonnet and shawl from a peg she had appropriated to her special use, and proceeded to invest herself for her departure.

"Weel! I s'pose ye'll expect me to come when ye send for me," said she, turning round in the doorway with a grotesque distortion of her face intended for an ironical smile.

"That is just as you please, Aunt Patty. We shall be happy to see you whenever you choose to come. [Good-bye]."

"Good bye," said Mrs. McNab in a quacking, quavering, half resentful tone, as she closed the door behind her.

Adèle went immediately to the adjoining pantry, called Bess, a tidy looking mulatto, gave her directions for the morning work and then went upstairs to relieve her mother. Mrs. Dubois made signs to her that she preferred not to resign her post. But Adèle silently insisted she should do so.

After her mother had left the room, she placed herself near the bedside that she might observe the countenance and the breathing of the invalid. His face was pale as that of death. His breath came and went almost imperceptibly. The physician had excluded every ray of sunshine and a hush, like that of the grave, reigned in the apartment. In her intercourse with the people of the settlement, Adèle had often witnessed extreme illness and several dying scenes; but she had never before felt herself so oppressed and awestruck as now. As she sat there alone with the apparently dying man, she felt that a silent, yet mighty struggle was going on between the forces of life and death. She feared death would obtain the victory. By a terrible fascination, her eyes became fixed on the ghastly face over which she fancied she could perceive, more and more distinctly, shadows cast by the hand of the destroyer. Every moment she thought of recalling her mother, but feared that the slightest jarring movement of the atmosphere might stop at once that feeble respiration. So she remained, watching terror stricken, waiting for the last, absolute silence—the immovable repose.

Suddenly, she heard a long, deep-drawn sigh. She saw the head of the sufferer turn gently on one side, pressing the pillow. A color—the faintest in the world, stole over the features. The countenance gradually settled into a calm, natural expression. The respiration became stronger and more regular. In a few moments, he slept as softly as a little child.

Adèle's heart gave one bound, and then for a moment stood still. She uttered a sigh of relief, but sank back in her chair, wearied by excess of emotion. She felt instinctively that the crisis had been safely passed, that there was hope for the invalid.

Then, for a long time, her mind was occupied with thoughts respecting death and the beyond.

Suddenly a shadow, flitting across the curtained window, recalled her to the present scene.

Ah! what a mercy, she thought, that Aunt Patty did not kill him before I discovered her beautiful mode of nursing sick people. No wonder he has been crazed all this time, with those strange manœuvres of hers!

On the previous night, Adèle had been the last of the family to retire. Stealing noiselessly past the door of the sick-room, which was somewhat ajar, her steps were arrested by hearing Aunt Patty, whose voice was pitched on a very high key, singing some old Scotch song. Thinking this rather a strange method of composing the nervous system of a delirious patient, she stood and listened. Up, far up, into the loftiest regions of sound, went Aunt Patty's cracked and quavering voice, and then it came down with a heavy, precipitous fall into a loud grumble and tumble below. She repeated again and again, in a most hilarious tone, the words—

> "Let us go, lassie, go,
> To the braes of Balquhither,
> Where' the blaebarries grow.
> 'Mang the bonnie Highland heather."

In the midst of this, Adèle heard a deep groan. Then she heard the invalid say in a feeble, deprecating tone—

"Ah! why do you mock me? Am I not miserable enough?"

Mrs. McNab stopped a moment, then replied in a sharp voice, "Mockin' ye! indeed, it's na such thing. If ye had an atom o' moosic in ye, ye wad ken at ance, it's a sweet Scotch sang I'm singin' to ye. I've sung mony a bairn to sleep wi' it."

There was no reply to this remark. All was quiet for a moment, when Adèle, fancying she heard the clinking of a spoon against the side of a tumbler, leaned forward a little and looked through the aperture made by the partially opened door. The nurse was sitting by the fire, in her huge headgear, wrapped in a shawl and carefully stirring what seemed, by the odor exhaled, to be whiskey. Her face was very red and her eyes wide open, staring at the coals.

The sufferer uttered some words, which Adèle could not distinguish, in an excited voice.

"I tell ye, there isna any hope for ye," said Mrs. McNab, who, for some reason, not apparent, seemed to be greatly irritated by whatever remarks her patient made.

"There isna any hope for thum that hasna been elected. Ye might talk an' pray a' yer life and 'twould do ye na gude, I dinna ken where you've been a' yer life, not to ken that afore. With a' yer furbelowed claithes and jewelled watch and trinkets, ye dinna ken much aboot the gospel. And then, this new preacher a' tellin' the people they can be saved ony minut they choose to gie up their hearts to the Lord! [It's] a' tegither false. I was taught in the Kirk o' Scotland, that a mon might pray and pray a' his days, and then he wadna be sure o' bein' saved. That's the blessed doctrine I was taught. If ye are to be saved, ye will be. There noo, go to sleep. I'll read the ward o' God to ye."

Alas! for the venerable church of old Scotia, had she many such exponents of her doctrine as Mrs. McNab.

Having thus relieved her mind, the nurse swallowed the contents of the tumbler. She then rose, drew a chair towards a table, on which stood a shaded lamp, and took from thence a Bible; but finding her eyesight rather dim, withdrew to a cot in one corner of the room, threw herself down and was soon sleeping and snoring prodigiously.

Adèle, who had, during the enactment of this scene, been prevented from rushing in and deposing Mrs. McNab at once, only by a fear of exciting the patient to a degree of frenzy, stole in quietly, bathed his head with some perfumed water, smoothed his pillow and seated herself, near the fire, where she remained until morning.

Mr. Brown slept only during the briefest intervals and was turning restlessly and talking incoherently all night.

Soon after [day-dawn], Aunt Patty began to bestir herself, but before she had observed her presence, Adèle had escaped to her own room. Soon, hearing Micah's voice, she went to the kitchen. She found his message from Mrs. Campbell, just the excuse she needed to enable her to dispose of Mrs. McNab. She had become quite convinced that whatever good qualities that worthy woman might possess as a nurse, her unfortunate proclivities towards the whiskey bottle, united with her rigid theological tenets, rendered it rather unsafe to trust her longer with a patient, whose case required the most delicate care and attention.

The queer, old clock in the dining-room struck one. Adèle heard it. She was still watching. Mr. Brown still slept that quiet sleep. Just then, Mrs. Dubois entered, took her daughter's hand, led her to the door, and whispered —

"Now, take some food and go to rest. I will not leave him." Adèle obeyed.

CHAPTER XII

A Case of Conscience

Mr. Brown remained in a peaceful slumber during the afternoon. Mrs. Dubois aroused him occasionally in order to moisten his parched lips, and with her husband's aid and Mr. Norton's to change his position in the bed. At such times he opened his eyes, gazed at them inquiringly, feebly assented to their arrangements, then sank away into sleep again.

The members of the family felt a peculiar interest in the stranger. Mr. Dubois had described him as a man of intelligence, refined and elegant in his deportment and tastes. He had noticed in him an air of melancholy, which even ludicrous events on the journey had dissipated, but for the moment. The wild words he had uttered on the night of his arrival revealed some deep disquiet of mind. Away from home, hovering between life and death, and thrown on the tender mercies of strangers, Mrs. Dubois was filled with compassion and solicitude in his behalf.

Having confidence in Mrs. McNab's skill as a nurse, she had not suspected that her partiality for a hot dose at night would interfere with her faithfulness to her charge. Not having communicated with Adèle, she did not yet know why it had been deemed important to dispose of her so summarily, and she secretly wondered how it had been accomplished with so little ado. When informed, she approved Adèle's decisive action.

Mr. Norton had fully shared the interest felt by the family in the stranger, and was happy to relieve Mrs. Dubois in the evening and to remain by his bedside during the night. Since his first interview with Mr. Brown, on the day of his arrival, he had felt that, in [accordance with] the vows by which he had bound himself to the [Great] Master, the unfortunate stranger had a claim on him, which he resolved to fulfil at the earliest moment possible. He had had no opportunity as yet of executing his purpose, Mrs. McNab having guarded the door of the sick-room like a lioness watching her cubs. When she had by chance permitted him to enter, he had found her patient wandering in mind and entirely incapable of coherent conversation.

Meantime, he had prayed earnestly for his recovery and secretly felicitated himself with the hope of leading him to a rock of refuge — a tower of defence, which would secure him from sin and sorrow.

Mr. Brown continued to sleep so peacefully during the night that Mr. Norton, whose hopes for his recovery had been increasing every hour, was not surprised at the dawn of day to perceive his eyes open, examining the objects in the room, with the air of a person just awakened from a bewildering dream.

He gazed curiously at the heavy, carved bureau of dark wood, at the grotesque little table, covered with vials and cups, at the cabinet filled with specimens of foreign skill and art, at the Venetian carpet and, at last, his eyes remained fixed upon a black crucifix placed in the centre of the mantle. He uttered a deep sigh.

Mr. Norton, convinced that he had fully collected his scattered thoughts and become aware of the realities of his situation, stepped gently forward from his station behind the bed and taking Mr. Brown's hand, said, in a cheerful tone, "How do you find yourself, my dear sir?"

After a momentary surprise, Mr. Brown replied —

"Better, I think, sir, better."

"Yes sir. You *are* better. I thank God for it. And also for this hospitable roof and the kind care these people have taken of you in your illness. The Lord's angel must have guided your steps to this house, and mine also."

"This house, sir! whose is it?"

"It belongs to Mr. Dubois."

"Ah! I recollect. I came here with him and have been ill several days. And the country is --."

"Miramichi," said Mr. Norton. "A desperate region sir. A land where the darkness may be *felt*."

Just then a ray of red, burning sunshine shot into the room. The good man modified his remark, exclaiming, "Morally, sir, morally."

Observing a cloud of anxiety stealing over Mr. Brown's face, he went on.

"Now, my dear sir, let me tell you—you have been very ill for two weeks. The danger in your case is now over, but you are extremely weak, and need, for a time, the attention of the two lovely nurses, who watched over you yesterday and are ready to bestow kind care upon you again today. You must lay aside, for the present, all troubles of mind and estate, and devote yourself to getting well. When you are somewhat stronger, I have excellent things to tell you."

"Excellent things!" exclaimed Mr. Brown, excitedly—a flush overspreading his wan features. "Has the traitor been found?" Then with a profound sigh of disappointment, he uttered feebly—

"Ah! you do not know."

"I do not know what your particular trouble is, my dear sir, but I know of a way to relieve you of that, or any other burden that weighs on your spirits. I will inform you when you get stronger. What you need now is a cup of oatmeal gruel mingled with a tea-spoonful of wine, which shall immediately be presented to you by the youthful queen of this mansion."

He turned to go and call Adèle. But Mr. Brown motioned him to remain.

"Do you reside here, sir?" he asked, in accents indicating great prostration and despondency.

"No, sir. I arrived here only a few hours before you. I am from the State of -- . You are also from that region, and I shall not leave you until I see you with your face set towards your native soil. Now, my dear sir, be quiet. Perhaps your life depends on it."

"My life is not worth a penny to anybody."

"It is worth ten thousand pounds and more to your friends. Be quiet, I say."

And Mr. Norton went out of the room, gently but decisively. Mr. Brown's eyes followed him as he closed the door.

Already he felt the magnetic power of that good and sympathizing heart, of that honest, upright soul, which inspired by heavenly love and zeal, cast rays of life and happiness wherever it moved.

Moreover, he was too much prostrated in mind and body vigorously to grasp the circumstances of his situation, whatever they might be. Pain and debility had dulled his faculties and the sharpness of his sorrow also. The good missionary's cheery voice and heartfelt smile soothed, for the time, his wounded spirit. It was as if he had taken a sip of Lethe and had come into the land in which it always seemeth afternoon.

Soon [Adèle] opened the door and, approaching the table gently, placed upon it the gruel. When she turned her eyes full of sympathy and kindness upon him and inquired for his health, he started with a remembrance that gave him both pain and pleasure. She reminded him strangely of the being he loved more than any other on earth—his sister. He answered her question confusedly.

She then raised his head upon the pillow with one hand and presented the cup to his lips with the other. He drank its contents, mechanically.

[Adèle] proceeded noiselessly to arrange the somewhat disordered room, and after placing a screen between it and the bed, raised a window, through which the warm September atmosphere wandered in, indolently bathing his weary brow. As he felt its soft undulations on his face, and looking around the pleasant apartment observed the graceful motions of his youthful nurse, the scenes through which he had recently passed appeared like those of an ugly nightmare, and floated away from his memory. The old flow of his life seemed to come back again and he gave himself up to pleasant dreams.

Mr. Brown continued thenceforward to improve in health, though slowly. Mr. Norton slept on a cot in his room every night and spent a part of every day with him, assisting in his toilet, conversing with him of the affairs, business and political, of their native State, and reading to him occasionally from books furnished by Mr. Dubois's library.

He informed Mr. Brown of his mission to this wild region of Miramichi, and the motives that induced it. That gentleman admired the purity and singleness of purpose which had led this man, unfavored indeed by a careful classical culture, but possessing many gifts and much practical knowledge, thus to sacrifice himself in this abyss of ignorance and sin. He was drawn to him daily by the magnetism which a strong, yet heroic and genial soul always exercises upon those who approach it.

In a few days he had, without any effort of the good man and involuntarily on his own part, confided to him the heavy weight that troubled his conscience.

"Ah!" said Mr. Norton, his eyes full of profound sorrow, and probing the wound now laid open to the quick, "it was a terrible weakness to have yielded thus to the wiles of that artful foreigner. May Heaven forgive you!"

Surprised and shocked at this reception of his confession, Mr. Brown, who had hoped for consolation or counsel from his sympathizing companion, felt cut to the heart. His countenance settled into an expression of utter despair.

"Why have you sought so diligently to restore me to health — to a disgraced and miserable existence? You must have known, from the delirious words of my illness, of which you have told me, that life would be a worthless thing to me. You should have permitted me the privilege of death," said he bitterly.

"The privilege of death!" said Mr. Norton. "Don't you know, my dear sir, that a man unprepared to live is also unprepared to die? Every effort I have put forth during your illness has been for the purpose of saving you for a happy life here, and for a blissful immortality."

"A happy life here! For me, who have deeply offended and disgraced my friends and my pure and unstained ancestry!"

"It is true, in an hour of weakness and irresolution, you have sinned against your friends. But you have sinned all your life against a Being infinitely higher [than] earthly friends. Your conduct has disturbed family pride and honor, and thereby destroyed your peace. But, do you never think of your transgressions against God? For a world, I would not have had you present yourself before His just tribunal with your sins against Him unrepented of. Is there no other thought in your heart than to escape the misery of the present?"

Mr. Brown was silent. Mr. Norton continued.

"It is utter weakness and cowardice, in order to escape present discomfort and wretchedness, to rush from this world into another without knowing what we are to meet there."

A flush of resentment at these words covered the invalid's face. Just then Adèle knocked on the door, and said a poor woman below wished to see Mr. Norton.

He rose instantly, went towards Mr. Brown, and taking his thin hand between his own and pressing it affectionately, said, "Look back upon your past life—look into your heart. Believe me, my dear sir, I am your friend."

Then he went to obey the summons, and Mr. Brown was left alone.

The emotion of anger towards his benefactor soon passed away. He had been trained early in life to religious truth, and he knew that Mr. Norton presented to him the stern requisitions of that truth, only in friendliness and love. The good man was absent several hours, and the time was employed, as well as the solitude of several subsequent days, by Mr. Brown, in looking into his heart and into his past life. He found there many things he had not even suspected. He saw clearly that he had hitherto held himself amenable only to the judgment of the world. Its standard of propriety, taste, honor, had been his. He had not looked higher.

His friend Mr. Norton, on the contrary, held himself accountable to God's tribunal. His whole conversation, conduct, and spirit, showed the ennobling effect which that sublime test of character had upon him. In fine, he perceived that the basis of his own character had been false and therefore frail. The superstructure he had raised upon it had been fair and imposing to the world, but, when its strength came to be tried, it had given way and fallen. He felt that he had neglected his true interests, and had been wholly indifferent to the just claims of the only Being, who could have sustained him in the hour of temptation. He saw his past errors, he moaned over them, but alas! he considered it too late to repair them. His life he believed to be irretrievably lost, and he wished only to commit himself to the mercy of God, and die.

For a few days, he remained reserved and sunk in a deep melancholy.

At length, Mr. Norton said to him, "I trust you are not offended with me, my dear sir, for those plain words I addressed to you the other day. Be assured that though stern, they were dictated by my friendship for you and my duty towards God."

"Offended! my good friend. O no. What you said is true. But it is too late for me to know it. Through the merits of Christ, I hope for the pardon of my sins. I am willing to live and suffer if it is His behest. But you perceive my power to act for the cause of truth is gone. My past has taken away all good influence from my future course. Who will accept my testimony now? I have probably lost caste in my own circle, and have, doubtless, lost my power to influence it, even should I be received back to its ties. In society, I am a dishonored man. I cannot have the happiness of working for the truth — for Christ. My power is destroyed."

"You are wrong, entirely wrong, my dear sir. Have courage. Shall not that man walk erect and joyous before the whole world, whatever his past may have been, whose sins have been washed away in the blood of Christ and whose soul is inspired by a determination to abide by faith in Him forever? I say, yes. Do the work of God. He will take care of you. Live, with your eye fixed on Him, ready to obey His will, seeking His heavenly aid, and you can face the frowns of men, while serene peace fills your heart."

Thus cheered and strengthened from day to day, Mr. Brown gained gradually in health and hope. Especially did Mr. Norton strive to invigorate his faith. He justly thought it was only a strong grasp on eternal realities that could supply the place of those granite qualities of the soul, so lacking in this lovable, fascinating young man.

CHAPTER XIII

THE GROVE

In the meanwhile, three or four times during the week, Mr. Norton continued to hold meetings for the people in Micah's Grove.

There had been but little rain in the Miramichi region during the summer and autumn. In fact, none worthy of note had fallen for two months, except what came during the late equinoctial storm. The grass was parched with heat, the roads were ground to a fine dust, which a breath of wind drove, like clouds of smoke, into the burning air; the forest leaves, which had been so recently stained with a marvellous beauty of brown, crimson and gold, became dim and shrivelled; a slight touch snapped, with a sharp, crackling sound, the dried branches of the trees; even the [goldenrod] and the purple aster, those hardy children of autumn, began to hang their heads with thirst. All day long the grasshopper and locust sent through the hot, panting air their shrill notes, stinging the ear with discord. The heaven above looked like a dome of brass, and a thin, filmy smoke gathered around the horizon.

Even the rude settlers, with nerves toughened by hardship, unsusceptible of atmospheric changes, were oppressed by the long, desolating drought.

It was only when the shadows of afternoon began to lengthen and the sun's rays to strike obliquely through the stately trees of the Grove that they were able to gather there and listen to the voice of the missionary. He had so far succeeded in his work as to be able to draw the people together, from a considerable distance around, and their number increased daily.

On the opposite bank of the river, half way up a slight eminence, stood a small stone chapel. Tasteful and elegant in its proportions, it presented a picturesque and attractive appearance. There, once on each Sunday, the service of the Church of England was read, together with a brief discourse by a clergyman of that order.

Behind the chapel, and near the top of the hill, was a large stone cottage surrounded by pretty grounds and with ample stable conveniences. It was the Rectory.

The Chapel and Rectory had been built and the clergyman was sustained, at a somewhat large cost, by the Establishment for the purpose of enlightening and Christianizing the population of the Parish of --.

Unfortunately, the incumbent was not the self-sacrificing person needed to elevate such a community. Though ministering at the altar of God, he had no true religious feeling, no disinterested love for men. He was simply a man of the world, a *bon vivant*, a horse jockey and sportsman, who consoled himself in the summer and autumn for his exile in that barbarous region by filling his house with provincial friends, who helped him while away the time in fishing, hunting, and racing. The winter months he usually spent at Fredericton, and during that interval no service was held in the chapel. Of late, the few who were in the habit of attending the formal worship there, had forsaken it for the more animating services held in the Grove.

Not only the habitual church-goers, but the people of the parish at large, began to feel the magnetizing influence, and were drawn towards the same spot. For a week or more past, late in the afternoons on which the meetings were held, little skiffs might have been seen putting off from the opposite shore, freighted with men, women, and children, crossing over to hear the wonderful preachings of the missionary.

What attracted them thither? Not surely the love of the truth.

Most of them disliked it in their hearts, and had not even began to think of practising it in their lives. They were interested in the man. They were, in some sort, compelled by the magical power he held over them to listen to entreaties and counsels, similar to those to which they had often hitherto turned a deaf ear.

Mr. Norton spent much of the time with them, going from house to house, partaking of their rude fare, sympathizing in their joys and sorrows, occasionally lending them a helping hand in their toils, and aiding them sometimes by his ingenuity and skill as an artisan.

They found in him a hearty, genial, and unselfish friend. Hence when he appeared among them at the Grove, their personal interest in him secured a certain degree of order and decorum, and caused them to listen to him respectfully.

Even beyond this, he held a power over them by means of his natural and persuasive eloquence, enlivened by varied and graphic illustrations, drawn from objects within their ken, and by the wonderful intonations of his powerful and harmonious voice. He began his work by presenting to them the love of Christ and the winning promises of the gospel.

This was his favorite mode of reaching the heart.

On most of these occasions, Adèle went to the Grove. It varied her monotonous life. The strange, motley crowd gathered under the magnificent trees, sitting on the ground, or standing in groups beneath the tall arches made by the overlapping boughs; the level rays of the declining sun, bringing out, in broad relief, their grotesque varieties of costume; the gradual creeping on of the sobering twilight; the alternating expressions of emotions visible on the countenances of the listeners made the scene striking to her observing eye.

Another burning, dusty day had culminated. It was nearly five o'clock in the afternoon. Mr. Norton was lying upon a lounge in Mr. Brown's apartment. Both gentlemen appeared to be in a meditative mood. The silence was only interrupted by the unusual sound of an occasional sigh from the missionary.

"Why! friend Norton," at length exclaimed Mr. Brown, "have you really lost your cheerfulness at last?"

"Yes," replied Mr. Norton, slowly. "I must confess that I am wellnigh discouraged respecting the reformation of this people. Here, I have been preaching to them these weeks the gospel of love, presenting Christ to them as their friend and Saviour, holding up the truth in its most lovely and winning forms. It has apparently made no impression upon their hearts. It is true, they come in crowds to hear me, but what I say to them makes no permanent mark. They forget it the moment the echo of my voice dies upon their ears. The fact is, friend Brown, I am disappointed. I did hope the Lord would have given this people unto me. But," continued he, after a moment's pause, "what right have I to be desponding? God reigns."

"According to all accounts," replied Mr. Brown, "they must be a hard set to deal with, both mentally and morally. I should judge, from what Miss Adèle tells me of your instructions, that you have not put them upon the same rigid regimen of law and truth that you may remember you prescribed for my spiritual cure." Mr. Brown smiled. "Perhaps," he continued, "these men are not capable of appreciating the mild aspect of mercy. They do not possess the susceptibility to which you have been appealing. They need to have the terrors of the law preached to them."

"Ah! that is it, friend Brown, you have it. I am convinced it is so. I have felt it for several days past. But I do dislike, extremely, to endeavor to chain them to the truth by fear. Love is so much more noble a passion to enlist for Christ. Yet they must be drawn by some motive from their sins. Love often follows in the wake and casts out fear."

"I remember," said Mr. Brown, "to have heard Mr. N --, the famous Maine lumber-merchant, who you know is an infidel, say that the only way the lumbermen can be kept from stealing each other's logs is by preaching to them eternal punishment."

"No doubt it is true," replied the good man, "and if these souls cannot be sweetly constrained into the beautiful fields of peace, they must be compelled into them by the terrors of that death that hangs over the transgressor. Besides, I feel a strong presentiment that some great judgment is about to descend upon this people. All day, the thought has weighed upon me like an incubus. I cannot shake it off. Something terrible is in store for them. What it may be, I know not. But I am impressed with the duty of preaching a judgment to come to them this very afternoon. I will do it."

A slight rattling of dishes at the door announced the arrival of Bess, with a tray of refreshment for Mr. Brown, and, at the same moment, the tinkling of a bell below summoned Mr. Norton to the table.

Half an hour later, the missionary, with a slow pace and the air of one oppressed with a great burden, walked to the Grove. He seated himself on a rustic bench and with his head resting on the trunk of an immense elm, which overshadowed him, sat absorbed in earnest thought, while the people gathered in a crowd around him.

At length, the murmuring voices were hushed into quiet. He rose, took up his pocket Testament, read a portion of the tenth chapter of Hebrews, offered a prayer, and then sang in his trumpet tones Charles Wesley's magnificently solemn hymn, commencing—

"Lo! on a narrow neck of land
'Twixt two unbounded seas, I stand
Secure! insensible!"

He then repeated a clause in the chapter he had just read to them. "If we sin wilfully after that we have received a knowledge of the truth, there remaineth no more sacrifice for sins, but a certain fearful looking for of judgment and fiery indignation, which shall devour the adversaries."

He began his discourse by reminding the people of the truths he had presented to them during the weeks past. He had told them faithfully of their sinfulness before a holy God, and pointed out the way of safety and purification through a crucified Saviour. And he had earnestly sought to induce them, by the love this Saviour bore them, to forsake their transgressions and exercise trust in Him. He now told them, in accents broken with grief, that he had every reason to fear they had not followed his counsel, and observing their hardness of heart, he felt constrained to bring them another and different message—a message less tender, but coming from the same divine source. He then unfolded to them the wrath of the Most High, kindled against those who scorn the voice of mercy from a dying Saviour.

They listened intently. His voice, his manner, his words electrified them. His countenance was illumined with an awful light, such as they had not before witnessed there. His eye shot out prophetic meanings. At the close, he said, in a low tone, like the murmur of distant thunder, "what I have told you, is true—true, as that we stand on this solid ground—true, as that sky that bends above us. This book says it. It is, therefore, eternal truth. I have it impressed upon my mind that a judgment, a swift, tremendous judgment, is about to descend upon this people on account of their sins. I cannot shake off this impression, and, under its power, I warn you to prepare your souls to meet some dreadful calamity.

"I know not how it will come — in what shape, with what power. But I feel that death is near. It seems to me that I see many before me who will soon be beyond the bounds of time. I feel constrained to say this to you. I beg you prepare to meet your God."

When he ceased, a visible shudder ran through the multitude. They rose slowly and wended their way homeward, many with blanched faces, and even the hardiest with a vague sense of some startling event impending.

<h1 style="text-align:center">CHAPTER XIV</h1>

<h1 style="text-align:center">JOHN AND CÆSAR</h1>

At four o'clock in the afternoon on the following day Mrs. Dubois sat in the Madonna room. Her fingers were employed upon a bit of exquisite embroidery, over which she bent with a contracted brow, as if her mind was filled with anxious thought.

Adèle, robed in a French silk of delicate blue, her rich, dark hair looped up in massive braids, sat listlessly, poring over a volume of old French romance.

Suddenly rising, she threw it hastily aside, exclaiming as she went towards an open window, "O! this interminable drought! It makes me feel so miserable and restless. Does it not oppress you, *ma chère mère?*"

Mrs. Dubois started suddenly, as Adèle spoke.

"Ah! yes. It is very wearisome," she replied.

"*Ma mère*, I have disturbed you. Of what were you thinking when I spoke?"

"Thinking of the chateau de Rossillon and its inmates. It is very long since we have had news of them. I am much troubled about the dear friends. It would be like rain on the parched ground could I once more hear my uncle's voice. The good, kind old man!"

"Never fear, *ma mère*. You shall hear it. I have a plan that will soon take us all to Picardy. You smile, but do I not accomplish my little schemes? Do not ask me, please, how I shall do it. The expedition is not wholly matured."

"Not wholly matured, indeed!" said Mrs. Dubois, with an incredulous smile.

"Nevertheless, it will take place, *ma mère*. But not this week. In the meantime, I am going to invite the gentlemen, who are doubtless moping in Mr. Brown's room, as we are here, to come in and examine that curiously illuminated missal of yours. How agreeable Mr. Brown is, now that he is getting well! Don't you think so? And Mr. Norton is as good and radiant as a seraph! No doubt, they are pining with homesickness, just as you are, and will be glad of our society."

Adèle left the room, and soon returned, accompanied by the two individuals, of whom she had gone in search.

She placed Mr. Brown, who looked quite superb in his brilliantly flowered dressing-gown, in a corner of a sofa. Having examined the missal with interest for a time, he handed it to Mr. Norton, and was soon engaged in an animated conversation with Mrs. Dubois, respecting various works of ancient art they had both seen in Europe.

Adèle watched with pleasure the light kindling in her mother's eyes as she went back, in memory and thought, to other days.

Mr. Norton gazed at his friend Brown, transfigured suddenly from the despairing invalid, who had lost all interest in life, to the animated being before him, with traces indeed of languor and disease upon his person, but glowing now with life, thought, and emotion. "A precious jewel gathered for the crown of Him, who sits on the throne above," he whispered to himself.

Felicitating himself with this thought, he divided his attention between the conversation of Mrs. Dubois and Mr. Brown, and the marvels of skill, labor, and beauty traced by the old monk upon the pages before him.

"I must say, Miss Adèle, that these lines and colors are put on most ingeniously. But I cannot help thinking those ancient men might have been better employed in tracing the characters of divine truth upon the hearts of their fellow-beings."

"True," said Adèle, "had they been free to do it. But they were shut up from the world and could not. Illuminating missals was far better than to pass their lives in perfect idleness and inanition."

"Don't you think, my dear," said the missionary, who had wisely never before questioned any member of the family on the points of religious faith, "that the cloister life was a strange one to live, for men who professed to have the love of God in their hearts, with a whole world lying in sin around them, for a field to labor in?"

"Yes, I do, and I think too many other things are wrong about the

Roman Church, but it pains my mother to hear me speak of them," said Adèle, in a low tone, glancing at her mother.

"Is it so?" exclaimed the good man. His face lighted up with a secret satisfaction. But he fixed his eyes upon the book and was silent.

Just then, someone knocked on the parlor door. Adèle opened it and beheld Mrs. McNab—her broad figure adorned with the brilliant chintz dress and yellow bandanna handkerchief, filling up the entire doorway, and her face surrounded by the wide, full frill, its usual framework, expressing a curious mixture of shyness and audacity.

It was her first call at the house since Adèle's summary process of ejection had been served upon her, and it was not until that young lady had welcomed her cordially and invited her to come in that she ventured beyond the threshold. She then came forward, made a low courtesy, and seating herself near the door, remarked that Bess was not below, and hearing voices in the picture parlor, wishing to hear from the patient, she had ventured up.

"An' how do ye find yersel' Mr. Brown?" said she, turning to that gentleman. "But I needna ask the question, sin' yer looks tell ye're amaist weel."

Mr. Brown assented to her remark upon his health, and expressed to her his obligations for her attentions to him during his illness.

"Them's naethin," she replied with a conscious air of benevolence. "'Tis the buzziness o' my life to tak' care o' sick bodies."

"How are Mrs. Campbell's children?" inquired Mrs. Dubois.

"All got weel, but Katy. She's mizerble eneugh."

"Has she not recovered from the measles, Mrs. McNab?"

"The measles are gone, but sunthin' has settled on her lights. She coughs like a woodchuck. An' I must be a goin', for I tole Mrs. Cawmell I wadna stay a bit, but wad come back, immediate."

As she rose to go, she caught a sight of several objects on the lawn below that rooted her to the spot.

"Why ther's Mummychog," she exclaimed, "leading a gran' black charger wi' a tall brave youth a walkin' by his side. Wha can he be?"

At that moment a low, clear laugh rang out upon the air, reaching the ears of the little company assembled in the parlor.

At the sound, Mr. Brown's pale face changed to a perfectly ashen hue, then flushed to a deep crimson. He started to his feet, and exclaimed, "John Lansdowne! brave fellow!"

It was even so. John and Cæsar had reached their destination.

CHAPTER XV

Travelling in New Brunswick

The following morning, Mr. Norton, Mr. Somers, alias Mr. Brown, and John Lansdowne were sitting together, talking of the route from -- to Miramichi.

"You must have had a tedious journey, Mr. Lansdowne," observed the missionary.

"By no means, sir. Never had a more glorious time in my life. The reach through the forest was magnificent. By the way, Ned, I shot a wolf. I'll tell you how it was, sometime. But how soon shall you feel able to start for home?"

"In two or three weeks, Dr. Wright says," replied Mr. Somers.

"You must not take the road again, young gentleman," remarked Mr. Norton, "until we have had a fall of rain. The country is scorched with heat beyond anything I ever knew. Fine scenery on the St. John River, Mr. Lansdowne."

"Wonderfully fine and varied! Like the unfolding of a splendid panorama! In fact, it nearly consoled me for the sleepless nights and horribly cooked dinners."

"Ah! well——. I've had some experience while passing up and down in these parts. In some localities, the country is pretty well populated," said Mr. Norton with a broad smile.

"I can certify to that geographical fact," said John, laughing. "One night, after retiring, I found that a large and active family of mice had taken previous shares in the straw cot furnished me. A stirring time they had, I assure you. The following night, I was roused up from a ten horse-power slumber by a little million of enterprising insects — well — their style of locomotion, though irregular, accomplishes remarkable results. By the way, I doubt that story of a pair of fleas, harnessed into a tiny chariot and broken into a trot."

"So do I," said Mr. Norton. "'Tis a libel on them. They couldn't go such a humdrum gait."

"That reminds me," said Mr. Somers, "of a very curious and original painting I saw in England. It represented the ghost of a flea."

"Ridiculous!" exclaimed John. "You are romancing, Ned."

"I am stating a fact. It was painted by that eccentric genius, Blake, upon a panel, and exhibited to me by an acquaintance, who was a friend of the artist."

"What was it like?" said John.

"It was a naked figure with a strong body and a short neck with burning eyes longing for moisture, and a face worthy of a murderer, holding a bloody cup in its clawed hands, out of which it seemed eager to drink. The shape was strange enough and the coloring splendid—a kind of glistening green and dusky gold—beautifully varnished. It was in fact the spiritualization of a flea."

"What a conception!" exclaimed Mr. Norton. "The artist's imagination must have been stimulated by intense personal sufferings from said insect. The savage little wretch. How did you manage the diet, Mr. Lansdowne?" continued the missionary, a smile twinkling all over his face.

"Ah! yes, the *table [d'hôte]*. I found eggs and potatoes safe, and devoted myself to them; I was always sure to get snagged when I tried anything else."

"Verily, there is room for improvement in the mode of living among His Majesty's loyal subjects of this [province]. I should say, that in most respects, they are about half a century behind the age," said Mr. Norton.

"How did you ascertain I was here, John?" inquired Mr. Somers.

"I learned at Fredericton that you had left with Mr. Dubois, and I obtained directions there for my route. Really," added John, "you are fortunate to have found such an establishment as this to be laid up in."

"Yes. God be thanked for the attention and care received in this house and for the kindness of this good friend," said Mr. Somers, laying his hand affectionately on the missionary's arm.

"But this Mummychog," said John, breaking into a clear, musical laugh, "that I came across last night. He is a curiosity. That, of course, isn't his real name. What is it?"

"He goes by no other name here," replied Mr. Norton.

"I met him," said John, "a few rods from here, and asked him if he could inform me where Mr. Dubois lived. 'Well, s'pose I ken,' he said. After waiting a few minutes for some direction, and none forthcoming, I asked, 'will you have the goodness to show me the house, sir?' 'S'pose you hev particiler business there,' he inquired. 'Yes. I have, sir.' 'Well! I s'pose ye are goin' fur to see *hur?*'

"'Hur!'" I exclaimed, my mind immediately reverting to the worthy ancient, who assisted Aaron in holding up the hands of Moses on a certain occasion, mentioned in the old Testament. 'Hur! who is Hur? I am in pursuit of a gentleman — a friend of mine. I know no other person here.' 'O well! come then; I'll show ye.' As he was walking along by Cæsar's side, I heard him say, apparently to himself, 'He's a gone 'un, anyway.'"

"He is a queer specimen," said Mr. Norton. "And now I think of it, Mr. Somers, Micah told me this morning that a good horse will be brought into the settlement, by a friend of his, in about a week. He thinks, if you like the animal, he can make a bargain and get it for you."

"Thank you for your trouble about it, my dear sir," replied Mr. Somers.

"Two weeks then, Ned," said John, "before the [doctor] will let you start. That will give me ample opportunity to explore the length of the Miramichi River. What are the fishing privileges in this region?"

"Fine — remarkably good!" said the missionary.

In the course of a few minutes, John, with the assistance of Mr. Norton, arranged a plan for a fishing and hunting excursion, upon which, if Micah's services could be obtained, he was to start the next day.

After inquiring for the most feasible way of transmitting a letter, he retired to relieve the anxiety of his parents by informing them of the success of his journey. As might have been expected after a somewhat detailed account of his travels, the remainder of his epistle home was filled with the effervescence of his excitement at having found Mr. Somers, and thus triumphantly accomplished the object of his expedition.

Beneath the flash and foam of John's youthful spirit there were depths of hidden tenderness and truth. He was warmly attached to his uncle. The difference in age between them was not great, and even that was considerably diminished by the peculiar traits of each. John possessed the hardier features of character. He had developed a strong, determined will and other granite qualities, which promised to make him a tower of defence to those that might shelter themselves beneath his wing. These traits, contrasting with his own, Mr. Somers appreciated and admired. They imparted to him a strengthening influence. John, on the other hand, was charmed with the genial disposition, the mobile and brilliant intellect of his uncle, and the ready sympathy he extended him in his pursuits. In short, they were drawn together in that peculiar, but not uncommon bond of friendship symbolized by the old intimacy of the ivy and the oak.

CHAPTER XVI

THE FLOWER UNFOLDING

There is nothing in human life more lovely than the transition of a young girl from childhood into womanhood. It suggests the springtime of the year when the leaf buds are partly opened and the tender blossoms wave in the genial sunshine; when the colors so airy and delicate are set and the ethereal odors are wafted gently to the senses; when earth and air are filled with sweet prophecies of the ripened splendor of summer. It is like the moments of early morn when the newly risen sun throws abroad his light, giving token of the majestic glories of noon-day, while the earth exhales a dewy freshness and the air is enchanted by the songs of birds, just wakened from their nests. It recalls the overture of a grand musical drama introducing the joyous melodies, the wailing minors, the noble chords and sublime symphonies of the glorious harmony.

The development of the maiden is like the opening of some lovely flower-bud. As life unfolds, the tender smile and blush of childhood mingle with the grace of maidenly repose; the upturned, radiant eye gathers new depths of thought and emotion; the delicate features, the wavy, pliant form, begin to reveal their wealth of grace and beauty.

Sometimes, the overstimulated bud is forced into intense and unnatural life and bloom. Sometimes, the development is slow and almost imperceptible. Fed gently by the light and dews of heaven, the flower, at length, circles forth in perfected beauty. Here, the airy grace and playfulness of a Rosalind, or the purity and goodness of a Desdemona is developed; there, the intense, passionate nature of a Juliet, or the rich intellect and lofty elegance of a Portia.

But, how brief is that bright period of transition! Scarcely can the artist catch the beautiful creation and transfer it to the canvas ere it has changed, or faded.

> "How small a part of time they share,
> That are so wondrous sweet and fair!"

Adèle Dubois had just reached this period of life. Her form was ripening into a noble and statuesque symmetry; the light in her eyes shot forth from darkening depths; a faint bloom was creeping into her cheek; a soft smile was wreathing those lips, wrought by nature, into a somewhat haughty curve; the frank, careless, yet imperious manner was chastening into a calmer grace; a transforming glory shone around her, making her one of those visions that sometimes waylay and haunt a man's life forever.

Her physical and intellectual growth were symmetrical. Her mind was quick, penetrative, and in constant exercise. Truthful and upright, her soul shone through her form and features as a clear flame, placed within a transparent vase, brings out the adornments of flower, leaf, and gem, with which it is enriched.

In a brown stone house, in the city of P --, State of --, there hangs in one of the chambers a picture of Adèle, representing her as she was at this period of her life. It is full of beauty and elegance. Sun-painting was an art unknown in the days when it was executed. But the modern photographist could hardly have produced a picture so exquisitely truthful as well as lovely.

CHAPTER XVII

THE DEER HUNT

Early in the morning, John Lansdowne, having donned his hunting suit and taken a hasty breakfast, seized his rifle and joined Micah, already waiting for him on the lawn in front of the house.

He was equipped in a tunic-like shirt of dressed buckskin with leggings and moccasins of the same material, each curiously embroidered and fringed. The suit was a present from his mother—procured by her from Canada. His head was surmounted by a blue military cap and his belt adorned with powder pouch and hunting-knife. Micah, with a heavy blanket coat of a dingy, brown color, leggings of embroidered buckskin, skull cap of gray fox skin, and Indian moccasins, wore at his belt a butcher knife in a scabbard, a tomahawk, otter-skin pouch, containing bullets and other necessaries for such an expedition.

In the dim morning light they walked briskly to a little cove in the river, where Micah's birchen canoe lay, and found it already stored with supplies for the excursion. There were bags of provisions, cooking utensils, a small tent, neatly folded, Micah's old Dutch rifle, fishing tackle, and other articles of minor account.

"Ever traviled much in a canoo?" inquired Micah.

"None at all," replied John.

"Well, then I'll jest mention, yeou needn't jump into it, like a catameount rampagin' arter fodder. Yeou step in kinder keerful and set deown and don't move reound more'n ye ken help. It's a mighty crank little critter, I tell ye. 'Twould be tolable unconvenient to upset and git eour cargo turned into the stream."

"It would indeed!" said John. "I'll obey orders, Mummychog."

John entered the canoe with tact, apparently to Micah's satisfaction, and soon they were gliding down the river, now, owing to the long-continued drought, considerably shrunk within its banks.

Just as night gave its parting salute to the advancing day, the voyagers passed into a region densely wooded down to the water's edge. Oaks, elms, and maples, birches of different sorts, willows and cranberry, grew in wild luxuriance along the margin, tinged with the rich hues of autumn. A thousand spicy odors exhaled from the frostbitten plants and shrubs, filling the senses with an intoxicating incense. When the rising sun shot its level rays through the trees, the clear stream quivered with golden arrows.

John viewed the scenes through which they glided with eager eye.

Micah's countenance expressed intense satisfaction. He sat bolt upright in the stern of the canoe, steering with his paddle, his keen bullet eyes dancing from side to side examining every object as they passed along. Both were silent.

At length, Micah exclaimed, "Well, Captin', this is the pootiest way of livin' I know on, any heow. My 'pinion is that human natur was meant to live reound on rivers and in the woods, or vyagin' on lakes, and sech. I never breathe jest nateral and lively till I git eout o' between heouse walls into the free air."

"'Tis a glorious life, Micah! I agree to it."

"Hark!" said Micah! "Got yer piece ready? Maybe you'll hev' a chance to bring sumthin' deown. I heerd an old squaw holler jest neow."

"I'm ready," said John. "But I didn't hear any sound. What was it like?"

"O! kinder a scoldin' seound. Cawcawee! cawcawee! Don't yer hear the critter reelin' of it off? Ha! 'tis dyin' away, though. We shall hear it agin, by and by."

"An old squaw," said John, as the excitement the prospect of a shot had raised in his mind subsided. "Do you have such game as *that* in Miramichi? I've heard of witches flying on broomsticks through the air, but didn't know before that squaws are in the habit of skylarking about in that way."

"Well, ye'll know it by observation before long," said Micah, with a slight twitch of one eye. "Them's ducks from Canada, a goin' south'ard, as they allers do in the fall o' the year. They keep up that ere scoldin' seound, day and night. Cawcawee! cawcawee! kind of an aggravatin' holler! But I like it, ruther. It allers 'minds me of a bustin' good feller that was deown here from Canada once."

"How remind you of him?" inquired John.

"Well, he cam' deown on bissiniss, but he ran [afoul] o' me, and we was eout in the woods together, consid'able. He used to set eoutside the camp, bright, starlight nights, and sing songs, and sech. He had a powerful, sweet v'ice, and it allers 'peared to me as ef every kind of a livin' thing hushed up and listened when he sung o' nights. He could reel off most anything you can think on. There was one kind of a mournful ditty he sung, and once in a while he brung in a chorus — cawcawee! cawcawee — jest like what them ducks say, only, the way he made it seound, was soft and meller and doleful-like. I liked to hear him sing that, only he was so solemn arter it, and would set and fetch up great long sythes. And once I asked him what made him so sober and take on so, arter singin' it. He said, Micah, my good lad, when I war a young man, I had a little French wife that could run like a hind and sing like a wild bird. Well, she died. The very last thing she sung was that 'ere song. When I see how he felt, I never asked him another question. He sot and sythed a spell and then got up, took a most oncommon swig of old Jamaky and turned into his blanket."

Just as Micah ended this account, John caught sight of a large bird at a distance directly ahead of them, and his attention became entirely absorbed. It took flight from a partly decayed tree on the northern bank, and commenced wheeling around, above the water. The canoe was rapidly nearing this promising game.

Micah said not a word, but observed, in an apparently careless mood, the movements of his young companion.

Suddenly, the bird poised himself for an instant in the air, then closed his wings and shot downward. A whizzing sound! then a plash, and he disappeared beneath the surface, throwing up the water into sparkling foam-wreaths. He was absent but a moment, and then bore upward into the air a large fish.

John's shot took him on the wing, and he dropped dead, his claws yet grasping the fish, on the water's edge.

"Ruther harnsum than otherwise!" exclaimed Micah. "You've got your dinner, Captin'."

And he put the canoe rapidly towards the river-bank to pick up the game.

They found it to be a large fish-hawk, with a good-sized salmon in its fierce embrace. It was a noble specimen of the bird, tinted with brown, ashy white, and blue, with eyes of deep orange color.

"Well, that are a prize," said Micah. "Them birds ain't common in these parts, bein' as they mostly live on sea-coasts. But this un was on his way seouth, and his journey has ended quite unexpected."

Saying which, he threw both bird and fish into the canoe, and darted forward on the river again.

"When shall we reach the deer feeding-ground you spoke of, Micah?"

"O! not afore night," said Micah. "And then we mustn't go anyst it till mornin'."

"I suppose you have brought down some scores of deer in your hunting raids, Micah?"

"Why, yes — takin' it by and large, I've handled over consid'able many of 'em. 'Tis a critter I hate to kill, Captin', though I s'pose it seounds soft to say so. Ef 't wan't for thinkin' they'll git picked off, anyway, I dunno but I should let 'em alone altogether."

"Why do you dislike to kill them?"

"Well, to begin with, they're a harnsum critter. They hev sech graceful ways with 'em, kinder grand ones tew, specially them bucks, with their crests reared up agin the sky, lookin' so bold and free like. And them bright little does — sometimes they hev sech a skeerd, tender look in their eyes — and I've seen the tears roll out on 'em when they lay wounded and disabled like, jest like a human critter. It allers makes me feel kind o' puggetty to see that."

They made a noon halt, in the shadows cast by a clump of silver birches, and did ample justice to the provision supplied from the pantry of the Dubois house.

At four o'clock they proceeded onward towards the deer hunt. John listened with unwearied interest to Micah's stories of peril and hair-breadth 'scapes, by flood, field, and forest, gathering many valuable hints in the science of woodcraft from the practised hunter.

Just at dark, they reached a broad part of the stream and selected their camping-ground.

The tent was soon pitched, a fire of brushwood kindled and the salmon broiled to a relish that an epicure could not have cavilled at. The table, a flat rock, was also garnished with white French rolls, sliced ham, brown bread, blocks of savory cheese, and tea, smoking hot.

The sylvan scene—the moon shedding its light around, the low music of the gently rippling waves, the spicy odor of the burning cedar, the snow-white clouds and deep blue of the sky mirrored in the stream, made it a place fit at least for rural divinities. Pan might have looked in—ah! he is dead—his ghost then might have looked in upon them from behind some old gnarled tree, with a frown of envy at this intrusion upon his ancient domain.

On the following morning, at the first faint glimmering of light, Micah was alert. He shook our young hero's shoulder and woke him from a pleasant dream.

"Neow's the time, Captin'," said Micah, speaking in a cautious undertone, "neow's the time, ef we do it at all, to nab them deer. While your gittin' rigged and takin' a cold bite, I'll tell ye the lay o' things. Ye see, don't ye, that pint o' land ahead on us, a juttin' out into the stream? Well, we've got to put the canoe on the water right away, hustle in the things, and percede just as whist and keerful as we ken, to that pint. Jest beyend that, I expect the animils, when day's fairly up, will come to drink. And there's where we'll get a shot at 'em."

"But what makes you expect they'll come to drink at that particular place, Micah?"

"You see that pooty steep hill that slopes up jest back o' the pint o' land, don't ye? Well, behind that hill, which is steeper 'n it looks to be, there's a largish, level piece of greound that's been burnt over within a few years, and it's grown up to tall grass and got a number o' clumps of young trees on it, and it's 'bout surreounded by a lot o' master rocky hills. That's the feedin' greound. There's a deep gorge cut right inter that hill, back 'o the pint. The gorge has a pooty smooth rocky bed. In the spring o' the year there's a brook runs through there and pours inter the river jest below. But it's all dry neow, and the deer, as a gen'al thing, scramble eout of their feedin' place into this gorge and foller it deown to the river to git their drink. It brings 'em eout jest below the pint. We have got neow to cross over to the pint, huggin' the bank, so the critters shan't see us, and take a shot from there. Git yer piece ready, Captin. Ef there's tew, or more, I'll hev the fust shot and you the second. Don't speak, arter we git on to the pint, the leastest word."

"I understand," said John, as he examined his rifle to see that all was right.

"Now for it," said Micah, as having finished their arrangements, they entered the canoe.

Silently, they paddled along, sheltered from observation by the little wooded promontory and following as nearly as possible the crankling river as it indented into the land. In a few minutes, they landed and proceeded noiselessly to get a view of the bank below.

After a moment's reconnoitre, John turned his face towards Micah with a look of blank disappointment.

But Micah looked cool and expectant. He merely pointed up the rocky gorge and said under his breath—

"'T aint time to expect 'em yet. The wind, what there is on it, is favorable tew—it blows right in our faces and can't kerry any smell of us to 'em. Neow hide yourself right away. Keep near me, Captin', so that we ken make motions to each other."

In a few moments they had secured their ambuscade, each lying on the ground at full length, concealed by low, scrubby trees. By a slight turn of the head, each could command a view up the gorge for a considerable distance.

Just as the sun began to show his broad, red disc in the east, new light shot forth from the eyes of the hunters as they perceived a small herd coming down the rocky pathway. The creatures bounded along with a wild and graceful freedom until they reached the debouche of the pass into the valley. There they paused—scanned the scene with eager eyes and snuffed the morning breeze. The wind brought no tale of their enemies, close at hand, and they bounded on fearlessly to the river's brink.

It was apparently a family party, a noble buck leading the group, followed by a doe and two young hinds. They soon had their noses in the stream. The buck took large draughts and then raising his haughty front, tossed his antlers, as if in defiance, in the face of the god of day.

Micah's eye was at his rifle. A crack and a whizz in the air. The noble creature gave one mighty bound and fell dead. The ball had entered his broad forehead and penetrated to the brain.

At the report of the rifle, the doe, who was still drinking, gave a bound in the air, scattering the spray from her dripping mouth, wheeled with the rapidity of lightning, and sprang towards the gorge. But John's instantaneous shot sped through the air and the animal fell dead from her second bound, the ball having entered the heart. In the midst of their triumph, John and Micah watched with relenting eyes the two hinds, while they took, as on the wings of the wind, their forlorn flight up the fatal pathway.

Having slung their booty on the boughs of a wide-branching tree, and taken some refreshment from the supplies in the canoe, Micah declared himself good for a scramble up the hill to the feeding-ground, a proposition John readily accepted.

Over rock, bush and brier, uphill and down, for five hours, they pursued their way with unmitigated zeal and energy. They scaled the hill, cut by the gorge — approaching, cautiously, its brow, overlooking the deer haunt. But they could perceive no trace of the herd.

"It's abeout as I expected," said Micah, "them two little hinds we skeered gin the alarm to the rest on 'em and they've all skulked off to some covit or ruther. S'pose Captin', we jest make a surkit reound through the rest of these hills, maybe we'll light on 'em agin."

"Agreed," responded John.

They skirted the enclosure, but without a chance for another shot. As, about noon, they were rapidly descending the gorge on their way back to the promontory, the scene of their morning success, Micah proposed that they should have "a nice brile out of that fat buck at the pint, and then put for the settlement."

"Not yet," said John. "Why, we are just getting into this glorious life. What's your hurry, Mummychog?"

"Well, ye see," said Micah, "I can't be gone from hum no longer neow, any heow. Next week, I'll try it with ye agin, if ye say so."

John acceded reluctantly to the arrangement, though his disappointment was somewhat mitigated by the prospect of another similar excursion.

The meal prepared by Micah, for their closing repast, considering the circumstances, might have been pronounced as achieved in the highest style of art. Under a bright sky, shadowed by soft, quivering birch-trees, scattering broken lights all over their rustic table, never surely was a dinner eaten with greater gusto.

Life in the forest! ended all too soon. But thy memories live. Memories redolent of youth, health, strength, freedom, and beauty, come through the long years, laden with dews, sunshine, and fragrance, and scatter over the time-worn spirit refreshment and delight.

As our voyagers were paddling up stream in the afternoon, in answer to questions put by John to Micah, respecting the Dubois family, he remarked—

"Them Doobyce's came to the kentry, jest ten year before I did. Well, I've heerd say, the [squire] came fust. He didn't set himself up for anything great at all, but explored reound the region a spell, and was kinder pleasant to most anybody he came across. Somehow, or 'nuther, he had a kind of a kingly turn with him that seemed jest as nateral as did to breathe, and ye could see that he warn't no ways used to sech a wildcat sort of a place as Miramichi was then."

"I wonder that he remained here," said John.

"Well, the pesky critters reound here ruther took to him, and he bought a great lot o' land and got workmen and built a house, and fetched his wife and baby here. So they've lived here ever since. But they're no more like the rest o' the people in these parts than I'm like you, and it has allers been a mystery to me why they should stay. But I s'pose they know their own bissiniss best. They're allers givin' to the poor, and they try to make the settlers more decent every way, but 'taint been o' much use."

After a long, meditative pause, Micah said, "Neow Captin', I want yeou to answer me one question, honestly. I aint a goin' to ask any thing sarcy. Did ye ever in yer life see a harnsumer, witchiner critter than Miss Adèle is?"

Micah fixed his keen eye triumphantly upon our hero, as if he was aware beforehand that but one response could be made. John, surprised by the suddenness of the question, and somewhat confused, for the moment, by a vague consciousness that his companion had found the key to his thoughts, hesitated a little, but soon recovered sufficiently to parry the stroke.

"You don't mean to say, Micah, that there's any person for beauty and bewitchingness to be compared with Mrs. McNab?"

"Whew-ew," uttered Micah, while every line and feature in his countenance expressed ineffable scorn. He gave several extra strokes of the paddle with great energy. Suddenly, his grim features broke into a genial smile.

"Well, Captin'," he said, "ef yeou choose to play 'possum that way, ye ken. But ye needn't expect *me* to believe in them tricks, cos I'm an old 'un."

John laughed and replied, "Mummychog, Miss Adèle Dubois is a perfect beauty. I can't deny it."

"And a parfeck angel tew," said Micah.

"I don't doubt it," said John, energetically. "When shall we reach the settlement, Micah?"

"Abeout three hours arter moonrise."

And just at that time our voyagers touched the spot they had started from the day before, and unloaded their cargo. They were received at the Dubois house with the compliments due to successful hunters.

CHAPTER XVIII

THE PERSECUTION

On the following afternoon, Mr. Norton preached to a larger and far more attentive audience than usual. The solemn warnings he had uttered and the fearful presentiments of coming evil he had expressed on the last occasion of assembling at the Grove had been communicated from mouth to mouth. Curiosity, and perhaps some more elevated motive, had drawn a numerous crowd of people together to hear him.

He spoke to them plainly of their sinful conduct, particularizing the vices of intemperance, profanity, gambling, and Sabbath-breaking, to which many of them were addicted. He earnestly besought them to turn from these evil ways and accept pardon for their past transgressions and mercy through Christ. He showed them the consequences of their refusal to listen to the teachings and counsels of the book of God, and, at last, depicted to them, with great vividness, the awful glories and terrors of the day of final account,

> "When the Judge shall come in splendor,
> Strict to mark and just to render."

As his mind dilated with the awful grandeur of the theme, his thoughts kindled to a white heat, and he flung off words that seemed to scorch and burn even the callous souls of those time-hardened transgressors. He poured upon their ears, in tones of trumpet power and [fullness], echoed from the hills around, the stern threatenings of injured justice; he besought them, in low, sweet, thrilling accents, to yield themselves heart and life to the Great Judge, who will preside in the day of impartial accounts, and thus avert his wrath and be happy forever.

At the close, he threw himself for a few moments upon the rustic bench appropriated to him, covered his face with his hands and seemed in silent prayer. The people involuntarily bent their heads in sympathy and remained motionless. Then he rose and gave them the evening benediction.

Mr. Somers, his nephew, and Adèle had been sitting under the shade of an odorous balm poplar, on the skirt of the crowd, at first watching its movements, and then drawn away from these observations by the impressive discourse of Mr. Norton.

"What a clear, melodious voice he has!" said John in an undertone to Adèle, as the missionary finished the opening service.

"Wait until you hear its trumpet tones, Mr. Lansdowne. Those will come, by and by. They are magnificent. Please listen." And Adèle placed a finger upon her lips, in token of silence.

John listened, at first, in obedience to her request, but he soon became enchained by the speaker.

After the discourse was concluded, the trio remained sitting as if spellbound, quite unobservant of the crowd, slowly dispersing around them.

"What would that man have been, Ned," at length exclaimed John, "had he received the culture which such munificent gifts demand? Why, he would have been the orator of our nation."

"Ay, John," replied Mr. Somers, "but it is the solemn truth of his theme that gives him half his power."

"It is as if I had heard the *Dies iræ* chanted," said Adèle.

As they walked on towards the house in silence they encountered a company of persons, of which Mr. Dubois and the missionary were the centre. These two were conversing quite composedly, but the surrounding groups seemed to be under some excitement.

At the dispersion of the gathering at the Grove, as Mr. Norton was on his way to the quiet of his own room, Mr. Dubois had presented to him the bearer of a dispatch from Fredericton. The messenger said he had been instructed to announce that the Provincial Court was in session in that city, and that a complaint had been lodged with the grand jury against Mr. Norton, and he was requested to meet the charge immediately.

Mr. Norton was surprised, but said very calmly—

"Can you inform me, sir, what the charge is!"

"It is a charge for having preached in the Province of Brunswick without a license."

"Can you tell me by whom the charge was brought?"

"By the reverend Francis Dinsmoor, a clergyman of the Established Church, of the Parish of --."

"Yes, sir. I understand. He is your neighbor on the other side of the river, Mr. Dubois. Well, sir," continued Mr. Norton, "I suppose you have just arrived and stand in need of refreshment. I will confer with you, by and by."

The messenger retraced his steps towards the house.

In the meantime, a few rough-looking men had overheard the conversation, taken in its import, and now came about Mr. Dubois and Mr. Norton, making inquiries.

Tom Hunkins, more noted for profanity, hard drinking, and gambling than any man in the settlement, and whom Mr. Norton at the risk of making him a violent enemy, had on one occasion severely reprehended for the pernicious influence he exerted in the community—here interposed a word of counsel. He was just speaking, when Adèle, Mr. Somers, and John, joined the group.

"Neow ef I may be so bold," said Tom, "I wouldn't go anyst the cussed court. It's nothin' at all, but the meanness and envy o' that rowdy priest over the river there. He's jest mad, cos the people come over here to git fodder instid o' goin' to his empty corncrib. They like to hear yer talk better than they do him, and that's the hull on it. I'd let the condemed critter and court whizz, both on 'em. I would't go aynst 'em."

"But Mr. Hunkins," said Mr. Norton, "I must attend to this matter. I am exposed to a fine of fifty pounds and six months' imprisonment for breaking a law enacted by the Assembly of His Majesty's Province."

"I'll tell ye what ye can do, parson. I'll take and put ye right through to Chartham this very night, and ye ken take a schooner that I know is going to sail tomorrow for Eastport. That 'ill land ye safe in the State of Maine, where ye ken stay till the Court is over, and the fox has gone back to his hole, and then we'll give ye a lift back agin and ye ken go on with yer preachin'."

"I thank you for your kind feeling towards me, Mr. Hunkins, but I must go to Fredericton. The case is just this. I knew, before I came to Miramichi, that the government was not particularly favorable to dissenting ministers, and also that the Assembly had passed this law. But I had heard of the condition of this people and felt constrained to come here by my desire to serve Christ, my Master and my King. By so doing, I took all the risks in the case. Now, if I, for conscience's sake, have violated an unjust law, I am willing to pay the penalty. I have not wittingly done harm to any of His Majesty's subjects, or endeavored to draw them away from their loyalty. I will therefore go with the messenger to Fredericton and meet this charge. I am not afraid of what evil-minded men can do unto me."

"That is right, Mr. Norton," exclaimed Adèle, who had been listening attentively to his words. "Will you not go with him, father?"

After a moment's meditation, Mr. Dubois replied, "If it is Mr. Norton's wish. I have a friend who is a member of the Assembly. A favorable statement of the case from him would doubtless have much weight with the jury."

"Thank you, sir, thank you. Such an arrangement would doubtless be of great service to me. I should be exceedingly grateful for it."

Micah, who had been hitherto a quiet listener to the colloquy, now gave a short, violent cough, and said, "Captin', it's kinder queer I should happen to hev an arrand reound to Fredericton tomorrow. But I've jest thought that as long as I'm a goin' to be in the place, I might as well step in afore the jury and say what I know abeout the case."

"Thank you, Micah. I believe you have been present whenever I have discoursed to our friends, and know precisely what I have said to them."

"Well, I guess I dew, pooty nigh."

The affair being thus arranged, the party separated.

Mr. Norton informed the messenger of his intention, early in the morning, to depart with him for Fredericton.

He then retired to his room, spent an hour in reflecting upon the course he had adopted, examined faithfully the motives that influenced him, and finally came to the conclusion that he was in the right path. He firmly believed God had sent him to Miramichi to preach the gospel, and resolved that he would not be driven from thence by any power of men or evil spirits. He then committed himself to the care of the Almighty Being, and slept securely under the wing of [His] love.

In the meantime, there was a high breeze of excitement blowing through the settlement, the people taking up the matter and making common cause with Mr. Norton. He seemed to have fairly won their good will, although he had not yet induced them, except in a few instances, to reform their habits of life. They ventilated their indignation against the unfortunate clergyman of the Parish of -- in no measured terms.

There was, however, one exception to the kind feeling manifested by the settlers, towards the missionary at this time, in the person of Mrs. McNab. She informed Mrs. Campbell, as they were discussing the matter before retiring for the night, that it was just what she had expected.

"Na gude comes o' sech hurry-flurry kind o' doctrenes as that man preaches. I dinna believe pussons can be carried into the kingdom o' heaven on a wharlwind, as he'd have us to think."

"Well," said Mrs. Campbell, who had been much impressed with Mr. Norton's teachings, "I don't think there's much likelihood of many folks round here [bein'] kerried that way, or any other, into the kingdom. And I shall always bless that man for his kindness to the children when they were so sick, and for the consoling way in which he talked to me at that time."

"His doctrenes are every way delytarious, and you'll find that's the end on't," said Mrs. McNab.

To this dogmatic remark Mrs. Campbell made no reply.

Sitting in the Madonna room that evening, John remarked to Mr. Somers, "I have a growing admiration for your missionary. Did you notice what he said in reply to the man who counselled him to fly into Maine and so evade the charge brought against him? Small things sometimes suggest great ones. I was reminded of what Luther said, when cited before the diet of Worms, and when his friends advised him not to go. 'I am lawfully called to appear in that city, and thither I will go, in the name of the Lord, though as many devils as tiles upon the houses were assembled against me.'"

"Ay, John. There are materials in the character of that man for the making of another Luther. Truth, courage, power—he has them all."

CHAPTER XIX

THE LIEUTENANT-GOVERNOR

The next morning at an early hour, Mr. Dubois and Mr. Norton, accompanied by the bearer of the [dispatch], started for Fredericton. They were joined by Micah, whose alleged urgent business in that city proved to be nothing more nor less than to lend his aid towards getting the missionary out of what he called "a bad fix!"

Proceeding up the Miramichi River a short distance, they came to the portage, where travelling through the wilderness twenty miles to the Nashwauk they passed down that stream to its junction with the St. [John] River, opposite Fredericton.

After throwing off the dust of travel and resting somewhat from their fatigue, the two gentlemen first named went to call on Col. Allen, the friend of whom Mr. Dubois had spoken, who was a resident of the Capital.

He was a man of wealth and consideration in the province. Having listened attentively to the statement made by Mr. Dubois respecting the arrest of Mr. Norton, he promised to do all in his power to secure for him a fair trial.

Although a high churchman in principle and feeling, he was yet candid and upright in his judgments, and happened, moreover, to be well acquainted with the character of the clergyman of the Parish of --, who had brought the charge against Mr. Norton. He made a few inquiries respecting the evidence the missionary could produce of good character in his native State.

"It will be well," he remarked, "to call on his Excellency, the Governor, and put him in possession of these facts. It is possible the case may take some shape in which his action may be called for. It will do no harm for him to have a knowledge of the circumstances from yourselves, gentlemen. Will you accompany me to the

115

Government House?"

The Government House, a large building of stone, is situated near the northern entrance to the city. With its extensive wings, beautiful grounds and military appointments, it presents an imposing appearance. In the rear of the mansion, a fine park slopes down to the bank of the river, of which it commands frequent and enchanting views.

The three gentlemen alighted at the entrance to the grounds, opening from the broad street, and after passing the sentry were conducted by a page to the Governor's office. His Excellency shortly appeared and gave them a courteous welcome. In brief terms Col. Allen presented to him the case.

The Governor remarked in reply that the law prohibiting persons from publicly preaching, or teaching, without a license, had been passed many years ago in consequence of disturbances made by a set of fanatics, who promulgated among the lower classes certain extravagant dogmas by which they were led on even to commit murder, thinking they were doing [God's] service. The purpose of the law, he said, having been thus generally understood, few, if any clergymen, belonging either to the Established Church or to Dissenting congregations, had applied for a license, and this was the first complaint to his knowledge, that had been entered, alleging a violation of the law. He said, also, that from the statement Col. Allen had made, he apprehended no danger to Mr. Norton, as he thought the charge brought against him could not be maintained.

"I advise you, sir," said he, turning to the missionary, "to go to the Secretary's office and take the oath of allegiance to the government. Mr. Dubois states you are exerting a good influence at Miramichi. I will see that you receive no further annoyance."

"I thank your Honor," Mr. Norton replied, "for your kind assurances, and I declare to you, sir, that I have the most friendly feelings towards His Majesty's subjects and government, as I have given some proof in coming to labor at Miramichi. But, sir, I cannot conscientiously take an oath of allegiance to your government when my love and duty are pledged to another. I earnestly hope that the present amicable relations may ever continue to exist between the two powers, but, sir, *should* any conflict arise between them, the impropriety of my having taken such an oath would become too evident."

"You are right. You are right, my good sir," replied the Governor. "I promise you that as long as you continue your work in the rational mode you have already pursued, making no effort to excite treasonable feelings towards His Majesty's government, you shall not be interfered with."

His Excellency then made numerous inquiries of Mr. Dubois and Mr. Norton, respecting the condition of society, business, means of education and religious worship in the Miramichi country. He already knew Mr. Dubois by reputation, and was gratified to have this opportunity of meeting him. He inquired of the missionary how he happened to light upon New Brunswick as the scene of his religious labors, and listened to Mr. Norton's account of his "call" to Miramichi with unaffected interest.

The next day the case was brought before the [jury]. The charge having been read, Mr. Dubois appeared in behalf of the missionary, testifying to his good character and to the nature of his spiritual teachings. He also presented to the [jury] three commissions from the Governor of the State of --, which Mr. Norton had in his possession, one of them being a commission as Chaplain of the Regiment to which he belonged. Inquiry being made whether Mr. Norton's preaching was calculated to disaffect subjects towards the government, no evidence was found to that effect. On the contrary, witnesses were brought to prove the reverse.

Mr. Mummychog, aware before he left Miramichi that a number of his compeers in that region, who had been in the habit of coming to the Grove to hear Mr. Norton discourse, were just now at Fredericton on lumbering business, had been beating up these as recruits for the occasion, and now brought forward quite an overpowering weight of evidence in favor of the defendant. These men testified that he had preached to them the importance of fulfilling their duties as citizens, telling them that unless they were good subjects to the civil government, they could not be good subjects in Christ's kingdom. They testified, also, that they had frequently heard him pray in public for the health, happiness, and prosperity of His Majesty, and for blessings on the Lord Lieutenant-Governor.

After a few minutes of conversation, the [jury] dismissed the charge.

The party retired, much gratified at the favorable conclusion of what might, under other circumstances, have proved to the missionary an annoying affair. Mr. Norton warmly expressed his gratitude to Mr. Dubois, as having been the main instrument, in securing this result. He also cordially thanked Micah and his friends for their prompt efforts in his behalf.

"Twant much of a chore, any heow," said Micah. "I never could stan' by and see any critter put upon by another he'd done no harm to, and I never will."

As they returned to the hotel, Mr. Dubois remarked that this journey to the Capital, after all, might not be without good results.

"You made," he said to Mr. Norton, "an extremely favorable impression on the minds of several gentlemen who wield power in the province, and should you be subjected to future persecutions, you will probably be able to secure their protection."

"Possibly—possibly. I am grateful if I have in anyway secured the good will of those gentlemen. I was particularly impressed by their dignity, affability, and readiness to oblige yourself. But, my dear sir, it is better to trust in the Lord than to put confidence in princes."

CHAPTER XX

MR. LANSDOWNE SUBMITS TO THE INEVITABLE

In the meanwhile, a change had come upon John Lansdowne. Only a few weeks ago he was a careless youth of keen and vigorous intellectual powers, satiated with books and tired of college walls, with the boy spirit in the ascendant within him. His eye was wide open and observant, and his ringing laugh was so merry that it brought an involuntary smile upon anyone who might chance to hear its rich peals. His talk was rapid, gay, and brilliant, with but the slightest dash of sentiment, and his manner frank and fearless.

But now his bearing had become quiet and dignified; his conversation was more thoughtful and deep-flowing, less dashing and free; he spoke in a lower key; his laugh was less loud but far sweeter and more thrilling; his eyes had grown larger, darker, deeper, and sometimes they were shadowed with a soft and tender mist, not wont to overspread them before. The angel of Love had touched him, and opened a new and living spring in his heart. Boiling and bubbling in its hidden recess, an ethereal vapor mounted up and mantled those blazing orbs in a dim and dreamy veil. A charmed wand had touched every sense, every power of his being, and held him fast in a rapturous thrall, from which he did not wish to be released. Under the spell of this enchantment, the careless boy had passed into the reflective man.

Stories are told of knights errant, in the times of Merlin and the good King Arthur, who, while ranging the world in quest of adventures, were bewitched by lovely wood fairies or were lulled into delicious slumber by some [Siren's] song, or were shut up in pleasant durance in enchanted castles. Accounts of similar character are found, even in the pages of grave chroniclers of modern date, to say nothing of what books of fiction tell, and what we observe with our own eyes in the actual world. The truth is, Love smites his victims just when and where he finds them. Mr. Lansdowne's case, then, is not an unprecedented one. The keen Damascus blade, used to pierce our hero and bring him to the pitiful condition of the conquered, had been placed in the hand of Adèle. Whether Love intended to employ that young lady in healing the cruel wound she had made, remains to be seen.

At the beginning of their acquaintance, they had found a common ground of interest in the love of music.

They both sang well. Adèle played the piano and John discoursed on the flute. From these employments, they passed to books. They rummaged Mr. Dubois's library and read together, selected passages from favorite authors. Occasionally, John gave her little episodes of his past life, his childish, his school, and college days. In return, Adèle told him of her term at Halifax in the convent; of the routine of life and study there; of her friendships, and very privately, of the disgust she took, while there, to what she called the superstitions, the mummeries and idolatry of the Catholic church.

When Mr. Somers had acquired strength enough for exercise on horseback, Mrs. Dubois, [Adèle], and John were accustomed to accompany him. Daily, about an hour after breakfast, the little party might have been seen [setting] off for a canter through the forest. In the evening, the group was joined by Mr. Dubois and the missionary. The atmosphere being exceedingly dry, both by day and night, they often sat and talked by moonlight on a balcony built over the large, porch-like entrance to the main door of the house.

Thus John and [Adèle] daily grew into a more familiar acquaintance.

During the absence of Mr. Dubois at Fredericton, Mr. Somers announced to John that he felt himself strong enough to undertake the ride through the wilderness, and proposed that, as soon as their host returned, they should start on their journey home.

With increasing strength, Mr. Somers had become impatient to return to the duties he had so summarily forsaken.

He wished to test, in active life, his power to maintain the new principles he had espoused and to ascertain if the nobler and holier hopes that now animated him would give him peace, strength, and buoyancy, amid the temptations and trials of the future.

John, for several days, had been living in a delicious reverie, and was quite startled by the proposition. Though aware how anxiously his parents were awaiting his return, and that there was no reasonable excuse for further delay, he inwardly repudiated the thought of departure. He even indicated a wish to delay the journey beyond the time Mr. Somers had designated. A piercing look of inquiry from that gentleman recalled him to his senses, and after a moment of hesitation he assented to the arrangement. But the beautiful dream was broken. He was thrown at once into a tumult of emotion. Unwilling to expose his agitation to the observation of others, he went directly to his room and locked himself in.

After sitting half an hour with his face buried in his hands, the chaos of his soul formed itself into definite shape. His first clear thought was this—"Without Adèle my life will be a blank. She is absolutely necessary to my existence. I must win her." A very decided conclusion certainly for a young gentleman to reach, who when he arrived at this house but a few weeks before, seemed to be enjoying a liberal share of hope and happiness. The question arose, Does she care for me? Does she regard me with any special interest beyond the kindness and courtesy she accords to all her father's guests? On this point, he could not satisfy himself. He was torn by a conflict of doubt, hope, and fear. He thought her not averse to him. She conversed, sang, and rode with him as if it were agreeable to her. Indeed she seemed to enjoy his society. But she was equally pleased to converse and ride with Mr. Somers and good Mr. Norton. He was unable to determine the sentiments she really cherished and remained tossed to and fro in painful suspense and agitation.

A couple of hours passed and found him in the same state. Mr. Somers came and tapped upon his door. Unwilling to awaken a suspicion of any unusual discomposure, John opened it and let him in.

"Hope I don't intrude," said Mr. Somers, "but I want you to look at the horse Mummychog has brought for me."

"Ah! yes," said John, and seizing his hat he accompanied his friend to the stables.

Their observations over, they returned to the house.

"You have had a fit of solitude, quite unusual, my boy," said Mr. Somers, planting his hand on John's shoulder.

"Yes, quite. For a novelty, I have been collecting my thoughts." John meant to speak in a gay, indifferent tone, and thought he had done so, but this was a mistake.

Besides he had in fact a decidedly conscious look.

"If you have any momentous affair on hand, I advise you to wait until you reach *home* before you decide upon it, my boy," said Mr. Somers, with a light laugh, but a strong emphasis upon the word, home.

And he passed upstairs, leaving John standing bewildered in the hall-door.

"Ah! Ned has discovered it all," said he to himself. But he was too much occupied with other thoughts to be annoyed by it now.

Mr. Somers's last remark had turned the course of his meditations somewhat. He began to question what opinion his parents might have in regard to the sentiments he entertained towards Adèle, and the plan he had formed of endeavoring to secure her love. He knew they considered him as yet hardly out of boyhood. He had indeed, until within a few weeks, looked upon himself in that light.

Not yet freed from college halls—would they not think him foolish and precipitate? Would they approve his choice?

But these queries and others of like character he disposed of summarily and decisively. He felt that, no matter how recently he had passed the limits of boyhood and become a man, it was no boy's passion that now swayed his whole being it seemed to him that, should he make the effort, he could not expel it from his soul. But he did not wish to make the effort. Adèle was worthy [of] the love of any man.

It had been his fortune to find a jewel when he least expected it. Why should he not avail himself of the golden opportunity and secure the treasure? Would his parents approve his choice? Certainly, Adèle was "beautiful as the Houries and wise as Zobeide." Considerations of policy and expediency, which sometimes appear on the mental horizon of older people, were quite unknown to our young hero.

So he returned to the only aspect of the case that gave him real disquiet. He had fears respecting Adèle's sentiments towards himself, and doubts of his ability to inspire in her a love equal to his own. But he must be left for the present to adjust himself to his new situation as best he can.

CHAPTER XXI

TROUBLED HEARTS

On the afternoon of the day following, Adèle was sitting alone in the parlor. She held a book in her hand, but evidently it did not much interest her, as her eyes wandered continually from its pages and rested, abstractedly, upon any object they happened to meet.

She felt lonely, and wondered why Mr. Lansdowne did not, as usual at that hour, come to the parlor. She thought how vacant and sad her life would be after he and Mr. Somers had departed from Miramichi. She queried whether she should ever meet them again; whether, indeed, either of them, after a short time, would ever think of the acquaintances they had formed here, except when recalled by some accident of memory or association. She feared they might wholly forget all these scenes, fraught with so much interest and pleasure to her, and that fear took possession of her heart and made her almost miserable. She strove to turn her mind upon her favorite project of returning with her parents to France. But, notwithstanding her efforts, her thoughts lingered around the departing gentlemen and the close of her acquaintance with them.

Suddenly she heard Mr. Lansdowne's step approaching the room. Conscious that her heart was at this moment in her eyes, she hastily threw the book upon the table. Taking her embroidery, she bent her attention closely upon it, thus veiling the tell-tale orbs with their long dark lashes.

She looked up a moment, as he entered, to give him a nod of recognition. A flash of lightning will reveal at once the whole paraphernalia of a room, even to its remotest corners; or disclose the scenery of an entire landscape in its minutest details, each previously wrapt by the darkness in perfect mystery; so, one single glance of the eye may unveil and discover a profound secret that has hitherto never been indicated by either word or motion. By that quick glance, Adèle saw Mr. Lansdowne's face, very pale with the struggle he had just gone through, and a strange light glowing from his eyes that caused her to withdraw her own immediately.

Her heart beat rapidly — she was conscious that a tide of crimson was creeping up to her cheek, and felt herself tremulous in every limb as Mr. Lansdowne approached and drew a seat near her. But pride came to her aid. One strong effort of the will, and the young creature, novice as she was in the arts of society, succeeded in partially covering the flutter and agitation of spirit caused by the sudden discovery of her lover's secret.

"When do you expect your father's return, Miss Adèle?" inquired Mr. Lansdowne.

"In a day or two," was the reply.

"Do you know that my uncle and I will be obliged to leave our newly-found friends here soon after your father gets home?"

"I know," replied Adèle, with apparent calmness, "that Mr. Somers's health has greatly improved and I supposed you would probably go away soon."

"Pardon me, Miss Adèle," said John, in a voice that betrayed his emotion, "but shall you miss us at all? Shall you regret our absence?"

Again Adèle's heart bounded quickly. She felt irritated and ashamed of its tumult.

By another strong effort, she answered simply, "Certainly, Mr. Lansdowne, we shall all miss you. You have greatly enlivened our narrow family circle. We shall be very sorry to lose you."

How indifferent she is, thought John. She does not dream of my love.

"Miss Adèle," he exclaimed passionately, "it will be the greatest calamity of my life to leave you."

For a moment, the young girl was silent. His voice both thrilled and fascinated her. Partly proud, partly shy, like the bird who shuns the snare set for it, only fluttering its wings over the spot for an instant and then flying to a greater distance, Adèle bestirred her powers and resolved not to suffer herself to be drawn into the meshes. She felt a new, strange influence creeping over her to which she was half afraid, half too haughty to yield without a struggle.

"Mr. Lansdowne, I am happy to learn you place some value on our friendship, as we do on yours. But surely, your own home, such as you have described it to me, must be the most attractive spot on earth to you."

"Is it possible," said Mr. Lansdowne vehemently, taking her hand and holding it fast in his, "that you cannot understand me — that you do not know that I love you infinitely more than father, or mother, or any human creature?"

Surprised at the abruptness of this outburst, bewildered and distressed by her own conflicting emotions, Adèle knew not what to say, and wished only to fly away into solitude that she might collect her scattered powers.

"Mr. Lansdowne, I am not prepared for this. Let me go. I must leave you," she exclaimed.

Suddenly drawing her hand from his, she fled to her own room, locked the door and burst into a passionate flood of tears. Poor child! Her lover with his unpractised hand had opened a new chapter in her life too precipitately. She was not prepared for its revelations, and the shock had shaken her a little too rudely.

John remained sitting, white and dumb, as if a thunderbolt had fallen upon him.

"Gone! gone!" he exclaimed at length, "she does not love me! And, fool that I was, I have frightened her from me forever!"

He bowed his head upon the table and uttered a groan of despair.

Mr. Lansdowne returned to the solitude of his own room, sufficiently miserable. He feared he had offended Adèle past healing. Looking over the events of the week, he thought he could perceive that she had been teased by his attentions, and that she wished to indicate this by the coolness of her manner and words to him during their recent interview. And he had recklessly, though unwittingly, put the climax to her annoyance by this abrupt disclosure of his love. He berated himself unmercifully for his folly. For a full hour, he believed that his blundering impetuosity had cost him the loss of Adèle forever.

But it is hard for hope to forsake the young. It can never wholly leave any soul, except by a slow process of bitter disappointment. John saw that he had made a mistake. The strength and tumult of his passion for Adèle had led him thoughtlessly into what probably appeared to her an attempt to storm the citadel of her heart, and in her pride, she had repulsed him.

He bethought him that there were gentler modes of reaching that seat of life and love. He became a tactician. He resolved he would, by his future conduct, perhaps by some chance word, indicate to Adèle that he understood her repulse and did not intend to repeat his offence. He would not hereafter seek her presence unduly, but when they were thrown together would show himself merely gentle and brotherly. And then — he would trust to time, to circumstances, to his lucky star, to bring her to his side.

In the meantime, after her tears had subsided, Adèle found, somewhat to her surprise, that this sudden disturbance of her usual equilibrium came from the very deep interest she felt for Mr. Lansdowne. And, moreover, she was annoyed to find it so, and did not at all like to own it to herself. Naturally proud, self-relying, and in the habit of choosing her own path, she had an instinctive feeling that this new passion might lay upon her a certain thralldom not congenial to her haughty spirit. This consciousness made her distant and reserved when she again met Mr. Lansdowne at the tea-table.

In fact, the manner of each towards the other had wholly changed.

John was calm, respectful, gentle, but made no effort to draw Adèle's attention. After tea he asked Mrs. Dubois to play backgammon with him.

Adèle worked on her embroidery, and Mr. Somers sat beside her, sketching on paper with his pencil various bits of ruin and scenery in Europe, mixed up with all sorts of grotesque shapes and monsters. Mr. Lansdowne appeared, all the evening, so composed, so natural, and simply brotherly, that when Adèle went to her room for the night the interview of the afternoon seemed almost like a dream. She thought that the peculiar reception she had given to his avowal might have quite disenchanted her lover. And the thought disturbed her. After much questioning and surmising, she went to sleep.

The next day and the next, Mr. Lansdowne's manner towards Adèle continued the same. She supposed he might renew the subject of their last conversation, but he did not, although several opportunities presented when he might have done so. Occasionally, she strove to read his emotions by observing his countenance, but his eyes were averted to other objects. He no longer glanced towards her. "Ah! well," said Adèle to herself, "his affection for me could not be so easily repulsed, were it so very profound. I will care nothing for him." And yet, somehow, her footstep lagged wearily and her eye occasionally gathered mists on its brightness.

It was now the eve of the fifth of October. An unnatural heat prevailed, consequent on the long drought; the horizon was skirted with a smoky haze and the atmosphere was exceedingly oppressive. Mrs. Dubois, who was suffering from a severe headache, sat in the parlor, half buried in the cushions of an easy-chair. Adèle stood beside her, bathing her head with perfumed water, while Mr. Somers, prostrated by the weather, lay, apparently asleep, upon a sofa.

"That will do, Adèle," said Mrs. Dubois, making a slight motion towards her daughter. "That will do, *ma chère*, my head is cooler now. Go out and watch for your father. He will surely be here to-night."

Adèle stepped softly out through the window upon the balcony.

A few minutes after, Mr. Lansdowne came to the parlor door, looked in, inquired for Mrs. Dubois's headache, gazed for a moment at the serene face of the sleeper on the sofa, and then, perceiving Adèle sitting outside, impelled by an irresistible impulse, went out and joined her.

She was leaning her head upon her hand with her arm supported by a low, rude balustrade that ran round the edge of the balcony, and was looking earnestly up the road to catch the first glimpse of her father. Her countenance had a subdued, sad expression. She was indeed very unhappy. The distance and reserve that had grown up so suddenly between herself and Mr. Lansdowne had become painful to her. She would have rejoiced to return once more to their former habits of frank and vivacious conversation. But she waited for him to renew the familiarity of the past.

She turned her head towards him as he approached, and without raising her eyes, said, "Good evening, Mr. Lansdowne." He bowed, sat down, and they remained several minutes in silence.

"I suppose," said John, at length, making a desperate effort to preserve a composure of manner entirely at variance with the tumultuous throbbings of his heart, "you are confident of your father's return to-night?"

"O, yes. I look for him every moment. I am quite anxious to hear the result of the expedition."

"I am, also. I hope no harm will come to our good friend, Mr. Norton. Do you know whether he intends to spend the winter here, Miss Adèle?"

"I think he will return to his family. But we shall endeavor to retain him until we go ourselves."

"*You* go, Miss Adèle," exclaimed John, unable to conceal his eager interest, "do you leave here?"

"We go to France next month."

"To France!" repeated the young man.

"My father and mother are going to visit their early home. I shall accompany them."

John, aroused by information containing so much of importance in regard to Adèle's future, could not restrain himself from prolonging the conversation. Adèle was willing to answer his inquiries, and in a few minutes they were talking almost as freely and frankly as in the days before Mr. Lansdowne's unfortunately rash avowal of his passion.

Suddenly a thick cloud of dust appeared in the road, and Mr. Dubois, Mr. Norton, and Micah, were soon distinguished turning the heads of their horses towards the house.

Adèle uttered an exclamation of joy, and bounded from her seat. As Mr. Lansdowne made way for her to reach the window, she glanced for a moment at his face, and there beheld again the strange light glowing in his eyes. It communicated a great hope to her heart.

She hastened past him to greet her father.

CHAPTER XXII

A Memorable Event

The morning of the sixth of October dawned. The heat of the weather had increased and become wellnigh intolerable. At breakfast, Mr. Dubois and Mr. Norton gave accounts of fires they had seen in various parts of the country, some of them not far off, and owing to the prevalence of the forest and the extreme dryness of the trees and shrubs, expressed fears of great devastation.

They united in thinking it would be dangerous for the two gentlemen to undertake their journey home until a copious rain should have fallen.

During the forenoon, the crackling of the fires and the sound of falling trees in the distant forest could be distinctly heard, announcing that the terrible element was at work.

Mr. Dubois, accompanied by Mr. Norton and John, ascended the most prominent hills in the neighborhood to watch the direction in which the clouds of smoke appeared. These observations only confirmed their fears. They warned the people around of the danger, but these paid little heed. In the afternoon, the missionary crossed from the Dubois house on the northern side of the river, to the southern bank, and explored the country to a considerable distance around.

In the evening, when the family met in the Madonna room, cheerfulness had forsaken the party. The languor produced by the heat and the heavily-laden atmosphere, solicitude felt for the dwellers in the forest, through which the fire was now sweeping, a hoarse rumbling noise like distant thunder occasionally booming on their ears, and gloomy forebodings of impending calamity, all weighed upon the dispirited group.

Mr. Norton said it was his firm conviction that God was about to display His power in a signal manner to this people in order to arouse them to a sense of their guilt.

Before separating for the night, he requested permission to offer up a prayer to heaven. The whole circle knelt while he implored the Great Ruler of all to take them as a family under his protecting love, whether life or death awaited them, and that He would, if consistent with His great and wise plans, avert His wrath from the people.

The night was a dismal, and for most of the family, a sleepless one. The morning rose once more, but it brought no cheering sound of blessed rain-drops. The air was still hot and stifling.

About noon, the missionary came in from a round of observation he had been making and urged Mr. Dubois to take his family immediately to the south bank of the river. The fires were advancing towards them from the north, and would inevitably be upon them soon. He had not been able to discover any appearance of fire upon the southern side of the river. It was true the approaching flames might be driven across, but the stream being for some distance quite wide, this might not take place. In any event, the southern side was the safest at the present moment. He had faith in the instinct of animals, and for several hours past he had seen cattle and geese leaving their usual places of resort and swimming to the opposite shore.

Mr. Dubois, also convinced that there was no other feasible method of escape, hastened to make arrangements for immediate departure.

A mist, tinged with deep purple, now poured in from the wilderness and overspread the horizon. A dark cloud wrapped the land in a dismal gloom. The heat grew nearly insupportable. Rapid explosions, loud and startling noises, filled the air, and the forest thrilled and shook with the raging flames. Soon a fiery belt encircled them on the east, north, and west, and advancing rapidly, threatened to cover the whole area. The river was the only object which, by any possibility, could stay its course.

Then followed a scene of wildest confusion. The people, aroused at last to their danger, rushed terrified to the river, unmoored their boats and fled across. Hosts of women, whose husbands were absent in the forest, came with their children, imploring to be taken to the other side. The remainder of the day was occupied in this work, and at the close of it, most of those living in the Dubois [Settlement] had been safely landed on the southern shore; and there they stood huddled together in horror-stricken groups, on the highest points they could reach, watching the terrible, yet majestic scene.

Mr. Somers had been occupied in this way all the afternoon and was greatly exhausted. As the darkness of night shut down upon the scene, he landed a party of women and children, who rushed up, precipitately, to join those who had crossed before. He had handed the last passenger over the edge of the boat when a sudden faintness, produced by the excessive heat and fatigue, overpowered him. He tottered backward and fell, striking his head violently upon some object in the bottom of the boat. It was a deathblow.

There he lay, with face upturned towards the lurid glare that lit up the darkness. The boat nestled about in the little cove, rocked upon the waves, presenting the pale countenance, now half in shadow, now wholly concealed by the overhanging shrubs, and now in full relief, but always with a sweet, radiant, immovable calm upon the features, in strange contrast to the elemental roar and tumult around him.

In the meantime, the fires drew nearer and nearer the northern bank of the river. A strong breeze sprang up and immense columns of smoke mounted to the sky. Then came showers of ashes, cinders and burning brands. At last, a tornado, terrible in fury, arose to mingle its horrors with the fire. Thunderbolt on thunderbolt, crash on crash rent the air. At intervals of momentary lull in the storm, the roar of the flames was heard. Rapidly advancing, they shot fiery tongues into every beast lair of the forest, into every serpent-haunted crevice of the rock, sending forth their denizens bellowing and writhing with anguish and death; onward still they rushed licking up with hissing sound every rivulet and shallow pond, twisting and coiling round the glorious pines that had battled the winds and tempests hundreds of years, but now to be snapped and demolished by this new enemy.

With breathless interest, the inhabitants of the settlement watched the progress of the flames. The hamlet where they lived was situated on a wide point of land, around which the Miramichi made an unusually bold sweep. Micah's Grove partly skirted it on the north.

From the Grove to the river, the [forest trees] had been cleared, leaving the open space dotted with the houses of the settlers. The fire pressed steadily on toward the Grove. The destruction of that forest fane, consecrated so recently to the worship of God, and the burning of their homes and earthly goods seemed inevitable. The people, with pale, excited faces, awaited this heart-rending spectacle.

Just at this moment, the tornado, coming from the [north] with terrific fury, drawing flames, trees, and every movable object in its wake, whirling forward with gigantic power, suddenly turned in its path, veered towards the east, swept past the Grove and past the settlement, leaving them wholly untouched, and took its destructive course onward to the ocean. The people were dumb with amazement. Ruin had seemed so sure that they scarcely trusted the evidence of their senses.

They dared not even think they had been saved from so much misery. For a time, not a word was uttered, not a muscle moved.

Mr. Mummychog was the first to recover his voice.

"'Tis a maracle! and nuthin' else," he exclaimed, "and we've jest got to thank Captin' Norton for it. He's been a prayin' ut we might be passed by, all 'long and 'tis likely the Lord has heerd him. 'Tain't on eour own acceounts, my worthy feller-sinners, that we've been spared. Mind ye remember *that*."

The people in their joy gathered around the missionary, and united with Micah in acknowledging their belief that his prayers had averted from them this great calamity. For a moment, their attention was distracted from the still raging horrors of the scene by the sense of relief from threatened danger.

It was during this brief lull of intense anxiety and expectation that our friends first became aware of the absence of Mr. Somers. They had supposed, of course, that he was standing somewhere among the groups of people, his attention riveted, like their own, upon the scene before them. Adèle first woke to the consciousness that he was not with them.

She turned her head and explored with earnest gaze the people around. She could see distinctly by the intense red light nearly every countenance there, but did not recognize that of Mr. Somers. A painful anxiety immediately seized her, which she strove in vain to conceal. She approached near where Mr. Lansdowne stood by the side of her mother, gazing after the fire, placed her hand lightly on his arm, and asked, "Can you tell me where Mr. Somers is to be found?"

"Mr. Somers! yes — Ned. Where is he?" he exclaimed, turning, half bewildered by her question, and looking in her face.

In an instant, the solicitude her features expressed passed into his own, the same sudden presentiment of evil possessed him.

Drawing Adèle's arm hurriedly into his, he said, "please go with me to seek him."

Hastening along, they went from one to another, making inquiries. It appeared that Mr. Somers had not been seen for several hours.

Immediately, the whole company took the alarm and the search for him commenced.

John and Adèle, after fruitless efforts among the houses, at length took their way to the [river-bank]. As they were hastening forward, a woman standing upon a rock overhanging the path they pursued told them that Mr. Somers brought herself and children over in the boat, just at dark — that she had not seen him since, and she remembered now that she did not see him come up from the river after he landed them.

"Lead us to the spot where you left the boat," said Adèle. "Go on as quickly as you can."

The woman descended from her perch upon the rock and plunged before them into the path.

"I remember now," she said with sudden compunctions at her own selfish indifference, "that the gentleman looked pale and seemed to be dreadful tired like."

Neither John nor Adèle made reply, and the woman hurried on. In a few minutes, a sudden turn in the path brought them to the little cove where the boat still lay.

The woman first caught sight of the wan face in the bottom of the boat, and uttered a scream of horror. The lips of the others were frozen into silence by the dread spectacle.

Scarcely a moment seemed to have passed before John rushed down into the water, reached the boat, raised thence the lifeless form, bore it to the shore and laid the dripping head into the arms of Adèle, who seated herself on the grass to receive it.

"Go quickly," she said to the woman, "go for Dr. Wright. I saw him only a moment ago. Find him and bring him here."

John threw himself upon his knees and began chafing Mr. Somers's hands. "He is dead! he is dead!" he whispered, in a voice hoarse and unnatural with fear and anxiety.

"Let us hope not," said Adèle in a tone of tenderness. "Perhaps it is only a swoon. We will convey him to some shelter and restore him." And she wrung the rain from his curls of long brown hair.

John's finger was upon Mr. Somers's wrist. "It will break my mother's heart," he said, in the same hoarse whisper. At that moment, Dr. Wright's voice was heard. He placed himself, without a word, upon the grass, looked at the pale face, unfastened the dripping garments, thrust his hand in beneath them, and laid it upon the young man's heart.

"He is dead!" said Dr. Wright. "Friends, get a bit of canvas and a blanket and take him to some house till day breaks."

John, stupefied with horror and grief, still knelt by Mr. Somers, chafing his hands and wringing the water from his wet garments. At length, Mr. Dubois gently roused him from his task, telling him they would now remove their friend to a house, where he might be properly cared for.

"Let me lift him," said Micah to the young man. But John shook his head and stooping, raised Mr. Somers and laid him on the canvas as gently as if he were a sleeping infant.

Mr. Dubois, the missionary, John, and Micah conveyed the precious charge. The [doctor], with Mrs. Dubois and Adèle, followed in melancholy silence. The crowd came behind. The terrific events of the night had made the people quiet, thoughtful, and sympathetic.

Once, after the prolonged, clinging gaze of each upon the face of the sleeper, the eyes of the missionary and John met.

"My dear young man," said Mr. Norton, in a low, emphatic voice, "God has taken him in mercy. The dear friend whom we loved is himself satisfied, I doubt not. May the Eternal Father grant us all at the end of our course here a like blessed deliverance. Amen."

John looked in the good man's face as if he but half understood his words, and fixed his eyes again upon Mr. Somers.

At length, the party reached a house near the [river-bank], where they deposited the dead.

Mrs. McNab, who had followed close on their footsteps when they reached the door, drew Adèle aside and said, "Naw, Miss Ady, I want the preevaleege o' trying to resoositate that puir gentelman. It wad be like rasin' the dead, but there'll be nae harm in tryin', to be sure."

"He is dead. The doctor says so, Aunt Patty." And Adèle turned away quickly.

But Mrs. McNab caught her shawl and held it.

"Naw, Miss Ady, dinna turn awa' fram a puir body that was overtook ance or twice with the whiskey, when a was tired and worrit for want o' sleep. I wad nae ha' hurt a hair o' the gentelman's head. An' I wad like the preevaleege o' wrappin' some blankets round him an' puttin' some bottles o' hot water to his feet."

Adèle, who had listened more patiently than she was wont, now turned and, glancing at Aunt Patty, saw that she really looked humble and wishful, and two great tears were in her eyes.

"Well, I will see," said she, struck with this new phase of Mrs. McNab's countenance. She went into the apartment, where they had just laid Mr. Somers upon a bed.

In a few minutes, she returned.

"The doctor says it will be of no use, Aunt Patty. But Mr. Lansdowne would like to make an attempt to restore him. So come, mamma and I will help you."

Notwithstanding Mrs. McNab's subdued state of mind and her genuine, unselfish wish to do all in her power to bring consciousness to the stricken form, she could not avoid, as she made one application after another, making also a few indicative observations to Mrs. Dubois.

"Did ye hear what the preacher said to the young mon as we cam' alang? He's a mighty quick way o' desmeesin a' bonnie creetur like this out o' the warld and sayin' he's satisfied aboot it."

"That was not what the missionary said, Mrs. McNab," replied Mrs. Dubois. "He said that Mr. Somers is happy now. He is in Paradise, and we must not wish him back. He is satisfied to be with Jesus and the angels and his own mother. That is what he meant. And does he not *look* satisfied? See his blissful countenance!"

Mrs. Dubois leaned over him a moment, and thinking of his sister, Mrs. Lansdowne, parted his hair with her pale, slender fingers and imprinted a kiss on his forehead.

All efforts to restore warmth or life to that marble form were in vain, and at length they covered his face gently until the day-dawn.

John sat by the bedside, his head buried in his hands, until morning. He thought over all his past companionship with this youthful Uncle Ned, of his pleasantness, wit and fascination, of his generous spirit, of his love for his mother and himself, and wondered at the awful strangeness that had thus fallen, in a moment, between them. Then the thought of his mother's bitter grief swept over him like a flood and nearly unmanned him. Like the drowning man, his brain was stimulated to an unwonted activity. He lived over again his whole life in a few minutes of time. This dread [power], who had never crossed his path before, shocked him inexpressibly. Who of the young, unstricken by sorrow, ever associates death with himself or with those he loves till the Arch Reaper comes some day and cuts down and garners his precious treasure?

John had heard of death, but he had heard of it just as he had heard of the poisonous Upas-tree, growing on some distant ocean island, or of an evil star, under whose baleful influence he might never fall.

The young live as if this life were immortal. So much the more bitter their experience when they wake up from the delusion.

The others of the party were gathered in an adjoining room, gazing silently at the scene without. It was fearful, yet sublime. The whole northern side of the Miramichi [River], for over one hundred miles, had become involved in one mighty sheet of flame, which was sweeping on in swift destruction to the Gulf of St. Lawrence. The river boiled with the fierce heat and tossed its foaming waters, filled with its now lifeless inhabitants, to the shore. The fire was fed by six thousand square miles of primeval forest—a dense growth of resinous trees—by houses and barns filled with crops, and by thriving towns upon the river's bank.

Above all, the people could not put aside the horrible truth that hundreds of men, women, and children—their friends and their acquaintances—were perishing by the all-consuming element. They could not exclude from fancy, the agonized and dying shrieks of those dear to them, and the demoniac light shone on countenances, expressing emotions of pity, grief, horror, and despair.

While the missionary sat there waiting for the day, he recalled with startling distinctness the wild dream he dreamed on that first night he spent at the Dubois [house]. Of course, his belief in foregleams of future events was confirmed by the scenes transpiring around him.

Mrs. Dubois sat near him, her countenance expressing profound grief.

"The dear young man!" she said. "How sad and awful thus to die!"

"My dear madam," said Mr. Norton, "let us not mourn as those who have no hope. Our beloved friend, brilliant and susceptible, aspiring and tender, was illy fitted for the rude struggle of life. It is true he might have fought his way through, girt with the armor of Christian faith and prayer, as many others, like him, have done. But the fight would have been a hard one. So he has been kindly taken home. Sad and awful thus to die? Say, rather, infinitely blest the God-protected soul, thus snatched away from this terrific uproar of natural elements into the sphere of majestic harmonies, of stupendous yet peaceful powers."

At daybreak the little community took to their boats, crossed the river and re-entered once more the dwellings they had but a few hours before left, never expecting to return to them again. Some went home and gathered their families in unbroken numbers around them. Others, whose husbands and sons had been absent in the forest at the time of the breaking out of the fire, over whose fate remained a terrible uncertainty, gathered in silence around lonely hearths. The terrors of the past night were, to such, supplemented by days and even weeks of heartbreaking anxiety and suspense, closed at last by the knowledge of certain bereavement.

All had been deeply impressed with the horror of the scene, and sobered into thoughtfulness. A few felt truly grateful to the Most High for their wonderful preservation.

CHAPTER XXIII

THE SEPARATION

With the morning light and the return to the settlement, Mr. Lansdowne awoke to a consciousness of the duty immediately before him: that of making arrangements for the safe conveyance home of the precious form now consigned to his care.

His friends at the Dubois house manifested the deepest sympathy in his affliction, and aided him in every possible way. In making his journey he concluded to take a boat conveyance to Chatham and a trading vessel thence to his native city.

The missionary, who since the early spring had been laboring up and down the rivers St. John and Miramichi, now concluded to return to his family for the coming winter. Such had been his intention and his promise to Mrs. Norton when he left home. He was induced to go at this particular time partly by the hope of rendering some service to Mr. Lansdowne during his journey, and partly in order to see Mrs. Lansdowne and impart to her the particulars of her brother's residence and illness at Miramichi. A scheme of mercy on the part of the good man.

On the return of Mr. Dubois to his house, he found a package of letters, which, in the confusion and anxiety of the previous day, had remained unopened. There was one from the Count de Rossillon, announcing the death of the Countess. He wrote as if deeply depressed in mind, speaking of the infirmities of age weighing heavily upon him and of his loneliness, and imploring Mr. Dubois to come, make his abode at the chateau and take charge of the estate, which, at his death, he added, would pass into the possession of Mrs. Dubois and Adèle.

Mrs. Dubois's heart beat with delight and her eyes swam with tears of pleasure at the prospect of once more returning to her beloved Picardy. Yet her joy was severely chastened by the loss of the Countess, whom she had fondly loved.

Adèle felt a satisfaction in the anticipation of being restored to the dignities of Rossillon, which she was too proud to manifest.

Mr. Dubois alone hesitated in entertaining the idea of a return. His innate love of independence, together with a remembrance of the early antipathy the Count had shown to the marriage with his niece, made the thought repellant to him. A calmer consideration, however, changed his view of the case. He recollected that the Count had at last consented to his union with Mrs. Dubois, and reflected that the infirmities and loneliness of the Count laid on them obligations they should not neglect. He found, also, that his own love of home and country, now that it could at last with propriety be gratified, welled up and overflowed like a newly sprung fountain.

The tornado had spent itself, the fire had rushed on to the ocean, the atmosphere had become comparatively clear and the weather cool and bracing.

On the evening before the departure of Mr. Norton and Mr. Lansdowne, the family met, as on many previous occasions, in the Madonna room. In itself, the apartment was as cheerful and attractive as ever, but each one present felt a sense of vacancy, a shrinking of the heart. The sunny changeful glow of one bright face was no longer there, and the shadows of approaching separation cast a gloom over the scene.

These people, so strangely thrown together in this wild, obscure region of Miramichi, drawn hither by such differing objects of pursuit, bound by such various ties in life, occupying such divergent positions in the social scale, had grown by contact and sympathy into a warm friendship toward each other. Their daily intercourse was now to be broken up, the moment of adieu drew nigh, and the prospect of future meeting was, to say the least, precarious. Was it strange that some sharp pangs of regret filled their hearts?

Mr. Lansdowne, who had up to this time been wholly occupied with his preparations for departure, was sitting, in an attitude betokening weariness and despondency, leaning his arms upon a table, shading his face with his hand. A few days of grief and anxiety had greatly changed him. He looked pale and languid, but Adèle thought, as she occasionally glanced at him from the sofa opposite, that she had never seen his countenance so clothed with spiritual beauty.

Mr. Dubois, who had not yet spoken to his friends of his intention to remove to France, now broke the heavy silence by announcing his purpose to leave, in the course of a week, and return with his family to Picardy.

Mr. Lansdowne started suddenly and uttered a slight exclamation. Adèle looked at him involuntarily. He was gazing at her intently. The strange light again glowed in his eyes. Her own fell slowly. She could not keep her lids lifted beneath his gaze.

After the plans of Mr. Dubois had been discussed, mutual inquiries and communications respecting future prospects were made until the evening hours were gone.

"If my life is spared, I shall come here and spend another season as I have spent the one just closing," said Mr. Norton.

Thus they parted for the night.

In the morning there was time for nothing but a few hasty words.

Adèle's face was very pale. Mr. Lansdowne, looking as if he had not slept for many hours, took her hand, bent over it silently for a moment, then walked slowly to the boat without turning his head.

During days and weeks of tranquil pleasure in each other's companionship, these two young beings had unconsciously become lovers. No sooner had they awakened to a knowledge of this fact, [that] a great danger and an unlooked-for sorrow, while deepening the current of their existence, had also deepened their affection. Was that formal, restrained adieu to be the end of all this?

CHAPTER XXIV

CHATEAU DE ROSSILLON

In the year 1828, three years after the occurrences related in the last chapter, Adèle Dubois, grown into a superb beauty, stood near the Aphrodite fountain in front of the chateau de Rossillon feeding from her hand a beautiful white fawn. It was a warm, sunny afternoon in June. Majestic trees shaded the green lawn, and the dark brown hue of the old chateau formed a fitting background for the charming tableau. Adèle was enveloped in a cloud of white gauzy drapery, a black velvet girdle encircling her waist fastened by a clasp of gold and pearls. Her hair was laid in smooth bands over her brow, then drawn into one mass of heavy braids upon the back of the head, and secured by a golden arrow shot through it.

One who by chance had seen Adèle in the wilds of Miramichi, at the age of sixteen, would at once recognize the lady feeding the fawn as the same. At a second glance, the hair would be seen to have grown a shade darker and a gleam more shining, the large sloe-colored eyes more thoughtful and dreamy, the complexion of a more transparent whiteness, and the figure to have ripened into a fuller and richer symmetry.

Nothing could surpass the exquisite moulding and fairness of the arm extended alternately to feed and caress the pet animal before her. No wonder the little creature looked up at her with its soft, almost human eyes, and gazed in her face as if half bewildered by her beauty.

With a proud and stately grace, she moved over the sward, up the marble steps and passed through the great saloon of the chateau. Was there not a slight air of indifference and *ennui* in her face and movements? Possibly. It has been noticed that people who are loved, petted, and admired, who have plenty of gold and jewels, who sit at feasts made for princes, and have the grand shine of splendor always gleaming round them, are more likely to carry that weary aspect than others. Queens even do not look pleased and happy more than half the time. The fact was that Adèle of Miramichi, having spent much time in Paris during the last three years, where she had been greatly admired, now that the novelty was over, had become tired of playing a part in the pageantry of courtly life and longed for something more substantial.

As she crossed the saloon, a page informed her that Mrs. Dubois wished her presence in the library. She immediately obeyed the summons.

This apartment, one of the pleasantest in the chateau, was a favorite with the Count; and as age and infirmity crept upon him, he grew more and more attached to it, and was accustomed to spend there the greater part of his time, amused and soothed by the attentions of Mrs. Dubois and Adèle. It was a lofty, but not very large apartment, the walls nearly covered with bookcases of oak, carved in quaint old patterns and filled with choice books in various languages. Several finely executed statues were placed in niches, and one large picture, by Rubens, gathered a stream of sunshine upon its gorgeous canvas.

The Count was sitting, buried in the purple cushions of an easy-chair, fast asleep, and as Adèle entered the room, her mother held up her finger, warningly.

"*Ma chère*," said Mrs. Dubois in a low tone, "here is a packet of letters for you, from Paris."

Adèle took them from her mother's hand, indifferently. She read and crushed together a note bearing the impression of a coat of arms.

"Count D'Orsay and sister wish to come here next week," she said with a half sigh.

"*Eh, bien! ma chère*, they are agreeable people. I shall be glad to see them."

"Yes," replied Adèle, "Gabrielle is very lovely. Nevertheless, I regret they are coming."

"Do you know, Adèle, how highly your father esteems the young Count?"

"Yes, mamma, and that is one reason why I do not wish him to come now to Rossillon. You know he loves me, and my father approves. I can never marry him. But I esteem and respect him so much that it will give me infinite pain to say nay."

Mrs. Dubois looked at Adèle very tenderly, yet gravely, and said, "*Ma fille*, do not throw away a true, devoted affection for the sake of a phantom one. I fear that, while you are dreaming and waiting, happiness will slip out of your path."

"Dreaming and waiting," repeated Adèle, a slight red color kindling on her cheek, "*am* I dreaming and waiting?"

"It seems to me you are, *ma chère*; I fear it will at last spoil your peace. I do not see how the Count D'Orsay can fail to win your heart. Do not decide hastily, Adèle."

"I have considered the affair a long time already. I have looked into my heart and find nothing there for Count D'Orsay but simple respect, esteem, and friendship. It would be a wrong to him, should I consent to marry him, without a warmer, deeper sentiment. It is of no use thinking about it longer. The subject must be closed. I know I shall not change, and his affection is too true and pure to be tampered with. I shall tell him all frankly next week."

"*Eh, bien!*" said Mrs. Dubois with a sigh, and returned to her letters.

Adèle, who felt quite unhappy to disappoint her mother's hopes in the case, looked thoughtful. They were both silent for several minutes.

"Here is a letter from the good missionary," suddenly whispered Mrs. Dubois, holding up to her daughter several sheets of large paper, well covered. "See, what a nice long one. Now we shall hear the news from our old home."

She began to read the missive in a low tone, looking occasionally to see if her voice disturbed the sleeper, and Adèle, whose countenance had instantly brightened upon the mention of the letter, drew her seat nearer to her mother and listened intently.

MIRAMICHI RIVER, APRIL, 1828

DEAR FRIENDS—

I am again on the memorable spot. You can scarcely imagine my interest in retracing the scene of my brief mission here, in the summer and autumn of 1825, or the deep emotion with which I revisit your former residence, the house under whose roof you so kindly sheltered and entertained one, then exiled, like yourselves, from home. I shall ever rejoice that Providence threw me into your society, and bestowed upon me the precious gift of your friendship.

Three years have passed since those eventful weeks we spent together on the banks of this beautiful river, and you will be interested to know what changes have taken place here during that time.

Traces are still distinctly visible of the awful fire, but Time, the great healer of wounds, and Nature, who is ever striving to cover up the desolations of earth, are both at work, silently but diligently overlaying the hideous black disfigurement with greenness and beauty. The Miramichi and its picturesque precincts are now more alive than ever with a hardy and active population. New villages are springing up on the banks of the river, and business, especially in the branches of lumbering and fishing, is greatly increasing. There is also a marvellous change in the moral aspect of the country. It is ascribed in a great degree to the deep impression made upon the minds of the people by the conflagration, and doubtless this is the fact. It must be that God had a retributory end in view in that great event. It was a judgment upon the community for its exceeding wickedness. Nothing short of a grand, widespread illumination like that could have penetrated the gross darkness that hung over the land.

The way has been thus prepared for the reception of the truth; and whereas formerly the people, if they came at all to hear the preaching of God's word, were only drawn by motives of vain curiosity, or the desire of novelty, they now come in great numbers and with a sincere desire, as I believe, to be instructed in the way of salvation. Last year, I came to this region early in the spring and labored until late in the autumn, preaching up and down the river, from house to house and from grove to grove, and found the people, almost everywhere, ready to hear. Many were baptized in the flowing waters of the Miramichi, made a profession of their faith in Christ, and have since exhibited in their daily lives good and in some cases shining evidence of their sincerity.

You may perhaps be interested to know that yesterday, which was the Sabbath, I discoursed, as in days gone by, in Micah's Grove. The people came in from a great distance around, and it was estimated that there were not less than eight hundred present.

My soul was completely filled with a sense of God's unbounded love to the human family, and my heart was enlarged to speak of the wonderful things belonging to His goodness and mercy towards us as a race. I was like a bottle filled with new wine, my heart overflowing with the remembrance of God's love. Conviction was carried in a most signal manner to the souls of many present. The whole assembly seemed for a time to be overshadowed by the immediate Divine presence.

It is remarkable that though the people do at the present time seem to be under profound religious impressions, yet there are scarcely any traces of the delusion and wildfire usually accompanying such seasons among a somewhat uncultivated and undisciplined population. That great fire sobered them, perhaps.

But, my dear friends, I know you are impatient to hear some details respecting the state of affairs at the "Dubois Settlement," so called from the grateful attachment felt by the inhabitants for a distinguished family once residing there. The new people who have established themselves here of late are acquainted with the family just alluded to, of course only by tradition, but so deep has been the impression made upon the minds of the new comers by Mrs. McNab, Micah Mummychog, and others of the worth, benevolence, power, and present grandeur of said family, that these persons are more than willing; they feel honored in retaining the name of Dubois in this parish. The above is written to elucidate to your minds the fact, obvious enough here, that you are not forgotten.

Now, you will wish to hear what has befallen some of the queer notabilities of the [settlement]. By courtesy, I begin with Mrs. McNab. You will remember her as the general oracle and adviser of a certain portion of the female population in the neighborhood, and as greatly opposed to some of the "doctreenes," as she called my instructions to the people. Well, she remains in her entireness and individuality, her costume as grotesque and her speech as Scotch as ever.

You will be surprised, however, to learn that she has a far more favorable opinion of your humble servant than formerly. I have had some difficulty in accounting for this change in her disposition. It seems, however, that she had early taken a prejudice against Yankees, and had got an idea, in the beginning, that I had some wily and sinister intentions toward the people, connected with my labors here. No developments of that kind having been made, she began to look more complacently upon my efforts, and she thinks now that the way in which I have endeavored to lead the community is not so bad after all.

"The warst thing I had agen ye was this," she said to me not long since. "My meenister o' the Kirk at Dumfries used to preach that a pusson might repent o' his sins, an' pray and pray a' his life lang, but wad nae ken, in this warld, whether or nae he was to be saved. Whereas, ye ken ye told the people that ef they repented o' their sins and believed in Christ and gave the evidence o' gude warks they might settle right doon, and ken they'd be saved, anyhow. I ca' that a peskalent doctreen, an a loose ane to promoolgate. Though I must confess, ye hae na dune the meeschief I luked for."

I did not think it best to go into a discussion of our theological differences, lest it should stir up the waters of strife, and therefore waived the subject.

Mrs. McNab occupies two comfortable rooms at Mrs. Campbell's house, from whence she issues forth, whenever occasion calls, to perform the duties of nurse, counsellor, and supervisor-general of the domestic affairs of the community. The tea-drinkings in her parlor seem to be occasions of great social enjoyment to the fortunate neighbors invited. After the regular gossip of the day has been discussed, she entertains her company with the same old stories of her former life in Scotland, among its grand families, and to these she has added, for the benefit of those who have more recently come into the [settlement], accounts of the "Doobyce" family, characterizing its members by remarking that "Mr. Doobyce was a braw, princely mon, his wife a sweet, fair spoken leddy, an' Miss Ady was a born queen, ef there ever was ane. She had her ane way wi' everybody, an' e'en I mysel' hae gien up to her whiles."

Micah Mummychog, alias Jones, Miss Adèle's special devotee, never a bad-hearted person, has now become one of the influential men of the neighborhood, and sustains here every good word and work. About a year after the great fire, he had a long and dangerous illness, brought on by great exposure to cold while lumbering in the woods.

Mrs. McNab voluntarily went to his house and took care of him most assiduously, for many weeks, until his recovery. Micah said that "it looked remarkable kind in the old soul to come of her own accord and take keer of him when he'd allers plagued her so unmascifully."

He felt very grateful to her and paid her handsomely for her services. Nevertheless, he teases her yet occasionally and says "he dont know neow, which skeered him most, the great fire, or comin' to his senses one night when he was sick and seein' Aunt McNab with her head wropped up in its cotton night gear."

Subsequent to Micah's recovery, he went to the Kennebec River and visited his friends. After his return, he commenced trading, and is now doing quite an extensive business. He has entirely broken off from his old habits of swearing and gambling, and discountenances them among the people. He attends religious worship constantly, and sets a worthy example in keeping the Sabbath day.

He is also getting his ideas up on the subject of education. Not long since, he told me it was his opinion that "there warn't half school larnin' enuf among the people, and there'd oughter to be longer schools. There's Jinny Campbell, there, a bright leetle imp as ever was, and ef she'd had a chance would a taken to her books like a chicken to a dough dish. And there's others, most as smart as she is, all reound, that need schoolin'. I feel the want of it myself, neow [it's] tew late to git it."

A few days ago, Micah told me he expected to build a new house for himself soon.

"Ah! Micah," said I, "have you got tired of that comfortable old house of yours, where we have had so many nice suppers and [cosy] times together?"

"Well, no, Captin', I hain't, and I'm afeerd I shall never like another place as I dew that. But ye see, ef a feller is a goin' to git married, he's got to stir reound and dew what suits other folks as well as hisself."

"Married! Micah," I said, in complete astonishment, "are you going to be married?"

"That's jest the way I expected yeou'd look," said he, "when I told ye abeout it, because ye knew I used to talk agin it like fury. But ye see, Captin', I aint just as I used to be abeout some things. I'll tell ye heow it came reound, any heow, so as to sahtisfy ye I ain't crazy. Well, when I was a beginnin' to git better o' that terable sickness, the fust and only one I ever had in my life, Miss Campbell, she used to send Jinny up, with bits o' briled chicken, nice broth and sech, to kinder tempt my appetite like. The little critter used to bring 'em in and be so pitiful to me and say, do Micah try to eat this, so that you may git well; and she seemed so pooty, sincere and nateral like in all her ways that I took to her mightily, specially as I hadn't Miss Adèle to look arter and chore reound for any more. Once or twice, when she came to bring suthin, Ant McNab kinder advised her to do this and that, and the way the leetle critter spunked up and had her own way made me think o' Miss Adèle and pleased me some, I tell ye.

"Well, arter I got well, she seemed to be just as chipper and pleasant as ever, and was allers glad when I went to the heouse, and so it went on (I won't bother abeout the rest on't) till six months ago. As I was a walkin' hum from a meetin' at the Grove with her, she sed, 'what a pooty Grove that is, of yours, Micah;' Witheout a considerin' a half a minit, I sed, right away, 'Jinny, I'd give yeou that Grove and all I have beside, upon one condition.' I looked at her, arter I'd sed it, as skeered as I could be, fur fear she'd fly right at me fur sayin' sech a thing. But she didn't. She only colored up awfully and sed, in a fluttered kinder way, 'what condition, Micah?' 'Pon condition that you'd merry me, Jinny.' You may believe that arter I sed that, my heart stood still better'n a minit. She didn't say a word at fust, seemed ruther took by surprise, and then, all of a sudding, she turned her head and looked up inter my face as sarcy as ye ever see anything, and says she, 'Do yeou think I'd ever merry a man with sech a horrid name as Mummychog?' 'Is that all the objection you hev, Jinny?' ses I. Ses she, "Tis the greatest, I know of.' Then ses I, 'There ain't no diffikilty, for my name aint Mummychog, and never was. When I came deown to this kentry, I was a wild, reckless kind of a critter, and I thought I'd take some outlandish name, jest for the joke on it. I took Mummychog, and they allers called me so. But my real name is Jones.' 'Well, Mr. Jones,' ses she, lookin' sarcier than ever, 'I shall expect yeou to hev a sign painted with your real name on it and put up on your store, and yeou must build a new heouse before I merry yeou.' That sobered me deown a leetle. I sed, 'But Jinny, I don't want ye to merry me unless ye like me. I'll build a heouse and gin it tew ye, ef that's what ye want. But ye needn't merry me unless ye like me — neow remember.' She looked at me, jest as soon as I sed that, and caught up my big hand inter her little one, and ses she, 'O law, Micah, I'd merry ye ef yer name *was* Mummychog, and ye needn't build a heouse, nor nuthin'. I ken go right to the old place jest as well. I'd merry ye ef ye hadn't a cent, for I like ye better'n anybody else in the world, Micah.' And then she began to cry, and I hushed her up. And so, neow it's all settled."

"Well Micah," said I, after hearing this account of his courtship of Jenny Campbell, "I congratulate you on your choice; Jenny is a good girl and a pretty one. But isn't she rather young?"

"Well, yis. I thought yeou'd be speakin' o' that. I'm forty year old and she's abeout eighteen or so. Consid'able difference in eour ages. I told her abeout that t'other day, and she sed, well she didn't see but I 'peared abeout as young as she did. She didn't see much difference. So ef she's sahtisfied, I'd oughter be. But Captin', I'll tell ye, she's a curus leetle critter as ever ye see. She has spells of playin' off all kinds o' tricks on me and hectorin' me every way she ken, but the minit she sees me look sober, as ef I felt anyway bad, she leaves right off, and comes up and kisses me, and ses she didn't mean anything by it, and is as good as a kitten."

Alas! poor Micah! You see, Miss Adèle, he is in the meshes, and there we must leave him for the present. I have taken pains to give you the above in his own language, as it is so much more graphic than any I could employ.

My letter of Miramichi gossip has swollen, unconsciously, to an enormous size, and I fear I am getting tedious. Be patient a few minutes longer, dear friends, while I tell you of Mr. John Lansdowne.

I happened in the city of P -- last winter, on business, and just before leaving town I went to call on Mr. Lansdowne. Aunt Esther, Mr. John's nurse, an aged negro woman who has been a member of the household many years, answered my ring at the door. Finding that none of the family were at home, I was turning to leave when Aunt Esther begged me to come in, saying she reckoned they would soon be back, as they had already been several hours absent, adding, good soul, that "they'd all be dreffully disapinted not to see me."

I knew that several months prior to this, Mr. Lansdowne had been admitted to the practice of law and had become junior partner in business to the distinguished Mr. Eldon of P --. And I now gathered from Aunt Esther that the Supreme Court was in session, and that a great criminal case was being tried before the jury. Mr. Eldon had been taken ill, just before the trial came on, and had urged Mr. Lansdowne to take his place in Court, saying he could argue the case as well as himself. Mr. John, as Aunt Esther informed me, did it with great reluctance, though she didn't see why. "He always does everything he sets out to do, 'markable nice. But Massa and Missus felt kind of anxious, and they v'e gone into Court, with other gemmen and ladies, to hear how't goes. I feel no concern about it. I know he'll make a splen'id talk, anyhow, cos he always does."

After waiting half an hour, I was obliged to leave messages of regret with Aunt Esther and hasten home.

I observed in "The Eastern Gazette" of the following week a notice of Mr. Lansdowne's plea before the jury in the great case of "The Commonwealth *vs* Jenkins," in which he was eulogized in the highest terms. He was said to have displayed "great acumen, extensive legal acquirements, and magnificent powers of oratory." So, Aunt Esther's confidence about the "splen'id talk" was not without a reasonable basis.

I was highly gratified, myself, in reading the flattering paragraphs. You know we all greatly admired the young gentleman at Miramichi. He has a brilliant earthly future before him, should his life and faculties be spared.

Micah was much charmed with the intelligence I brought him of his old favorite.

"I ain't a mite surprised at what you v'e sed abeout the young man. Ever sence I took that trip inter the woods with him, I know'd he'd the genooine ring o' trew metal tew him. When he gits to be President o' the United States, I shall sell eout here and go hum to the Kennebec."

Please let me hear from you soon, my dear friends. It seems long since I have had tidings from you.

With an abiding gratitude for past kindness, shown by you to a weary wanderer from home, and with the warmest respect and friendship, I remain as ever,

Yours truly,
SAMUEL J. NORTON

Mrs. Dubois not having but one pair of eyes, and those being fully occupied with the contents of the above letter, and the Count de Rossillon remaining asleep during the entire reading, of course it could not be expected that they observed the changes that took place on Adèle's countenance. But an author, as is well known, has ways and means of observation not common to others, and here it may be remarked that that young lady's face had exhibited, during the last fifteen minutes, or more, quite a variety of emotions. It had at first been thoughtful and interested, then lighted with smiles, then radiant with enjoyment of the good missionary's sketches of Mrs. McNab and Micah. But the moment her mother read the name of John Lansdowne, her face was suffused with a deep crimson, and she listened almost breathlessly, and with glistening eyes, to the close.

"Oh! the good noble man!" said Mrs. Dubois, as she folded up the sheets. "It will please your father to read this; where is he, Adèle?"

"He rode away with Pierre, not long ago. Please let me take the letter. I must read it again," said Adèle, having conquered her emotion without her mother perceiving it.

She took it away to her own boudoir, and as she read the pages, the flowing tears fell fast. Why should she weep over such a cheerful letter as that? Why?

CHAPTER XXV

THE LAST SLEEP

Adèle had long since discovered that the events of greatest interest in her life had transpired before she entered the walls of Rossillon or mingled in the festivities of the Court at Paris.

The scenes that occurred at Miramichi, during Mr. Lansdowne's accidental residence there, were fraught with a power over her heart, continually deepening with the flight of time. Those golden days, when their lives flowed side by side, had been filled with the strange, sweet agitations, the aerial dreams, the bewitching glamour, the intoxicating happiness of a first and youthful love. Those days were imprinted yet more deeply in her memory by a consciousness that there was somewhat with which to reproach herself connected with them. Just when she had reached the top of bliss, her pride had sprung up, and, like a dark storm-cloud, had shadowed the scene. She could not forget that cold, sad parting from her lover.

And now, though the ocean rolled between them, and the spheres in which each moved were so widely separated and the years had come and gone, she was yet calculating and balancing the probabilities that they might meet again and the wrong of the past be cancelled.

Mr. Lansdowne had been plodding among musty law books and threading legal intricacies, with occasional interruptions caused by fits of impatience and disgust at the detail and tedium of study, until he had at length fought his way through and placed himself in the front rank of his profession. His brilliant achievement in the famous Jenkins case, in the outset of his career, had at once won for him a position at the bar which most young men have to toil years to obtain. His family was wealthy and influential. It was not strange that with these advantages, united to the possession of remarkable personal beauty, he should be the centre of a numerous group of friends and admirers. He was the object of pride among the older barristers and gentlemen of the bench, the cynosure of the young men, and the one among a thousand whom elegant mammas and smiling maidens wooed with their selectest influences.

Yet one great element of earthly happiness was wanting to his life. He could not forget the enchantment of those days spent in the far-off wilds of Miramichi. He turned continually to those scenes as the most prominent of his existence. There he had stepped from boyhood into manhood. There he had seen life in new and before untried forms. He had there witnessed a wonderful display of God's power through the terrible agency of the all-devouring flame, and there, for the first time, he had confronted death and sorrow. There, he had loved once and as he believed, forever. He recalled Adèle, as she first appeared before him — an unexpected vision of beauty, in all her careless grace and sweet, confiding frankness; in her moments of stately pride, when she chilled him from her side and kept him afar off; and in her moments of affectionate kindness and generous enthusiasm. In short, in all her changeful moods she was daily flitting before him and he confessed to himself that he had never met a being so rich in nature and varied in powers, so noble in impulse and purpose, so peerlessly beautiful in person.

Thus he lived on from day to day, remembering and yearning and dreaming — the ocean yawning between him and his love. Concealed in the depths of his soul, there was, however, a hope fondly cherished, and a purpose half formed.

A few weeks after the reception of Mr. Norton's letter, the Count de Rossillon died. Sitting, as usual, in his great purple-cushioned arm-chair, taking his afternoon nap, he expired so gently that Mrs. Dubois, who was reading by the window, did not know, or even suspect, when the parting between spirit and body occurred. Kindly, genial, and peaceful had been his last years, and his life went out calmly as the light of day goes out amid the mellow tints of a pleasant autumn sunset.

When Mrs. Dubois went to arouse him from what seemed an unusually long slumber, she found a volume of [Fénelon] spread open upon his knee, and, turning it, her eye ran over passages full of lofty and devout aspiration. These probably expressed the latest thoughts and desires of the good chevalier, for as she looked from the pages to his face, turned upward toward the ceiling, a smile of assent and satisfaction was still lingering there, although his breath had departed and his pulse was still.

Mrs. Dubois stooped to kiss the forehead of her uncle, but started back with a sudden thrill of fear. She gazed searchingly at him for a moment, and then she knew that Death, the conqueror, stood there with her, looking upon his completed work.

After the first shock of surprise was over, she remained gazing upon the spectacle in perfect silence. A truly devout Catholic, in her grief she leaned with all a woman's trust and confidingness upon the love and power of Christ, and something of the divine calmness which we associate with the character of the mother of our Lord, and which has been so wonderfully depicted to the eye by some of the older painters, pervaded her spirit.

As she thus stood, spellbound, entranced, her eyes fixed upon the noble features irradiated with a smile of content and peace, the long silvery locks parted away from the forehead and flowing around the head, like a halo, she thought it the countenance of a saint, and her poetic fancy created at once a vision of the Saviour, with an aspect grand, glorious, yet gracious and benign, placing with His right hand a golden jewelled crown upon her uncle's head. A cloud swept up over the gorgeous earthliness of the great Rubens picture, and from out its folds shone sweet and smiling angel faces, looking down upon the scene.

Mrs. Dubois never knew how long she remained thus absorbed. She was first aroused by hearing a voice saying, in tones of fervor, "How blessed it is to die!" And Adèle, who had entered the room a little time before, and had uttered these words, stepped forward and imprinted a kiss upon the pale uplifted brow of the sleeper.

CHAPTER XXVI

POMPEII

About this period, Mrs. Lansdowne, whose health had been declining for nearly a year, was urgently advised by her physician to seek a milder climate. John immediately offered himself as her *compagnon de voyage*, and manifested great alacrity in the preparations for their departure for Italy.

After a favorable sea passage, they landed at [Civitavecchia], and, with brief delays at Rome and Naples, went to Sorrento, intending to remain there several months.

This place combines the most striking peculiarities of Italian scenery. It stands on a wide and beautiful plain, shut in by the mountains and the sea. The fertile soil produces oranges, lemons, grapes, and figs of the richest quality and in great abundance. The coast line, a wall of volcanic rock, is broken into varied forms by the constant action of the waters. Here, they spent day after day, rambling about the old town, making excursions into the neighboring mountains, or crossing the bay to different points of interest. They delighted particularly in sailing under the shadow of the cliffs, watching the varying colors, blue, purple, and green, presented by the glassy surface, peering into the arched caverns, worn into the rock by the waves, and looking upward at the gay profusion of wild flowers, which, growing in every crevice, adorned its face with beauty. From the balcony of the house they occupied, they looked upon gardens, invisible from the street, so closely were they walled in from the view of the passer by, and beheld orange and lemon trees, with rounded tops of dark green foliage, golden fruit, and snowy blossoms. The soft air permitted them to sit during the evenings and listen to the whisper of the sea on the beach, to watch the sails of the fishing vessels gleaming in the moonlight, and gaze at the dark form of Vesuvius, with his lighted torch, brooding at a distance over the scene.

A month had thus passed away. A marked improvement had taken place in Mrs. Lansdowne's health, and John proposed that they should go to Naples and make an excursion thence to Pompeii.

One morning, they drove out from the swarming city toward those famous ruins, revealing to the curious so much of the old Roman civilization. After a drive of twelve miles past fields of lava and ashes, the accumulations from recent irruptions of Vesuvius, they arrived at the street of tombs, a fitting entrance to the desolated city. Here, the beautifully sculptured monuments, memorials of a departed generation, awoke in their hearts a peculiar interest. Through these they entered at once into the inner life of joys and sorrows of an extinct race.

"How terrible death must have been to these people, whose ideas of the future world were so vague and unsatisfying, and who had really no knowledge of immortality!" said Mrs. Lansdowne.

"Yes," replied John. "And with nothing brighter or more glorious to look forward to in the beyond, how reluctant they must have felt to leave these glowing skies, this delicious air, these scenes of beauty and art, for the darkness of the grave. I fancy it must have been harder for them than if they had been surrounded with the sombre tints, the chilling atmosphere, and the more subdued forms of life in our own clime."

Leaving the cemetery, they passed on through the narrow streets, paved with blocks of lava, on which were the traces of carriage wheels worn into the material more than eighteen hundred years ago. They went into the Pompeian houses, walked over the marble mosaic floors, looked at the paintings on the walls, examined the bronzes, the statues, the domestic utensils, the shop of the oil merchant, with his name on it still legible, until, in imagination, they began to people the solitude—bringing back the gay, luxurious, beauty-loving Pompeians again to live and revel in their former haunts.

At length, quite exhausted, Mrs. Lansdowne sank down on a seat in one of the porticoes, and John, placing himself by her side, tempted her to partake of a lunch he had provided for the occasion.

Soon, the pensive influences of the scene stole over them, and they sat for some time in perfect silence.

Mrs. Lansdowne first interrupted it by exclaiming, "John, what are you thinking of?"

"Thinking of! why I was thinking just then how those Pompeians used to sit in these porticoes and talk of the deeds of Cæsar and of the eloquence of Cicero, while those renowned men were yet living, and how they discussed the great combats in the amphitheatres of Rome. And what were you cogitating, my dear mother?" said he, smiling.

"Oh! I was thinking woman's thoughts. How slowly they excavate here! I have an extreme curiosity to know what there is, yet uncovered to the light of day, beyond that dead wall of ashes."

"If I were a magician, I would apply to your eyes some unguent, which should unveil what is there concealed," said John, smiling. "Will you go now to the theatre?"

He drew his mother's arm within his, and they moved on. That portion of the city appeared as if it had been partially destroyed by a conflagration.

Looking towards Vesuvius, he said, "I can easily imagine the sensations of those who gazed at the volcano on that terrible day and saw for the first time its flames bursting out, and throwing their horrid glare on the snow-capped mountains around. Fire is a tremendous element."

As he uttered the words, the scene of the great conflagration at Miramichi rose to his view.

"*Salve! Salve!*" exclaimed a rich, musical voice near him, just at that moment.

The word and the tone in which it was uttered thrilled him, like an electric shock. He looked, with a bewildered air, in the direction from whence the voice proceeded, and saw, standing before the threshold of one of the Pompeian houses, a tall, elegant female figure, habited in mourning.

Her eyes were fixed upon the word of salutation, written on the threshold, at the entrance. After contemplating it a moment, she turned her head involuntarily towards Mr. Lansdowne, who stood transfixed to the spot. Their eyes met in instant recognition. Neither moved — they were both paralyzed with sudden emotion.

Mrs. Lansdowne looked up in surprise.

"What is it, John?"

"It is," said he, recovering himself, "it is, that I am astonished to meet here, so unexpectedly, a friend whom I supposed to be in France — certainly not here."

He led his mother forward a few steps and presented her to Mademoiselle Dubois.

M. and Mdme. Dubois, who were standing a little apart, examining some objects of interest, while this scene of recognition transpired, now joined the group and were presented to Mrs. Lansdowne. During the remainder of the day, the two families formed one party.

They visited the ruined theatre, the Forum, the temples of Isis and Hercules, but the spell of Pompeii no longer bound the souls of John and Adèle. It is true, they walked on, sometimes side by side, sometimes with other forms between, absorbed, entranced; but a spirit more potent than any inhabiting the walls of the old Roman city had touched the powers of their being and woven its sorceries around them. The living present had suddenly shut out the past.

So, after three years, they had met. Such meetings are critical. In the lapse of time, what changes may occur! There is so much in life to mar the loveliest and noblest! In regard to character, of course no one can stand still. There is either a process of deterioration going on, or a work of intellectual and spiritual advancement. Memory and imagination glorify the absent and the dead. The lovers had been constantly exercising, respecting each other, their faculty of idealization. When they parted, they were young, with limited experiences of life, with slight knowledge of their own hearts. It was a dangerous moment when they thus met.

But there was no disappointment. Mr. Lansdowne gazed upon Adèle with emotions of surprise and astonishment at the change a few years had wrought in her and marvelled at the perfection of her beauty and manner.

Adèle, albeit she was not used to the reverential mood, experienced an emotion almost verging into awe, mingled with her admiration of the noble form, the dignity and stately grace of him who had so charmed her girlish days.

Thus the acquaintance, broken off in that cold, restrained morning adieu on the banks of the Miramichi, was renewed under the sunny, joyous sky of Italy. Their communion with one another was now no longer marred by youthful waywardness and caprice. During those long years of separation, they had learned so thoroughly the miseries attending the alienation of truly loving hearts that there was no inclination on the part of either to trifle now. Day by day, the hours they spent together became sweeter, dearer, more full of love's enchantment.

"Mademoiselle Dubois," said Mr. Lansdowne a few weeks after their recognition at Pompeii, "I think I did not quite do justice to that famous excavated city when I visited it. I was so occupied with the pleasure of meeting old friends that I really did not examine objects with the attention they deserve. Tomorrow I intend to revisit the spot and make amends for my neglect. Will you give me the pleasure of your company?"

"Thank you, Mr. Lansdowne, I shall be happy to go with you. A week spent there could not exhaust the interest of the place."

The two families were still at Naples and from that city Mr. Lansdowne and Adèle started again to visit Pompeii.

No evidence, as to the amount of antiquarian lore acquired on that day by our two lovers has yet transpired, but it is certain that, while wandering among the ruins, they came before the threshold of the door where Adèle was standing when first recognized by Mr. Lansdowne. There, he gently detained her, and explained how that ancient salute of welcome to the guest and the stranger, when uttered by her lips, had thrilled his heart; how it had been treasured there as an omen of good for the future, and how the memory of it now emboldened him to speak the words he was about to utter. There, within sight of Vesuvius and with the fiery memories of Miramichi hanging upon the hour, he renewed the avowal of his love, first made in the haste and effervescence of youthful passion.

And now, Adèle did not, as then, fly from his presence. She simply put her hand in his, and pronounced in sweet and almost solemn accents the irrevocable promise.

In the meantime, Mrs. Lansdowne had been cultivating the friendship of M. and Mdme. Dubois. She was gratified to have an opportunity of thanking them in person for their hospitality and kindness to her son and brother in Miramichi. Her profound gratitude for attentions to those so dear to her would have proved a bond of sufficient strength to unite her to these new acquaintances. But she was attracted to them also by traits of mind and character unfolded in their daily intercourse.

The discovery of John's attachment to Adèle explained many things in his conduct, during the last few years, that had appeared enigmatical. With this fact made clear to her mind, it may well be supposed that she observed the young lady with keen scrutiny. At the end of a week, John confessed his intention to win Adèle if possible for his wife. His mother had no objection to such an alliance, and only wished him success in his efforts.

Having spent six weeks together at Naples and Sorrento, the party pursued their travels leisurely, for several months, through Italy and Germany, until at length they reached France. After a visit at Paris, they located themselves quietly at the chateau de Rossillon, where preparations were soon commenced for the marriage.

It was observed that the lovers, supposed to be the parties most particularly interested, were remarkably indifferent in regard to these affairs. When needed for consultation on important arrangements, they were reported to be off, riding or driving or wandering in some remote part of the park, and when at last an opportunity occurred to present some point for their consideration, they seemed to have no particular opinions on the subject.

With a very decided taste of her own, in matters of dress, not less than in other things, Adèle could not be made to attend to the details of the *trousseau*, and at last the two older ladies took it into their own hands.

In the meantime, the lovers were leading a rapturous life in the past, the present, the future. In the past they remembered the morning glories of Miramichi; in the present they saw, daily, in each other's eyes, unfathomed depths of love; as to the future it shone out before them, resplendent with the light of an earthly Paradise.

At last, the wedding day came, and the parting between Adèle and her parents. It was a great sacrifice on the part of M. and Mdme. Dubois. But, remembering their own early trials, they made no opposition to Adèle's choice. They sought only her happiness.

CHAPTER XXVII

CONCLUSION

On a dark, stormy day, in the winter of 1845, at ten o'clock, a tall, stout, elderly man, muffled in fur, rang at the door of Mr. Lansdowne.

The house was large, of brown stone, and situated on H -- Street, in the city of P --.

As the servant opened the door, the hall light fell upon a face of strongly marked features, irradiated by an expression of almost youthful cheerfulness. To the inquiry if Mr. and Mrs. Lansdowne were at home, the servant replied that they were absent, but would return shortly.

"Miss Adèle is in the drawing-room sir," he added, immediately throwing open the door of that apartment to its widest extent, as if to insure the entrance of Mr. Norton, for it was no other than the good missionary of Miramichi. He was still the warmly cherished and highly revered friend of the entire family.

Adèle, a young lady of sixteen, was sitting on a low seat in the drawing-room, beneath a blaze of waxen candles, intently occupied with a new book. She gave a start on being recalled so suddenly from the fancy land in which she was roaming, but after a moment of bewilderment, flung aside her book, came quickly forward, put her arms around the neck of Mr. Norton, who bent down to receive them, and welcomed him with a cordial kiss.

"Every day more and more like your mother, Miss Adèle," said he, as, after returning her salutation, he held her at arm's length and surveyed her from head to foot.

"Papa and mamma will be home soon," said Adèle. "They went to dine at Mr. Holbrook's. It is time for their return."

"All right, my dear. And how are you all?"

The young lady led him to a large, cushioned arm-chair.

"How did you leave mamma Norton, Jenny, and Fanny?"

"All quite well. And they sent love," replied the missionary.

"How is Gray Eagle?"

"Ah! Gray Eagle is good for many a trot round the parish yet."

"I have not forgotten how he shot over the hills with me last summer. He began his scamper the moment I was fairly seated on his back. I hope he has sobered down a little since then," said Adèle.

"Yes, I remember. Gray Eagle knew well enough that the little sprite he carried liked a scamper as well as himself. The animal is quite well, I thank you, and is on good behavior. So are your other acquaintances, Cherry, the cow, and Hodge, the cat."

"I am glad to hear it. I had a charming visit at Rockdale last summer. Johnny and Gabrielle are wild to go there. But mamma and I, and all of us, were so disappointed because you would not consent to Fanny and Jenny coming to spend the winter with us. Mamma says she does not quite understand yet why you objected."

"Ah! well, my dear, I'll make it all right with your mamma. The fact is, I wish to get a few rational ideas into the heads of those precious little ladies before they are launched out into city life. Just a little ballast to keep them from capsizing in a gale."

"Mamma says they are both very much like you," said Adèle, archly.

"True, my dear. That makes it all the more necessary to look after them carefully."

After a few moments of chat, Adèle left the room to give orders for hastening supper.

During her absence, Mr. Norton, with his eyes fixed upon the glowing grate, fell into a fit of musing. Look at him a moment, while he sits thus, occupied with the memories of the past. Twenty years have passed since he was introduced to the attention of the reader, a missionary to a remote and benighted region. He is now sixty years old, and very few have passed through greater toil and hardships than he has endured in asserting the claims of the Redeemer to the gratitude and love of the race. Yet his health and vigor of mind are scarcely impaired, and his zeal continues unabated.

Beginning his journey early each spring and returning to his family late every autumn, he had spent sixteen successive summers in

Miramichi engaged in self-imposed labors. Each winter, he wrought at his anvil, and thus helped to maintain an honest independence.

Four years previous, a parish having become vacant in the town where he resided, it was urged upon his acceptance by the unanimous voice of the people. By his efforts, a great change had been wrought in the field of his past labors and a supply of suitable religious teachers having been provided there, he accepted the invitation as a call of Divine Providence, and had ministered to the spiritual wants of the people of Rockdale since.

Business called him occasionally to the city of P --. His visits there were always regarded by the Lansdownes as especial favors. The two families had frequently interchanged visits and had grown into habits of the closest intimacy.

Having been in the city several hours and dispatched the affairs which drew him thither, he had now come to look in upon his friends for the night, expecting to hasten away at [day-dawn].

There was something in his situation this evening, thus housed in warmth, light, and comfort, protected from the darkness and the storm without, and ministered unto by a lovely young maiden, that reminded him of a like scene that had occurred twenty years ago. He vividly recalled the evening, when, after a day of toil and travel on the banks of the distant Miramichi, he reached the house of Dubois, and how while the tempest raged without he was cheered by the light and warmth within, and was ministered unto by another youthful maiden, in form and feature so like her who had just left him, that he could almost imagine them the same. A glance around the apartment, however, dispelled the momentary fancy. Its rich and beautiful adornments afforded a striking contrast to the appointments of that humble room.

He was roused from his meditations by the ringing of the street bell, and in a moment Mr. and Mrs. Lansdowne came forward to welcome their early and long-tried friend.

The good man, who loved them with an affection akin to that which he felt for his own family, had preserved a watchful care over their earthly and spiritual welfare. Sometimes he feared that their wealth and fame might draw away their hearts from the highest good and impair the simplicity of their religious faith.

After the first cordial greetings, in accordance with his habit on occasions like this, he indulged in a careful scrutiny of his two friends.

Time had in no wise impaired the charms of Mrs. Lansdowne. Experience of life, maternal cares, and religious duties had added a softer light to her once proud beauty, and her old friend might well be pardoned a thrill of admiration as he gazed and thought within his heart that Mrs. Lansdowne, robed in black velvet, Mechlin lace, and the diamonds of the house of Rossillon, surpassed in loveliness the radiant Adèle Dubois, arrayed in the aerial garments of girlhood.

When also his keen eye had wandered over the face and figure of John Lansdowne, it returned from its explorations satisfied. No habits of excess had impaired the muscular strength and vigor of his form. Nor had ungoverned passion, avarice, political craft, or disappointed ambition drawn deep defacing [lines] to mar the noble beauty of his countenance.

"It is well with them still," ejaculated the good man mentally, "and may God bless them forever."

Afterword

Critical Apparatus and Notes for
Adèle Dubois: A Story of the Miramichi Valley

It is indeed true that the wider one's knowledge of history, the more fully and informed is one's engagement in the business of citizenship. That correlation between historical understanding and informed citizenship is especially vital today in the swirl of manufactured truths and alternative facts that surround us. Of course, no one is immune from those fictions, and no one ever was, but we can at least counter them by educating ourselves about the contextual conditions that both predate us and inform aspects of our present situation. Such is the reasoning behind the detailed historical analysis below. It is meant to deepen our understanding of the New Brunswick we inhabit today and the New Brunswick from which we come.

Authorship

Mary Langdon Bradbury was born on 2 April 1817 in York, Maine, just north of Portsmouth, New Hampshire. The eldest daughter of Jeremiah Bradbury and Mary Langdon Storer, she spent her formative years in the rural town of Alfred, Maine, where she acquired a "superior education" in a family "of rare domestic culture" that was known for its religious devotions and public standing.[1] That education and culture are evident in *Adèle Dubois*. Her father was a collector for US Customs and her mother was descended from high-ranking military and seafaring stock. At a young age, Mary Bradbury became deeply committed to the Congregational Church, studying at seminaries in Ipswich, Massachusetts, and Portland, Maine.[2] That calling, too, is everywhere present in the pages of her novel. On 5 April 1841,[3] she married Rev. William T. Savage, who had been a teacher in Alfred, Maine, and, after theological study, had been appointed pastor of the Congregational Church in the not-too-distant town of Amherst, New Hampshire. After a few years of difficult pastoral work, the young couple, in Rev. Savage's telling, "escaped … to the wilderness" of Houlton, Maine, a frontier garrison town on the Maine/New Brunswick border.[4]

Their arrival in Houlton in 1844 followed the signing of the Webster-Ashburton Treaty in 1842. The treaty had settled a long-standing US/British dispute over territory divided at the time of the Treaty of Paris in 1783, a dispute that eventually led to the Aroostook War (1838-39). Under the terms of the Webster-Ashburton Treaty, large northern and eastern portions of what is now the state of Maine became US territory, while Britain secured the important strategic corridor connecting Lower Canada to New Brunswick and Nova Scotia just south of the St. Lawrence River. *Adèle Dubois,* published twenty-three years after the treaty was signed, still takes for granted that the Maine/New Brunswick border is within an unmapped and "disputed" wilderness territory.[5] Consequently, the northeastern British North American lands that *Adèle Dubois*'s characters roam are treated as extensions of New England home territory. As observer William T. Baird explained, the residents of Houlton were "frequent visitors to Woodstock" and New Brunswick residents, in turn, went often "to Houlton to join in the sports, listen to the fourth of July spread-eagle orations, and return more or less tinctured with American proclivities." Not only that, but "the population [of Houlton in the 1840s] was made up largely of people from New Brunswick." The easy mixing of residents illustrated Joshua Smith's point that populations on both sides of the border "refused to accept the idea that the border created in 1783 meant that people on the other side of it were 'foreigners.'"[6]

That an essential part of Rev. Savage's pastoral duties included ministering to a wilderness of souls in a tangle of woods supports the likelihood that the Savages, too, pursued cross-border travel throughout western and central New Brunswick during their five years in Houlton—and accounts also for Mary Savage's familiarity with the area's topography. These factors address two essential questions about authorship: namely, was Mary Savage a New

Brunswick author and is *Adèle Dubois* a New Brunswick work? The considered answer to the second and more important of the two questions is yes. Though there is no evidence to suggest that Mary Savage was a resident of the province of New Brunswick, her life on the border and her familiarity with the vast expanse of a northern Maine that *included* New Brunswick, if unofficially, equipped her to write as knowingly about the province as any writer of her time. Her nineteenth-century fictional account of our province is therefore valuable.

As highly educated readers of northeastern US history, she and her Bangor-born husband were steeped in two well-known accounts that would have informed her fictional imaginings. The first was the journal account of Bangor surveyor Major Joseph Treat, who was commissioned by Maine's first governor, William King, to map the northeast wilderness shortly after Maine obtained statehood in 1820. Treat and his Indigenous guide John Neptune travelled through Wabanaki territory along the Penobscot and Allagash rivers to the St. John River, exploring northern Maine and western New Brunswick, and stopping along the way at sites of interest, such as the historically significant Mattawamkeag Point.[7] Henry David Thoreau followed suit in his own 1846 and 1853 journeys to the Houlton Military Road, those journeys recounted in *The Maine Woods* (1864). Mary Savage's *Adèle Dubois* contains two near-identical journeys of characters following a similar line from southern Maine, along the Mattawamkeag roads that Houlton-based garrison officers cut, and into western New Brunswick.

The point is that traversing what was considered a "soft" border in the northeastern Maine woods was not only part of the missionary work of the Savages, but also part of the imaginative culture in which the young couple found themselves at mid-century. Popular accounts of the Lewis and Clark expedition of 1804-6 had taken full effect. Along the north Atlantic, those accounts were manifest as a borderlands woodlore that was ubiquitous among the intellectual classes, much of that detailing a wild and inviting, if coarse, British North America. New York sports journalist Charles Hallock was one of many writers who fed the appetite for borderland intrigue. In an 1863 exposé for *Harper's New Monthly Magazine*, he employed romantic flourish to describe the "Arcadian forests" and "motley population" of settlers who inhabited the corridor between Aroostook and Madawaska counties, fixing the region in a timeless stasis of sixteenth-century dimensions.[8] While there is no direct evidence that Mary Savage read Treat's journals, Thoreau's *Maine Woods*, or Hallock's description of the Madawaska rustics in advance of writing *Adèle Dubois*, the contiguous timing and spatial similarities in those works offer insight into the forces that carried those authors on their journeys through the northern expanse. Such travelogues had become characteristic of the narrative signature of the Americas. Mary Savage's characters thus follow a pathway through backwoods and wilderness that had been previously staged by mapmakers and adventurers alike, the territory of their exploration always, in her words, appearing "in splendid and wasteful confusion."[9] On full display in *Adèle Dubois*, the objective is to tantalize and unsettle sophisticated readers, but to do so in ways that never stray far from the familiar. Here, for example, is her description of a burned area just inside what she terms "the British boundary" (New Brunswick):

> John rode over the glowing ground, the black monsters grimacing and scowling at him as he passed. What a nice eerie place this would be thought he for witches, wizards, and all Satan's gentry, of every shape and hue, to hold their high revels in.[10]

The passage reverberates with wonder at strangeness but not at the expense of the familiar, as the tone and imagery immediately recall Nathanial Hawthorne and Edgar Allan Poe, fellow New Englanders whose supernatural touches obviously delighted and influenced a young Mary Bradbury. New Brunswick's literary debt to those writers—and, more specifically, to gothic and Transcendentalist traditions that expressed a mix of colonial fear of the unknown and fetish for Indigenous ways of knowing—is clear. Those forces and tensions also excited Mary Savage's imagination, as they excited the imaginations of early New Brunswickers W.D. Kearney (*The Open Hand*, 1864), Arthur Slader (*The Conflagrations*, 1837), and "A Native of New Brunswick" (*The Lay of the Wilderness*, 1833). In other words, it didn't much matter which side of the Maine/New Brunswick border one was on: nineteenth-century literary taste had already selected a particular kind of treatment for the vast and still-wild northeast.

A final biographical connection to New Brunswick furthers the case for the American-authored *Adèle Dubois* being read with the provincial authority and attention it deserves. That connection involves Mary Savage's interest in the Miramichi, an interest cultivated by shared state and provincial histories and settlement patterns, and further developed through her marriage into the Savage family. In 1820, the New Brunswick government set aside fifty 200-acre plots of free land that ran laterally from Cape Tormentine to Port Elgin in the southeast corner of the province. The initiative was meant to attract immigrants at a time when New Brunswick was in the throes of an acute labour shortage, and Ireland, the likely source of those immigrants, was in a severe post-Napoleonic depression (1815-1821) — so severe, quipped family historian Rev. Edward Savage, that "the laboring classes ... quarrelled with the swine for their food."[11] "Almost immediately," wrote historians Houston and Smyth, "a community [of pre-famine Catholic Irish immigrants] took shape, built around numerous kin links, common origins, and common experiences."[12] New Brunswick's lieutenant governor, Sir Howard Douglas, sweetened the policy in 1824 by offering free tools, seeds, and other supports to the incoming Irish, the effort redoubling interest in New Brunswick as a popular destination. The result of such largess, observed Donald MacKay, "touched off a chain migration of [Irish] relatives and neighbours in the next few years," swelling the number of Irish in the province to 25 per cent of the population.[13] Whole families, neighbourhoods, and even communities relocated to New Brunswick, evidenced by the sudden appearance of villages like New Bandon on the province's northeast shore.

When the free land had been claimed and the settlement of Savagetown (known variously as Melrose or Emigrant Road) was established on the Tormentine peninsula, the Irish who kept arriving had to choose other places in the province to settle. One of the most attractive was the Miramichi, where scores of Catholic

Irish had been settling for decades. It was there that a line of the William Savage and Margaret Lane family took residence in the hope of prospering from opportunities afforded by "some of the best stands of pine in British North America."[14] That Savage line had originated in Bally-na-moche, Co. Cork, Ireland, where the patriarch William Savage was born circa 1750.[15] His descendants' residency in the Miramichi region of central New Brunswick was both memorable and temporary, however, for the Great Miramichi Fire of 1825 forced their exit soon after arrival in 1821-22.[16] A few returned to the Tormentine peninsula, while others went to Saint John, Irishtown (north of Moncton), Maine, and Illinois, the last two places also a preferred destination for Rev. William T. Savage's line into which Mary Bradbury had married. And while the William T. Savage paternal line was rooted in Boston long before the 1820's Tormentine immigration and 1825 Miramichi Fire, the fire's centrality in Savage family lore must have been highly significant for subsequent generations. At least *Adèle Dubois* suggests that it was, for the entirety of the novel is constructed as either pretext for or postscript of the fire.

The late-eighteenth-century genealogical record that would confirm a connection between the Savage families in Maine (*Adèle Dubois*) and Miramichi (Co. Cork, Ireland) is inconclusive. What is known about the Catholic Savages who went to the Miramichi in the 1820s is that they came from Murragh Parish, Co. Cork, and had wider, intergenerational connections in Kilkenny, Waterford, and Kerry.[17] Their line before parents William Savage (1750-1824) and Margaret Lane (1752-1830), and grandparents George Savage (1725-1800) and Elizabeth Hurst (1725-99), suggests Irish and English (Southwell, Nottinghamshire) residency. What is known about William T. Savage's Protestant line is that it descended from a Major Thomas Savage, who was born in North London circa 1608 and settled in the Boston area in his late twenties. Subsequent Savage generations spread out over New England but always considered Boston home. William T. Savage's paternal grandparents—John Savage (1739-98) and Mary Greenough (1746-92)—moved their family from Lincoln County to York, Maine, where Alexander Savage, William T.'s father, was born in 1780. As a young man, Alexander moved to Bangor, where he became town clerk and an original member of the Hammond Street Congregational Church.[18] All his children, including Rev. William T., were born in Bangor. Convergence of the Savage lines from Miramichi/Ireland and Bangor/Boston is possible, perhaps even probable, but difficult to trace.

In his genealogical analysis of the 1820's Savage family in southern New Brunswick, Rev. Edward Savage comes closest to establishing a connection, suggesting a direct, first-generational line between the 1820 Miramichi and Clark County, Illinois, families. More revealingly, he also draws a connection between descendants of the Miramichi Savage and Hennessey families in Bangor, Maine, where Daniel Hennessey was a well-known doctor at the time of the birth of the Savage children.[19] Subsequent to that, members of both lines either had interests or settled for a time around the Pemaquid lands (Lincoln County) of coastal Maine. Finally, there also may have been contacts in Whiteside and Cook counties in Illinois, where members of both lines settled in the 1840s. (Rev. William T. and his father, Alexander, died in Quincy, Illinois, southwest of Whiteside.)

All those intriguing possibilities aside, the greatest likelihood of connection is to be found in the shared heritage that historians Houston and Smyth identified: namely, that the families *knew of* each other through the "kin links, common origins, and common experiences" they shared. Most New Brunswick historians posit a similar confluence of interests, T.W. Acheson suggesting that the "common [Irish] ethnicity" that took root in the province in the 1820s consolidated scattered threads of history, ancestry, and other forms of tribal knowledge.[20] Whether as a result of the influence of the St. Patrick's and Sons of Erin societies, the political activities fomented at Saint John's Hibernian Hotel, the fact that the "first six bishops of New Brunswick were men of Irish birth or parentage," or "the role of the Irish language in helping to maintain a sense of identity" among the Catholic Irish immigrants to New Brunswick, Irishness became a dominant provincial narrative in the early decades of the nineteenth century.[21] What Acheson calls a new "faith in a structured conservative unitary society" was to become central in the "one reliable newspaper" that Irish Catholics and

Protestants on both sides of the Maine/New Brunswick border read.[22] That paper, the Saint John *Freeman,* was edited by "the most prominent Irish politician in New Brunswick," Timothy Warren Anglin, who tilted it toward the kin themes and linkages that sustained the diasporic Irish community.[23] What the Saint John *Freeman* did in New Brunswick to rouse Irish nationalism among Catholics, Thomas D'Arcy McGee's *American Celt* did in Boston and New York, both papers bringing Irish readers together across the Maine/New Brunswick border. The knowledge of shared heritage gleaned from pulpit, folk, and print exposures would certainly prime the pump of curiosity and explain the consequential nature of key events like the 1825 fire in familial and communal memory.

In that context it is reasonable to suppose that Mary Savage and her husband travelled to the Miramichi while living in the New Brunswick border town of Houlton. They were steeped in regional myth and family history, already frequent voyagers, and, despite Mary's fragile health, no armchair travellers. At a minimum, her husband's tribal connection to the fire as well as her own detailed representation of it in *Adèle Dubois* suggest that she was sufficiently preoccupied with the event that she had read Robert Cooney's eyewitness account in *Compendious History* (1832)—she clearly did, obviously fascinated by his treatment of the fire as "General Judgment" and of the region's renewal as "Phoenix"-like—and, from that, intrigued enough by his telling that she wished to explore it further in fiction.[24] As New Brunswick naturalist William Francis Ganong described in his compilation of accounts of the fire, stories of its wrath had reached an eager readership in Maine. One such widely circulated story published in Halifax in 1825 held that the eastern half of "the State of Maine" was so fully enveloped that the Penobscot River "resembl[ed] a sea of fire for thirty miles of its course."[25] Even without the Savage connection, the novelist in Mary Bradbury would have been intrigued.

Critical and Textual History

Bringing *Adèle Dubois* back to public notice from its long slumber began in archival discovery. Clues to when the process started on the Canadian side of the border are found in a June 1958 letter from New Brunswick poet and *Fiddlehead* editor Fred Cogswell to Ottawa-based Canadian literature scholar Robert McDougall. In the letter, Cogswell spoke of "that Klinck project," a reference to the *Literary History of Canada* that Carl F. Klinck and Northrop Frye had conceived in earlier discussions. Cogswell could not help being part of this pan-Canadian project because his two principal mentors, UNB's Alfred G. Bailey and Desmond Pacey, were associate editors. In answer to their invitation to contribute, Cogswell went to the Dalhousie University Library in May 1958 to read Maritime literature of the nineteenth century.[26] One of the reference books he consulted there was Lyle H. Wright's just-released bibliography *American Fiction 1851-1875*. In it, he came across a reference to the first-edition *Miramichi* and the later *Adèle Dubois*, both attributed to "Savage, Mrs. Mary L. [Bradbury]."[27] Early accession records indicate that the Dalhousie College library did not have a copy of the novel,[28] but, upon his return, Cogswell found a copy in UNB's Rufus Hathaway Collection of Canadiana. It had been purchased by the UNB library in February 1949, its author incorrectly recorded as A.K. Loring, the name of the publisher.[29] Cogswell asked UNB librarian M.J. Thompson to inquire further into the novel's authorship. The July 1958 correspondence between Thompson and Mildred O'Connor of the Boston Public Library is strong indication that Cogswell had located something of more-than-casual interest. Without "the moralistic and melodramatic trends ... [of the] amateur fiction" of the period, he would later write, *Miramichi* stood out because of its "local realism" and what it said about "living in New Brunswick during the middle years of the nineteenth century."[30] Its locally informed realism was in fact so compelling that Cogswell placed it next to Walter Bates's *The Mysterious Stranger* (1817) as one of the best examples of early realism in New Brunswick literary history.

When R.E. Watters's pioneering bibliography *A Check List of Canadian Literature and Background Materials, 1628-1950* came out the next year (1959), *Miramichi* and *Adèle Dubois* were not listed,[31] but Cogswell was on the case, mentioning the novel in his survey of Maritime fiction for the *Literary History of Canada* (1965) and again in his overview of New Brunswick literature for the centennial book *Arts in New Brunswick* (1967). The novel, it seemed, had resurfaced, but continued to be shrouded in mystery. After that flurry of brief notices, Cogswell abandoned further inquiry, as did his students and the contemporaries who were eagerly mining works of Canadian criticism for new research opportunities. The reason was likely that they could not unravel the novel's textual history or place its authorship and provenance in the broader borderlands contexts they deserved. The last paragraph of Mildred O'Connor's July 1958 letter to UNB's M.J. Thompson supports this conclusion, indicating that, despite trying, her research staff was unable to find information about Mrs. William T. Savage. What is now clear is that the obscurity surrounding *Adèle Dubois*'s textual history contributed to some of the enigma surrounding the novel. Untangling that clotted textual history is thus key to understanding how the novel fared in its time and why it languished for so long.

Released by Loring Publishers of Boston as a first edition in 1865, *Miramichi* was the first of three titles (see Figure 2). Only months after launch, the novel was re-issued with the same title in clearly marked second and third editions, and, shortly thereafter, re-issued with the longer title *Miramichi: A Story of the Miramichi Valley, New Brunswick* in Loring's Railway Library series (see Figure 3). It was then re-issued again circa 1868 under its final title *Adèle Dubois: A Story of the Lovely Miramichi Valley, in New Brunswick* (see Figure 1, 1868 title page).[32] The last re-issue is difficult to date because Loring did not provide a year on the title or copyright page; however, advance notices in the literary press indicate that *Adèle Dubois* arrived sometime in 1868.

Though the variant titles are at first confusing, an 1868 comment in *The Nation* offers a clue to why there were so many: "as [*Miramichi*] is not sufficiently interesting to make it probable that a second edition has been called for, and the present issue [*Adèle Dubois*] makes no mention of the former one, the unsold copies have probably been rechristened and put in a cheaper form upon the market."[33] This appears to have been the case, as extant versions of *Adèle Dubois* have different cover pages and lack the table of contents of the earlier issues, while remaining otherwise unchanged.

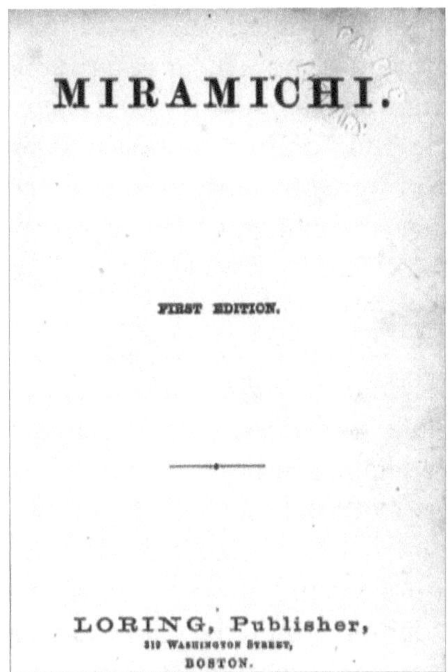

Figure 2

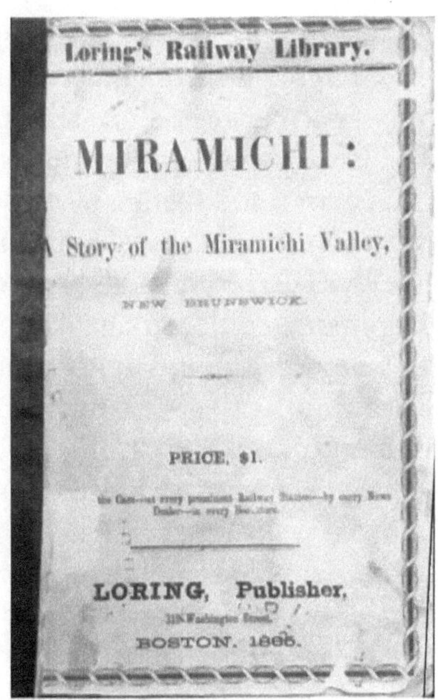

Figure 3

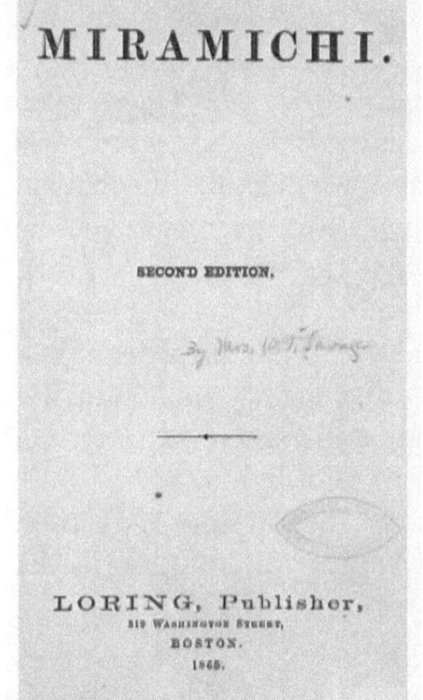

Figure 4

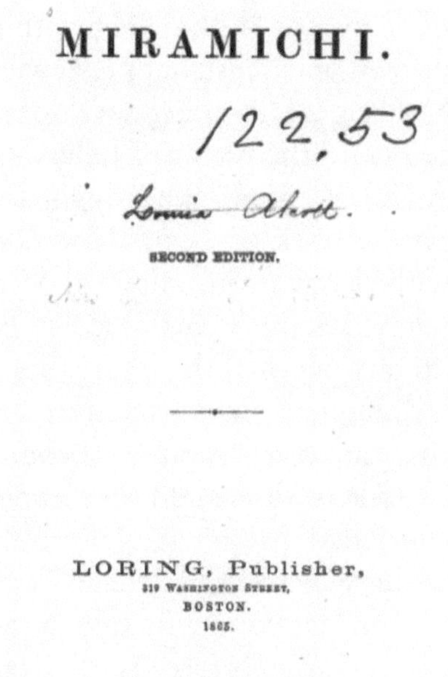

Figure 5

Errors are uncorrected, pagination and layout are identical, and, most tellingly, the original running title "Miramichi" appears at the top of each page of all re-issues, even the later-titled *Adèle Dubois*. The stereotype plates made for the 1865 edition by first printer J.E. Farwell and Company of Boston were obviously used again as copy-text for all subsequent printings, including by the last printer Rockwell and Rollins, also of Boston.[34] Loring was clearly retitling unsold first editions to get rid of inventory and recoup costs.

The lack of attribution across appellations supports this reasoning, as does the final title change to *Adèle Dubois*, a not-insignificant alteration that was likely a concession to the largely female demographic of Loring's readership. In short, the book had not sold well. That other Loring titles of the time, including those by women, *had* attribution,[35] suggests that Loring considered *Adèle Dubois* either a light work or its author too unknown to contribute to its marketing—all the more reason to put it on the market under different titles to different readerships, railway patrons being one. The critical response to the novel points to the same conclusion, as does the fact that there were more notices of publication than reviews, though the kind of extended reviews we know today were not common in the nineteenth century. Even Loring went against its own practice in not previewing or advertising *Adèle Dubois* in the back pages of its other novels of the time, those back pages preferring to herald the works of Julia C. Stretton, Menella B. Smedley, and A.D.T. Whitney. The only small gesture Loring made was to declare on the back cover of *Adèle Dubois* that the novel was "uniform with [Louisa May Alcott's] *Moods*," hoping, it seems, that it might piggyback on Alcott's success. Beyond that, what did appear in the literary pages of the local press struck dual tones of politeness and indifference. Reviewers were generally underwhelmed, observing that the novel "is rather above the average of light reading," while its style is "direct and simple; perhaps a trifle too simple." Another concluded that its value lay mostly in revealing "the little information we have concerning [the Miramichi region]."[36]

The last comment says something of importance to us today about *Adèle Dubois*. Among readers of the time, there seems to have been confusion about where the novel belonged. Was it a

New Brunswick novel? Clearly it was, but how could it be if it was written by an American? Was it an American novel? Well, its author was American, but it was situated elsewhere and focused on events that were at best peripheral to America. Without more obvious allegiances to anchor and categorize it, *Adèle Dubois* was therefore neither an American nor Canadian novel at a time when works of fiction were valued in terms of how well they indexed nationhood. An always self-interested America and a Canada on the eve of Confederation demanded nothing less. Identity was key. Had *Adèle Dubois* confined itself to the American side of the border, exploring northern Maine as knowingly as it explored central New Brunswick, its fortunes may have been different—as its fortunes may have differed if Mary Savage had been Canadian. If she had been, *Adèle Dubois* may have earned a place in Canada's nineteenth-century record as enduring as that of Sara Jeannette Duncan's *The Imperialist* (1904), another novel that explores the growing pains of emergent nationhood. For all its insight into pre-Confederation politics and social manners, then, *Adèle Dubois*'s achievement is to be found in its early life as a unique, rather misunderstood, hybrid thing. The transnational qualities that lend credence to it today hindered its appreciation at the time of its release. It deserved better, which is another reason why a critically informed reprint is warranted.

Situating the Fictional Story in Time, Space, and the Political Culture of the Time

Much of the action of the novel takes place "in the summer and autumn of 1825" along a stretch of the Miramichi River said to be "about sixty miles west from Chatham."[37] The location would be close to present-day Boiestown, where entry to central New Brunswick from the Taxis River was common in the early part of the nineteenth century. When two of the novel's characters travel to Fredericton to address a problem of law, they portage "through the wilderness [about] twenty miles" from the Miramichi to the Nashwaak watersheds, then follow the Nashwaak south to Fredericton.[38] The portage referred to is no doubt the Burnt Land Brook Portage, which early provincial historian Robert Cooney estimated was "23 miles" from the Nashwaak.[39] The "Dubois" surname offers more evidence for this general location. Pronounced "Doo-byce" by the Scots in the novel, the surname may be a veiled reference to Thomas Boies, founder of Boiestown and originally an American from Bedford, New Hampshire, not far from where Mary Savage and her husband settled immediately after marriage. Cooney explains that Boiestown was founded around 1821 and is considered one of the oldest villages in the northeast—in fact, a settlement of "principally adults from the United States."[40] Though Mary Savage's fictional Dubois is a Frenchman, the parallels between her patriarch and the historical Boies are striking, one of those similarities being that both lent their name to the settlements they founded.[41]

Equally striking is the ancestry she assigns to the fictional Dubois family. They are from Picardy, France, a region north of Paris that saw an exodus of citizens in the 1860s. Some of those who left went to northwestern New Brunswick and founded the village of Saint-Quentin, so named after a town of the same name in the Picardy region. The area of France they departed is perhaps best known for its most famous resident, the novelist and playwright Jules Verne, a writer fascinated by adventure, travel, and first contacts. Though some conflating of allusion is clearly present in Mary Savage's imagination, the fictional family name and ancestry she chooses, as well as the circumstance of their arrival from France, suggest that she was fully conversant with the history of Napoleonic France, including the fiction of Verne. The Bonapartists and "dethroned Bourbons" are mentioned in the novel, as is Amiens and "a fine, but not large estate, bordering on the River Somme" that is the maternal homeland from which Claude and Marie Dubois set off for "British America."[42] Significantly, the three principal locales in *Adèle Dubois*—Boiestown, Picardy, and southern Maine—reflect a deep knowledge and experience of intersecting emigration lines along the nineteenth-century Maine/New Brunswick border. That first-hand experience paints a picture of New Brunswick as a place connected to, albeit remote from, the global world.

The tenuousness of that connection is key, for the province's remoteness from the larger world in *Adèle Dubois* is not just a happenstance of geography but spiritual as well. The Miramichi region is described repeatedly as spiritually undeveloped—as wild, heathen, and morally reprehensible, "[a] land where the darkness may be *felt*."[43] Its people are likewise wayward and lawless, ignorant and debased. "They all drink, swear, gamble, and profane holy things," seeming "to have no respect for either God or man."[44] That representation functions as both plot device and historical marker. As plot device, it offers a point of entry for the forces that will put New Brunswickers on the right path; and, as historical marker, it uses the Miramichi as synecdoche for everything north of the civilities of Fredericton, thus further normalizing the north/south, French/English, Irish/Loyalist divisions of New Brunswick that historians have noted and which we still live with today.[45] The cultural geography of the novel is therefore accurate, even if it is ideologically laden with the views of an intellectual class that Mary Savage was reading at the time.[46] Importantly, those views still inform how residents of the province think of the "mutually exclusive parochialisms" that divide New Brunswick today.[47]

Into this Miramichi "abyss of ignorance and sin" comes horseback missionary Mr. Norton, a self-elected American evangelical called there, "almost audibly," to convert the godless.[48] Identified on the book jacket of the second issue of *Miramichi* as "an honest, religious Methodist blacksmith," he is more recognizably Baptist in modelling the progressive spiritual independence so admired by Maritime "Baptists, Methodists, and Congregationalists alike."[49] (The difficulty of categorizing his affiliation is actually a marker of his Free Will gospel.) He is lodging at the affluent Dubois home when Mr. Dubois brings in a mysterious traveller whom he has come across while journeying to Fredericton. Known only as Mr. Brown, the stranger falls into the delirium of typhoid fever as soon as he arrives. As the preacher Norton attempts to convert the heathens around him, the identity of Mr. Brown is slowly revealed, both actions bringing southern Maine and central New Brunswick together across the border they share.

He is, it turns out, Mr. Edward Somers, an American gentleman who has fled the southern Maine city of "P-" in disgrace.[50] Attempting to locate Mr. Somers and bring him home to the US is John Lansdowne, his nephew, who has also left P- and follows the same

Maine lumbering trails to the Miramichi through the Penobscot River Valley and Mattawamkeag. It is John Lansdowne's seventeen-day journey that is recounted in the novel, a journey so familiar in the tonality of its descriptions of the sometimes-malevolent, near-impenetrable northeast woods that New Brunswick readers may reasonably wonder if Charles G.D. Roberts was thinking of *Adèle Dubois* when he wrote *The Heart of the Ancient Wood* (1900) thirty-five years later.[51]

Against the parallel narratives of two Americans—one the preacher seeking entrance, the other the disgraced gentleman seeking escape—is the sixteen-year-old Adèle Dubois, daughter of the novel's patriarch. Strong-willed and full of modern attitudes, she is the object of the affections of the locals, none more smitten than Micah Mummychog, a fellow who "drinks and swears as hard as the rest of them."[52] To readers of Maritime literature, his unusual name and manner will suggest that the author was familiar with Thomas McCulloch and Thomas Chandler Haliburton. To the author's contemporaries, the name would have recalled the Atlantic killifish, the mummichog, a small minnow that swims in schools in brackish waters. In the nineteenth century, killifish were introduced to mosquito-infested ponds to rid them of larvae. With no individualism of its own, each mummichog follows its kind in despoiled streams only to eat and reproduce, exhibiting the same ignorant behaviour in a similar "kingdom of darkness" that the godless New Brunswickers do.[53] Though the comparison isn't flattering, the novel's overarching missionary aim requires that ignorance is constructed as the problem if redemption is to be the solution.

Adèle shines by contrast. She is the "perfect beauty"[54] that the era's penchant for romance demanded, and, as convention dictates, the young nephew from P- falls hard for her. Like the "knights errant, ... who, while ranging the world in quest of adventures, were bewitched by lovely wood fairies," he surrenders all his power to her.[55] In form, arc, and elevated language, then, the novel is a gothic romance as well as a morality tale, yet it inhabits both traditions uneasily. The Dubois house is affluent and warm, surrounded by a sinister forest where dwells a formidable darkness. The contrast of light and dark is ever-present, whether in personal conduct, social class (primitive vs. cultivated, new world vs. old), or moral law. Terror and horror are fixtures, as are superstitions, secrets, and ghosts. There is a Byronic hero on a quest, a colourful assortment of bandits and madmen, a European aristocracy in the last stages of decay,[56] a fair maiden playing coy, and even a salty old Scottish nurse who drinks whisky to excess. As well, fortuitous coincidences are commonplace.

Yet, despite its predominantly romantic features, the novel, as Fred Cogswell remarked, is also inflected with a good deal of unadorned realism and emotion that work against the atmospheric and the sublime. In fact, the novel takes issue with the romantic impulses that sustain it, equating those forces—most often appetite, idolatry, rigidity of belief, and superstition—with the spiritual adolescence of Catholic, Calvinist, and Anglican sensibilities. In doing so, the novel seeks to mute rural ignorance with the more austere rationalism of evangelical logic. Preacher Norton's particular brand of Baptist theology is thus akin to the progressive form that religious historians Stephen Marini and George Rawlyk identified in both New England and the Maritimes of the nineteenth century. That brand of Baptist thought was "experimental rather than doctrinal," explained Rawlyk, yearning to be "accommodationist rather than being narrowly rigid." It was also, wrote Marini, rooted in Biblical literalism and the intense, magnetic charisma of preachers like Norton and the real-life Robert Cooney, who filled lecture halls in Saint John in the 1840s and '50s.[57] Micah's Grove, the place where Norton holds his revivalist meetings of the "strange, motley crowd" of locals,"[58] is the ground where this progressive theology plays out—and where the differences between rural ignorance and evangelical logic are most clearly seen.

The name "Micah's Grove" is carefully chosen by Mary Savage to allude to both the Book of Micah and the many groves or gardens in the Hebrew Bible and Old Testament scriptures where faith and suffering collide. Much in the same way as the historical Micah prophesized the destruction of Jerusalem as retribution for its leaders' appetites and secular habits, *Adèle Dubois* hints repeatedly at the interconnection of the sins of established churches and the drought that is gripping the irreligious Miramichi, a drought that is sure to result in some sort of great reckoning, perhaps a cleansing fire that will burn all iniquity away. Following the lines of Micah's story, Mr. Norton is another in a long line of descendants of David that God has brought into the wilderness (the Miramichi) to bring consolation to people "from a considerable distance around."[59] And, as his precursor did, Norton fashions his grove into an ecumenical ground where order and beauty replace a darkness born of inattentive and self-interested church leadership. His disputes with the Dubois family over Catholic indulgence, with Mrs. McNab, the Scottish wit, over predestination, and with High Church Anglicanism over ritual and hierarchy serve ultimately to equate an enlightened ecclesiastical sovereignty with political autonomy. Not to be missed in that conflation is the argument that complete freedom and independence within both church and state is the most advanced form of each.

While Mr. Norton goes about winning converts to these ideas in his simple but heartfelt outdoor sermons, evidence of contrary spiritual truth and practice abound. The Catholic priest won't bury a poor Irish smuggler because he died in the commission of sin, and the Anglican minister is too much a "*bon vivant*, a horse jockey and sportsman" to care.[60] The indifference of established churches had indeed turned New Brunswickers into what Baptist preacher Edward Manning Saunders famously termed "adepts in wickedness."[61] The contrast presented is clear: an uncaring Catholicism, a self-satisfied Anglicanism, and a too-rigid and unquestioning Calvinism stunt the moral character of the region, suppressing its fuller development.

Adèle is placed outside those moral failures. As a representative of a generation best able to veer from indifference and decadence, she is the burgeoning country's best hope for an independent future, a future not found in the chicanery of politics or the church but rather in Mr. Norton's truer, small-r republican faith. "Eh! those horrible saints," Adèle says about her experience in a Halifax convent, "those teeth, those bones, those locks of hair in the cabinet. … I thought I was in some charnel-house. I could hardly breathe." Further asserting "disgust" at "what she call[s] the superstitions, the mummeries and idolatry of the Catholic church,"[62] she veers from the tradition of her parents to that of the evangelical preacher Norton, who, uncluttered, has the clarity of mind to predict what becomes the central event of the novel: the Great Miramichi Fire of 1825.[63] And though his cold evangelical logic is borne of a good deal of opportunism—the desire to cultivate a fear that will whip the rude settlers into compliance and subservience before the Lord—when the great calamity happens, his logic is seen to be irrefutable.[64] His non-institutional (in today's parlance, *transactional*) faith is therefore understood to be the better moral system for a new country coming into being.

So understood as improvement, Mary Savage's objective comes into plain view: what makes the Free Will gospel triumphal for Norton—namely, a radical independence of local congregations that enjoy complete freedom from denominationalism (an action labelled as "dissenting" ministry[65] in the novel)—also works as the most progressive form of political constitution, a view that becomes the central argument of the novel. Moreover, the providential inevitability of that independence complements the inevitability of the founders' belief in the manifest destiny of America to inhabit the continent. Such an alignment of religious and political views challenge distant forms of colonial and religious governance that threaten what is assumed to be the natural republicanism of the people. The novel is rhetorically powerful in its arguments for greater austerities in personal and community polity. Governance in any other form is thought to be harmful to church and state, for, as Mr. Norton declares, "it is better to trust in the Lord than to put confidence in princes."[66]

What we see in general terms in *Adèle Dubois* is the application of this Congregationalist thought to political theory. What we see more specifically is both the *fear* of a rogue Canadian state—that is, a non-republican parliamentary system tied constitutionally to a distant power—and the *dream* of a completely independent Canada freed of its tribal and archaic reliance on denominationalism and empire. In that dream is the American hope for pure democracy, the hope that New Brunswick and the Canadas might come to embrace the freedom of individuals governing themselves completely under Christ. This pure democracy of the individual to find Christ lies at the heart of Congregational and other evangelical traditions, and was central to the belief system of Mary Savage and her husband. In a critique of a sermon by Rev. Augustus Woodbury, William T.

Savage wrote the following in defence of pure freedom, espousing essentially the theology of Preacher Norton:

> No intelligent man, surely, can object to free discussion — to the *freest* discussion, indeed. For, must not each one adopt his own principles — establish his own faith — form his own creed, or else resign himself to mental imbecility and spiritual destitution? A belief merely hereditary and traditional cannot meet the wants of these times, or of any individual living in them.[67]

As we know from American constitutional history, the hope for Christian democracy puts a check on exercising power without the consent of the people (at least theoretically) and has given rise to a structural xenophobia of those forces outside its borders that don't share that view. The fact that this political narrative was even at issue in the novel reveals how a New Brunswick on the eve of Confederation was viewed from the Maine side of the border. The demarcation lines of the northeastern wilderness may have been settled by the Webster-Ashburton Treaty of 1842, but ideological ownership of the borderland was very much still contested — and trade, of course, still free, the Reciprocity Treaty in place, but weakening, when the novel came out in 1865. The novel is therefore as topical today as it was 160 years ago in its display of the same Christian-democratic values and cross-border anxieties around America-First trade and influence. We may live in a more restricted post-911 era, but the borderland narratives we hear daily are rife with identical persuasions and anxieties.

In the end (spoiler alert!), the formerly disgraced Edward Somers dies a hero in the fire and is redeemed; Micah Mummychog marries a local girl, reveals his true identity, and accepts a Baptist new birth; and Adèle and John Lansdowne, the American nephew, are married in Europe, returning to P- to start their now-Protestant life together. The novel closes twenty years beyond that in the presence of a new generation that enjoys the riches borne of the proper faith. A next-generation Adèle is introduced who possesses the same beauty and confidence as her mother, and Mr. Norton, the preacher, receives the blessing of living long enough to see his good works rewarded. Importantly, the corruptions of moral laxity that weakened an earlier Miramichi are now extinguished. "No habits of excess" remain, no "ungoverned passion, avarice, political craft, or disappointed ambition."[68]

The Great Miramichi Fire is therefore a cleansing event, a precursor in kind to the Halifax explosion in Hugh MacLennan's *Barometer Rising* (1941), the calamitous event that MacLennan re-imagined as creating the conditions for Canada's post-adolescence. If MacLennan's explosion moved Canada to an independent sense of itself within a larger commonwealth of nations, the Miramichi Fire, in Mary Savage's telling, was likewise liberating for a confederation of northern territories approaching formal association, an association whose ties and allegiances were not yet clearly determined in 1865.

As Canadians, we are familiar with the dominant Conservative and Loyalist sides of the border story—familiar with the boogeymen of American expansionism and Fenian raids—but there was, of course, another side, which *Adèle Dubois* presents. That side saw political and social opportunity in the loosely unified northern territories, particularly at a time when distant colonial leaders were increasingly in favour of cutting ties with the expensive, demanding, and largely defenceless colonies. The door seemed open for a much more populous and assertive America to lay claim. But, as evident in the pages of *Adèle Dubois*, America also saw an enervating moral disorder in the embryonic country that made it an unreliable partner in trade and other continental affairs. *Adèle Dubois* is therefore most profitably read in the context of the novelist's real time of the middle years of the 1860s instead of the novel's fictional time of 1825. After the American Civil War (1861-65), the restoration of the Union was foremost in the minds of those who believed in manifest destiny, the doctrine that the US was destined to expand across the whole North American continent—and not just by political decree but by "Divine Providence," wrote John Quincy Adams in 1811.[69] Territory north of the border was part of that grand vision, easy real estate that would make up for what the North had lost to the American South in the Civil War.

Adèle Dubois's appearance (as *Miramichi*) at the end of the Civil War and two years before Canadian Confederation hardly seems accidental in that context. "[S]ix thousand square miles of primeval forest" are transformed by the Great Fire, says the narrating voice.[70] The region's dark, iniquitous pre-history wiped out, New Brunswick (the *Canadian* province or *American* state?) is ready to be born. The ever-perceptive Mr. Norton sees this clearly a few years later, noting that the

> Miramichi and its picturesque precincts are now more alive than ever, with a hardy and active population. New villages are springing up... and business ... is greatly increasing. There is also a marvellous change in the moral aspect of the country. It is ascribed in a great degree to the deep impression made upon the minds of the people by the conflagration.

"That great fire," he concludes, "was a judgement upon the community for its exceeding wickedness." In effect, it "sobered them," reversing the fortunes of an "uncultivated and undisciplined population."[71] His meaning is clear if the novel is considered in its own time and circumstance: he means — or at least hopes — that New Brunswickers may finally take their place as North Americans rather than as hyphenated Europeans. A rapacious America needed that to be so — and, in the bargain, needed a partner of moral probity that was close to its own.

Conclusion

Part of Loring's intent in initiating the Railway Library series was to provide American, mostly Boston, travellers with a sense of the North American expanse. A preview of *Adèle Dubois* in *Literary Notices* captured that intention, billing the novel as an "interesting story" about "a [remote New Brunswick] region which, we cannot say the foot of man never trod, but the pen of the novelist has rarely if ever described."[72] In penning the novel, however, Mary Savage had no such intent, and she certainly, like Jules Verne, was no mere travel writer. Rather, as an educated American with strong ideological interests who had lived for a time on the edge of a country about to be born, she was using imaginative work to seed her own ideas of empire in Canadian soil—and, by extension, using a New Brunswick milieu to write a version of Canada into existence. There can be no doubt that she was doing so knowingly, for her novel betrays no desire to represent the different sides of the Confederation discussion that were raging in the Maritimes and Canadas at the time.

What she would have known politically about an emergent Canada in the 1850s and '60s were these basic facts: that A.R. Wetmore, Albert J. Smith, and many of their pre-1866 peers in New Brunswick were vehemently anti-Confederation; that the era of Reciprocity was still in place[73] and thus still called for the north-south railway link that had been the dream of Maine's Joseph Alfred Poor; and that American Secretary of State William Seward had renewed interest in the manifest destiny of the US to both control and occupy the continent. She would also have been aware of the whispered but well-known annexation sentiment issuing from the Reform Club in Saint John and the editorial pages of the Saint John *Morning News*. That paper's editor, George Fenety, was vocal in his opposition to "toadyism to British forms and systems, however oppressive and however ridiculous." Urging his New Brunswick readers to face geographic and economic facts, he declared that only "an imaginary line" separates the people of Maine and New Brunswick—and, more directly, that "we have sprung from the same stock, we speak the same language, profess the same literature, and [are] not lacking the enterprise of our neighbours." The only difference, he declared, is that New Brunswickers' talents have been "thwarted in the narrow confines of provincial life."[74] For Mary Savage, each of those factors would have pointed to the receptivity of New Brunswick to continental union, and ultimately to the "more perfect union"[75] that the preamble to the American constitution enshrines as the basis of the ecclesiastical republicanism that she embodied and invoked in her writing.[76]

The novel, then, is a valuable early record of the extent to which New Brunswick was crossed by a multitude of divergent national and ideological influences, including American, British, and French, as well as Protestant, Anglican, and Catholic thought systems. It also provides insight into overland transportation and trade corridors that were at the heart of our Confederation debate. It shows how the informal and black-market economies of the northeast prospered following the Portland Rum Riot of 1855, particularly from the ports of Chatham and Eastport. It suggests, as Béatrice Craig does in her book on the Madawaska/Maine border,[77] that mobility and sophistication were not only a privilege of urban Yankees and Loyalists, but known to rural folk as well. It offers important insight into the evangelical conservatism that infused imaginative culture in New Brunswick—and how that conservatism informed the political ethos that Hugh Thorburn and P.J. Fitzpatrick identified (and lamented) in our statecraft.[78] And, still politically, it shows how geographically and socially remote most areas of New Brunswick were (and perhaps continue to be) from the legislative and commercial centres of Fredericton and Saint John.[79]

Finally, in its imaginative constructions of the preternatural and multi-ethnic characteristics of the northeastern wilderness and its people, it presents New Brunswick quite differently from the genteel and moderate Loyalist bastion that Fredericton's Confederation Poets would celebrate in the 1880s and '90s. More realistically, but from an American perspective, it presents the province as a riotous and unformed land in need of the order and moral disciplines of ecclesiastical republicanism. As such, the book quite deliberately put New Brunswick on the American radar. Considered from the New Brunswick side of the border, it is remarkably prescient in announcing the fall of one empire and the rise of another, while also illustrating how provincial aspirations struggle to find ground under the weight of old allegiances and new allies. The novel, out of print for over 160 years, provides rare insight into a pre-Confederation New Brunswick viewed, courted, and curated from a distinctly American perspective that today we recognize, understand, and (rightly or wrongly) fear.

Acknowledgements

As a way into thanking supporters, I wish to comment briefly on a question posed by one of the readers of this introduction. The question was whether *Adèle Dubois*, a good but perhaps not exceptional novel about early New Brunswick, warrants the kind of comprehensive critical attention evident here. I have reflected on this question considerably, realizing that it may well be a question that other readers bring to this reprint. We are accustomed to asking such questions in New Brunswick because we have been trained for decades to believe that real worth, whether in art or enterprise, lies elsewhere. Others have insisted that that is so.

But it is not simply that we lack belief in the worth of what has been produced in or about New Brunswick as much as the fact that the lack of belief has become a first impulse that belies our better instincts. One of the ways to check that impulse—and, ultimately, to reverse its negative effects—is to undertake projects such as this reprint, which opens avenues to self-examination, contextual understanding, and other discoveries about the values and beliefs from which our multivalent society emerged. It hardly matters, then, if the objects of our inquiries meet some arbitrarily imposed standard of worth; what matters is that they trigger examination. What matters is that we actively seek opportunities to use history, art, and social enterprise as occasions for more general provincial study. We must therefore cultivate new habits of engagement, bringing critical tools and comprehensive analyses to bear on the political and social dimensions of our history and culture, regardless of how those have been judged by others. And we must be assertive in doing so, unafraid to face our past and unapologetic for the depth of our analyses. In a province with so little critical inquiry—we still, for example, do not have a comprehensive post-1867 scholarly history of New Brunswick—advancing on the consideration of worth should be of remote concern. More important are the engagements that open windows to the rich and complex parts of our past. That was exactly the advice that Nova Scotia's great cultural visionary Joseph Howe offered when he said that "a wise nation preserves its records, gathers up its muniments, decorates the tombs of its illustrious dead, repairs its great public structures and fosters national pride and love of country by perpetual references to the … past."[80] This critical reprint is one model of how such engagement can be done — one model of how a forgotten novel from history can be used as a point of entry into the examination of New Brunswick in the early and middle decades of the nineteenth century. Many more engagements are needed in many different forms and disciplines. All of which is to say that my first thanks must be to Chapel Street Editions, whose principals share this understanding and commitment to New Brunswick. Similar thanks also go to the four readers of this manuscript (ER, DV, JT, JM), whose provincial knowledge and decades of leadership, as well as frank and generous criticisms, strengthened it considerably.

In addition to the many librarians and archivists from UNB, Dalhousie, and Mount Allison who assisted with this reprint project over the years, I am also grateful to two outstanding research assistants. The first, Melissa Scanlan, was an undergraduate student of mine who helped crack the case of Mrs. William T. Savage's true identity. The second, Katherine MacDonald, also did stellar work as a research assistant during the final stages of her doctoral study. I am especially grateful to SSHRC for research funding that supported the work of these two talented research assistants.

This reprint is dedicated to Julianna Elizabeth Tremblay, a young artist and reader every bit as gifted as Mary Bradbury Savage.

Tony Tremblay
Fall 2025
Fredericton, NB

ENDNOTES TO AFTERWORD

1   Rev. Henry E. Parker, "An Address," 6; William T. Savage, "Appendix"
    to Rev. Parker's "An Address," 11. Jeremiah Bradbury was born in Saco,
    Maine, on 22 October 1779. He studied law and was admitted to the
    York County bar in 1805. In 1813 he was appointed collector of customs
    for the district of York, then, in 1820, clerk of the judicial courts of
    York County at Alfred, Maine. See William Berry Lapham, *Bradbury
    Memorial*, 112-14. The Bradbury family became well known in central
    Maine in the 1850s and '60s because of the political career of Bion
    Bradbury, Mary's oldest brother. In 1863 he was the nominee of the
    Democratic Party for governor. See Usher Parsons, *A Centennial History
    of Alfred*, 33.

2   William T. Savage, "Appendix," 11.

3   *The Maine Historical and Genealogical Recorder*, 207.

4   Ibid., 11. William Thomas Savage was born on 14 November 1812 in
    Bangor, Maine. He was the son of Alexander and Priscilla (Shaw) Savage.
    He graduated from Bowdoin College in 1833 then studied theology at
    Bangor Seminary, graduating 1837. In February 1840 he became
    pastor of the Congregational Church in Amherst, New Hampshire.
    He was dismissed in April 1843, and moved to Houlton, Maine, where,
    in addition to pastoral duties, he was a member of the State Board of
    Education for Aroostook County and superintendent of the public
    schools. He died in Quincy, Illinois, on 10 October 1888. See Lawrence
    Park, *Major Thomas Savage of Boston and His Descendants*, 43; and the
    Congregational Year Book, 1889, 36.

5   For historical detail on this "disputed territory," including the Maine/
    New Brunswick border area between Houlton and Woodstock, see the
    eyewitness accounts of Lieutenant Colonel William T. Baird in *Seventy
    Years of New Brunswick Life*, 85-96; 134-45. See also Craig, 76-78.

6   Baird, 138, 137, 141; Smith, 119. For more on the porous Maine/
    New Brunswick border, see Jacques Poitras, *Imaginary Line: Life on an
    Unfinished Border*. Poitras recounts centuries of population movements
    across the border, the major ones seeing an influx of Americans into New
    Brunswick during the 1860s (American Civil War) and 1970s (Vietnam
    War), and an exodus of New Brunswickers to Maine and "the Boston
    states" to feed the rapidly growing industrial expansion at the turn of the

twentieth century. Today, the movement west into Maine continues, with many New Brunswick nurses working on the other side of the border. For more on the history of New Brunswickers in Maine, see Hugh Thorburn, *Politics in New Brunswick*, 16-17, 24; and Betsy Beattie, "The 'Boston States,'" 252-263.

7 Pawling, *Wabanaki Homeland*. Mattawamkeag Point is located in eastern Maine where the Penobscot and Mattawamkeag rivers meet. For the Wabanaki and the settlers who followed their well-worn pathways, the Point was one of the key entrances into the Maine/New Brunswick borderland, the Mattawamkeag River a connector route to the province. By the early 1870s, the European and North American Railway (a cooperative British/US railway consortium) had completed a line from Bangor to Mattawamkeag to Vanceboro, which then went on to Saint John, New Brunswick.

8 Hallock, 690, 694.

9 *Adèle Dubois*, 38.

10 Ibid., 40.

11 Savage, "The Story of Melrose," 5.

12 Houston and Smyth, 198.

13 MacKay, 157, 154.

14 Spray, 56. See also Evans, 2-3.

15 Irwin. See also Rev. Edward Savage, 7.

16 See Evans (4, 9) for information about son William Savage's "location ticket" to New Brunswick.

17 Evans, 4; Rev. Edward Savage, 21.

18 Park, 21-22; 32-33.

19 Savage, "The Story of Melrose," 8, 14.

20 Acheson, 28. See also 29-35.

21 Toner, 63, 129.

22 Acheson, 54; Rev. Edward Savage, 29.

23 Toner, 67. See also Acheson's comments on the influential papers *The Mirror* and *The Loyalist*, 36-37, 44.

24 Cooney, 73, 87. Cooney's interpretation of the fire as judgment and renewal matches that found in an earlier account by Mrs. I.S. Prowse, raising the likelihood that Mary Savage was also familiar with her *Poems* (1830), which includes "The Burning Forest, a Tale of Miramichi, New Brunswick." Prowse's *Poems* was published by Loring's London affiliate Smith, Elder and Co. Cornhill. Her "Burning Forest" tells the

story of the 1825 fire in hyperbolic language, stressing the angry nature of the fire in ways matched even more closely by Mary Savage than Robert Cooney. It might also be noted that the Irish-born Cooney would have been an appealing figure for Mary Savage. Eight years after coming to New Brunswick in 1824 he converted from Catholicism to Methodism, travelling throughout the province in 1847 as an itinerant preacher—similar, then, to her Mr. Norton. He also had a church in St. Stephen and was honoured by theological institutes in Massachusetts, raising the probability that the Savages knew him personally or by reputation. See W.G. MacFarlane, *New Brunswick Bibliography*, 22-23.

25   Qtd. in Ganong, "Note 90," 411. Ganong was referring to Beamish Murdoch's often-sensational *A Narrative of the Late Fires at Miramichi, New Brunswick* (1825). In his investigations of the fire, including Murdoch's account, Ganong comments on the centrality and authority of Robert Cooney's version of events, writing that Cooney's "is the best-known description of the fire" and widely sourced. "Note 90," 411.

26   Cogswell letter to McDougall, 16 June 1958. Cogswell would eventually publish the chapter "Literary Activity in the Maritime Provinces (1815-1880)" in the *Literary History of Canada* (1965).

27   Wright, *American Fiction*, 289.

28   To confirm that *Miramichi* was not in the library's catalogue, I consulted Dalhousie College Library's Accession Books from the years 1860-1961. See "Dalhousie College Library Accession Records."

29   Library Accession Register for Accession 33897, 11 February 1949.

30   Cogswell, "Literary Activity," 110, 111.

31   Watters would eventually reference both *Miramichi* and *Adèle Dubois* in his expanded 1972 edition of *A Checklist of Canadian Literature*, 387.

32   A few curiosities in extant editions, now digitized, are worth mentioning. The first edition of *Miramichi*, held by the New Brunswick Museum in Saint John, New Brunswick, has the stamp "Ganong Library" in the upper right hand corner of the title page (see Figure 2). The book was in the possession of William Francis Ganong, a New Brunswick naturalist of wide renown on both sides of the Canada/US border, and was donated to the museum as part of Ganong's library. Noted on the front cover of the book is the detail "Ganong bought in Toronto, Oct 1913" (Longon). The second issue of the first edition (labelled Second Edition) of *Miramichi* was acquired by the Boston Library from the Boston Literary Society in November 1866. A copy of that edition (see Figure 4) was attributed, by penned signature, to "Mrs. W.T. Savage." It cannot be known for certain if that was her signature, but it probably is not, the greater likelihood being that the signature was put there as an identifier by a librarian trying to be helpful. Another copy of the same edition (see Figure 5) was owned by Louisa May Alcott and was signed in her

name, but, again, not in her own hand. Alcott published *Moods* (1864) and *Three Proverb Stories* (1868) in the same series. The Boston Library took *Miramichi* out of circulation in 1940. Harvard University Library acquired the book on 8 September 1941. Project Gutenberg suggests that Fredericton publisher James Hogg had an editorial role in the novel just before his death in 1866, though no evidence exists to support the suggestion. Hogg was publisher of *The New Brunswick Reporter and Fredericton Advertiser* at the time. No notice of *Miramichi* or *Adèle Dubois* appears in its pages between 1864 and 1868.

33   Notice, 296. One qualification needs to be made. "Cheaper" denotes quality, not price, as the price of the second issue was raised to $1 from $0.75. Re-issues subsequent to the first edition use cheaper cardboard or paper covers.

34   That the titles differed but the text did not was not unusual at the time. Loring and other publishers put out books in multiple issues and editions, partly to recoup initial costs, partly to market books to different audiences, and sometimes to announce American editions of previously published British books. When *Adèle Dubois* was released circa 1868, Loring's concurrent titles *Pique: A Tale of the English Aristocracy* and *Faith Gartney's Girlhood* were advertised as being in their 15th and 16th editions.

35   Adelaide (Kemble) Sartoris's *A Week in a French Country-House* (1867) carried its author's name on the title page, as did *Leslie Tyrrell* (1867) by Georgiana M. Craik and *Pen Photographs of Charles Dickens's Readings* (1868) by Kate Field.

36   Notice, 296; *Literary Notices*, 453. For all his excitement about the work, Cogswell was also critical, mentioning its "flaws in plotting, characterization, and style." "Literary Activity," 111.

37   *Adèle Dubois*, 148, 2. The distance from Boiestown to Chatham is closer to 75 miles, or 120 kms.

38   Ibid., 115.

39   Cooney, 103. The portage is southeast of present-day Astle.

40   Ibid., 111–12.

41   *Adèle Dubois*, 149.

42   Ibid., 59, 58, 63.

43   Ibid., 76. Italics in original.

44   Ibid., 19–20.

45   MacNutt, 179-81, 279–80.

46   William T. Baird embraced and circulated the same views a generation later in his offhand remarks about the Houlton/Woodstock borderland,

commenting that the "intensely Irish" ethnicity of one Woodstock officer made him "a wit and a good judge of poteen, or mountain dew" (155). These impressions were also central in the work of historian A.G. Bailey. See his "Creative Moments," 53-54. For more on the perceptions of the Irish as subspecies, see L.P. Curtis, *Apes and Angels*.

47 Thorburn, 3.

48 *Adèle Dubois*, 15, 78, 148.

49 Rawlyk, *Champions of the Truth*, 5.

50 Probable shorthand for Portland, Maine, P- is used either as a fashionable trope or to extend Mary Savage's desire for anonymity or universality. Whichever the case, Portland figured prominently in mid-nineteenth-century North Atlantic and New Brunswick history. A major manufacturing and railway transportation centre, it was home to many New Brunswickers who worked in its factories and shipyards. Most importantly, it was, with Eastport, Maine, the key port of entry into what New Brunswickers called "the Boston States." Passage to Eastport and Portland was frequent and cheap from St. Andrews and Saint John, with large numbers of European immigrants choosing those US destinations after temporary stays in New Brunswick. When the Grand Trunk Railway line to Montreal was completed in 1853, Portland also became one of the primary winter ports for Canadian exports.

51 See, for example, *Adèle Dubois*, 41, 102–104. Roberts's *Forge in the Forest* (1896) also comes to mind in the description of the hunting expedition. See *Adèle Dubois*, 100, 103.

52 *Adèle Dubois*, 20.

53 Ibid., 17.

54 Ibid., 107.

55 Ibid., 119.

56 Two of the final three chapters are set in Europe, a setting that reflects both the reach of the author's reading and her actual travel experiences. In 1860, Rev. Savage travelled in Britain, France, and Italy. His letters from that travel were published in the *Boston Recorder* in 1860. In 1866, after *Adèle Dubois* was published, Rev. Savage, his wife (the author), and his sister travelled throughout Europe and the Holy Lands of Asia Minor and Egypt. Again he wrote about his experiences—monthly articles on Egypt, Mount Sinai, and Palestine in the *Boston Review* in 1867. See *Congregational Year Book, 1889*, 36.

57 Rawlyk, "J.M. Cramp," 119; Marini, 20.

58 *Adèle Dubois*, 83, 85.

59 Ibid., 83.

60   Ibid., 44, 84.

61   Saunders, 100.

62   *Adèle Dubois*, 54, 120.

63   Having already established the likelihood that Mary Savage was familiar with I.S. Prowse's "The Burning Forest, a Tale of Miramichi, New Brunswick" (1830) — see note 24 — it is also possible that she had read Arthur Slader's "The Burning City" (*Conflagrations*, 1837), which recounts the Saint John fire of 1837 that nearly destroyed the city. Slader wrote of the Saint John fire as renewal in much the same way Mary Savage does in *Adèle Dubois*: as both spiritual and social restoration ("As the fictitious Phoenix from the fire … So shall our City's walls again aspire / In fairer form before our gladden'd eyes"; "From *seeming* ill educing *real* good" [Slader, *Conflagrations*, 27, 26]).

64   *Adèle Dubois*, 134.

65   Ibid., 112.

66   Ibid., 118.

67   William T. Savage, "'Who Is Right,'" 3. It should also be noted that such belief is currently driving Christian nationalism on the American right. See "Christian Nationalists."

68   *Adèle Dubois*, 172.

69   Adams wrote: "The whole continent of North America appears to be destined by Divine Providence to be peopled by one nation, speaking one language, professing one general system of religious and political principles, and accustomed to one general tenor of social usages and customs." Qtd. in McDougall, 78. Continentalism has a long history in the US. The political ideology emerged in the 1770s and became manifest in the Continental Congress, a legislative body that wanted to unite the Thirteen Colonies and, to do so, sought delegates from the then-Nova Scotia as vigorously as it sought delegates from the American South. The northeast was thus always within the American expansionist purview.

70   *Adèle Dubois*, 138.

71   Ibid., 148.

72   *Literary Notices*, 453.

73   The end of Reciprocity was announced in 1864, but only took effect in 1866. See Margaret Conrad and James K. Hiller, *Atlantic Canada*, 120.

74   Fenety, April-August 1849, *Morning News*. Qtd. in S.F. Wise, "The Annexation Movement," 68-70.

75   The first line of the Preamble of the American Constitution reads: "We the People of the United States, in Order to form a more perfect Union,

establish Justice, insure domestic Tranquility, provide for the common defence, promote the general Welfare, and secure the Blessings of Liberty to ourselves and our Posterity, do ordain and establish this Constitution for the United States of America."

76 Mary Savage's only other extended publication was an 1842 memoir entitled *Marcia*, which recounted the young life of her sister who died at the age of fourteen. The work is a deeply personal exposé of the devotional aspects of her young sister's life and of the Bradbury family generally. Mary Bradbury's husband espoused similar views in his writing, declaring often that "the evangelical truths embodied in the Congregational church have breathed *the breath of life* into New England" and that all believers "must become increasingly enterprizing [sic] for Christ," meaning that "the minds of men, in greatest numbers possible, be enlightened, purified, and saved." See William T. Savage, *A Review of Ten Years*, 8, 16.

77 Craig, 76.

78 Thorburn, *Politics in New Brunswick*; Fitzpatrick, "New Brunswick: The Politics of Pragmatism."

79 One poignant moment near the end of the novel presents his Excellency, the New Brunswick Governor, making earnest inquiries "respecting the condition of society, business, means of education and religious worship in the Miramichi country" (*Adèle Dubois*, 117). For more on the remoteness of areas of nineteenth-century New Brunswick, see Bailey, "Creative Moments," 53.

80 Qtd. in MacMechan, 46.

BIBLIOGRAPHY

"A Native of New Brunswick." [Moses Henry Perley?] *The Lay of the Wilderness: A Poem in Five Cantos*. Saint John, NB: Henry Chubb, 1833.

Acheson, T.W. "The Irish Community in Saint John, 1815-1850." *New Ireland Remembered: Historical Essays on the Irish in New Brunswick*. Ed. P.M. Toner. Fredericton, NB: New Ireland Press, 1989. 27-54.

Bailey, A.G. "Creative Moments in the Culture of the Maritime Provinces." *Culture and Nationality: Essays by A.G. Bailey*. The Carleton Library. No. 58. Toronto: McClelland and Stewart, 1972. 44-57.

Baird, William T. *Seventy Years of New Brunswick Life. Autobiographical Sketches*. St. John, NB: Press of Geo. E. Day, 1890.

Beattie, Betsy. "The 'Boston States': Region, Gender, and Maritime Out-Migration, 1870-1930." *New England and the Maritime Provinces: Connections and Comparisons*. Ed. Stephen J. Hornsby and John G. Reid. Montreal and Kingston: McGill-Queen's University Press, 2005. 252-63.

"Christian Nationalists—Wanting to Put God into US Government." *BBC News Online* 17 December 2022. https://www.bbc.com/news/world-us-canada-63902626

Cogswell, Fred. "The Development of Writing [in New Brunswick]." *Arts in New Brunswick*. Ed. R.A. Tweedie, Fred Cogswell, and W. Stewart MacNutt. Fredericton: Brunswick Press, 1967. 19-31.

---. Letter to Robert McDougall. 16 June 1958. Fiddlehead/ Cogswell Fonds. UA RG83. Correspondence 6/58, Ms 1.3532(b). Archives and Special Collections. University of New Brunswick Libraries. Fredericton, NB.

---. "Literary Activity in the Maritime Provinces, 1815-1880." *Literary History of Canada.* Gen. Ed. Carl F. Klinck. Toronto: University of Toronto Press, 1965. 102-24.

Congregational Year Book, 1889. Vol. 11. The National Council of the Congregational Churches of the United States.

Conrad, Margaret, and James K. Hiller. *Atlantic Canada: A Concise History.* Don Mills, ON: Oxford University Press, 2006.

Cooney, Robert. *A Compendious History of the Northern Part of the Province of New Brunswick, and of the District of Gaspé, in Lower Canada.* Halifax: Joseph Howe, 1832. Rpt. Chatham, 1896. https://archive.org/details/compendioushisto00coon/ page/110/mode/2up

Craig, Béatrice. *Backwoods Consumers and Homespun Capitalists: The Rise of a Market Culture in Eastern Canada.* Toronto: University of Toronto Press, 2009.

Curtis, Lewis P. *Apes and Angels: The Irishman in Victorian Caricature.* Devon, UK: David & Charles, 1971.

"Dalhousie College Library Accession Records." UA 23. Box 60-1,2,4 [1880-1924]; UA 23. Box 43-8 [1887-1908]; UA 23. Box 68-1,2,4,5 [1951-1961]; Dalhousie College Library Catalogue, No. 303 [pre-1880]. Archives and Special Collections. Killam Memorial Library. Dalhousie University Libraries. Halifax, NS.

Evans, Linda. "Melrose: An Irish Village Transplanted in New Brunswick." Irish Canadian Cultural Association of New Brunswick. Representative Settlements, Planned and Unplanned. https://newirelandnb.ca/culture/irish-trail/early-settlement/early-settlement-no-7-melrose.

Fitzpatrick, P.J. "New Brunswick: The Politics of Pragmatism." *Canadian Provincial Politics: The Party Systems of the Ten Provinces*. Ed. Martin Robin. Scarborough, ON: Prentice-Hall Canada, 1972. 116-33.

Ganong, William Francis. "Note 90: On the Limits of the Great Fire of Miramichi of 1825." *Bulletin of the Natural History Society of New Brunswick*. No. 24. Saint John: Barnes & Co., Printers, 1906. 410-18. https://archive.org/details/bulletinofnatura2419natu/page/410/mode/2up.

Hallock, Charles. "Aroostook and the Madawaska." *Harper's New Monthly Magazine* 27 (June-November 1863): 688-98.

Houston, Cecil J., and William J. Smyth. *Irish Emigration and Canadian Settlement Patterns: Patterns, Links, and Letters*. Toronto: University of Toronto Press, 1990.

Irwin, Julie. Profile Manager of "William Savage (1791-1880)." https://www.wikitree.com/wiki/Savage-6616.

Kearney, W.D. *The Open Hand; An Indian Tale of Maine and New Brunswick*. Presque Isle, ME: W.S. Gilman, 1864. https://ia800206.us.archive.org/4/items/cihm_45563/cihm_45563.pdf

Lapham, William Berry. *The Bradbury Memorial: Records of Some of the Descendants of Thomas Bradbury*. Portland, ME: Brown Thurston & Company, 1890.

Library Accession Register [UNB], Accession 33897. 11 February 1949. Early UNB Library Records. UA RG7. Archives and Special Collections. University of New Brunswick Libraries. Fredericton, NB.

Literary Notices. Adèle Dubois (November 1868): 453.

Longon, Jennifer. Correspondence with Author. 31 January 2023. Archives and Research Library, New Brunswick Museum. Saint John, NB.

MacFarlane, W.G. *New Brunswick Bibliography. The Books and Writers of the Province.* St. John, NB: Press of the Sun Printing Company, 1895.

MacKay, Donald. *Flight From Famine: The Coming of the Irish to Canada.* Toronto: McClelland and Stewart, 1990.

MacMechan, Archibald. *Headwaters of Canadian Literature.* 1924. New Canadian Library. No. 107. Toronto: McClelland and Stewart, 1974.

MacNutt, William S. *New Brunswick, A History: 1784-1867.* Toronto: Macmillan of Canada, 1984.

The Maine Historical and Genealogical Recorder. Vol. 4. Portland, ME: S.M. Watson, 1887.

Marini, Stephen. "New England Folk Religions, 1770-1815: The Sectarian Impulse in Revolutionary Society." PhD diss. Harvard University, 1976.

McDougall, Walter A. "Expansionism, or Manifest Destiny (So Called)." *Promised Land, Crusader State: The American Encounter with the World Since 1776.* New York: Houghton-Mifflin, 1997. 76-100.

Murdoch, Beamish [presumed author]. *A Narrative of the Late Fires at Miramichi, New Brunswick; with an Appendix Containing the Statements of Many of the Sufferers and a Variety of Interesting Occurrences, Together with a Poem Entitled, "Conflagration."* Halifax: P.J. Holland, 1825.

Notice. "Adèle Dubois: A Story of the Lovely Miramichi Valley, in New Brunswick." *The Nation* (8 October 1868): 296.

Park, Lawrence. *Major Thomas Savage of Boston and His Descendants.* Boston: Press of David Clapp & Son, 1914. https://archive.org/stream/majorthomassavag00park/ majorthomassavag00park_djvu.txt.

Parker, Rev. Henry E. "An Address in the Congregational Church at Franklin, N.H., January 4th, 1872, at the Funeral Services of Mrs. Mary Langdon Savage, Wife of the Rev. Wm. T. Savage, D.D." Concord, NH: Republican Press Association, 1872. 1-10.

Parsons, Usher. *A Centennial History of Alfred, York County, Maine.* Philadelphia: Collins, Printer, 1872.

Pawling, Micah A., ed. and intro. *Wabanaki Homeland and the New State of Maine: The 1820 Journal and Plans of Survey of Joseph Treat.* Amherst: University of Massachusetts Press, 2007.

Poitras, Jacques. *Imaginary Line: Life on an Unfinished Border.* Fredericton: Goose Lane Editions, 2011.

Rawlyk, George A. *Champions of Truth: Fundamentalism, Modernism, and the Maritime Baptists.* Sackville & Montreal: Centre for Canadian Studies/Mount Allison University and McGill-Queen's University Press, 1990.

---. "J.M. Cramp and W.C. Keirstead: The Response of Two Late-Nineteenth Century Baptist Sermons to Science." *Profiles of Science and Society in the Maritimes Prior to 1914.* Ed. Paul A. Bogaard. Victoria, BC: Acadiensis Press & Centre for Canadian Studies/Mount Allison University, 1990. 119-34.

Saunders, Rev. Edward Manning. *History of the Baptists of the Maritime Provinces.* Halifax, NS: Press of John Burgoyne, 1902.

Savage, Rev. Edward. "The Story of Melrose." Privately printed; copy from Université Saint Joseph Archives, Moncton, NB. FC 2499.M44 S3 1860a. Special Collections. Ralph Pickard Bell Library, Mount Allison University. Sackville, NB.

Savage, Mrs. William T. [Mary Bradbury] *Adèle Dubois: A Story of the Lovely Miramichi Valley in New Brunswick.* Boston: Loring, c. 1868. [Published as *Miramichi* in 1865.]

---. *Marcia*. Boston: Massachusetts Sabbath School Society, 1842.

Savage, Rev. William T. *A Review of Ten Years. A Discourse, Delivered in the Congregational Church, Franklin, N.H., April 3, 1859*. Concord, NH: Stream Printing Works of McFarland & Jenks, 1859.

---. "Appendix" to Rev. Henry E. Parker's "An Address in the Congregational Church at Franklin, N.H., January 4th, 1872, at the Funeral Services of Mrs. Mary Langdon Savage." 11-15.

---. "'Who Is Right,' or, 'An Examination of the Issue Taken by the Rev. Mr. Woodbury' with the Concord Young Men's Christian Association, by 'A Looker on in Vienna.'" Concord, NH: Steam Printing Works, 1853.

Slader, Arthur. *The Conflagrations: Comprising Two Poems...* Saint John, NB: D.A. Cameron, 1837. https://digitalarchive.tpl.ca/objects/341701/the-conflagrations-comprising-two-poems-as-follows-first.

Smith, Joshua M. "Humbert's Paradox: The Global Context of Smuggling in the Bay of Fundy." *New England and the Maritime Provinces: Connections and Comparisons*. Ed. Stephen J. Hornsby and John G. Reid. Montreal and Kingston: McGill-Queen's University Press, 2005. 109-24.

Spray, William A. "The Irish in Miramichi." *New Ireland Remembered: Historical Essays on the Irish in New Brunswick*. Ed. P.M. Toner. Fredericton, NB: New Ireland Press, 1989. 55-62.

Thorburn, Hugh G. *Politics in New Brunswick*. Toronto: University of Toronto Press, 1961.

Thoreau, Henry David. *The Maine Woods*. Boston: Ticknor & Fields, 1864.

Toner, P.M. "The Foundations of the Catholic Church in English-Speaking New Brunswick." *New Ireland Remembered: Historical Essays on the Irish in New Brunswick*. Ed. P.M. Toner. Fredericton, NB: New Ireland Press, 1989. 63-70.

---. "The Irish of New Brunswick at Mid Century: The 1851 Census." *New Ireland Remembered: Historical Essays on the Irish in New Brunswick*. Ed. P.M. Toner. Fredericton, NB: New Ireland Press, 1989. 106-32.

Watters, Reginald E. *A Checklist of Canadian Literature and Background Materials, 1628-1960*. 1959. 2nd ed. Toronto: University of Toronto Press, 1972.

Wise, S.F. "The Annexation Movement and Its Effect on Canadian Opinion, 1837-67." *Canada Views the United States: Nineteenth-Century Political Attitudes*. Ed. S.F. Wise and Robert Craig Brown. Toronto: Macmillan, 1975. 44-97.

Wright, Lyle H. *American Fiction 1851-1875: A Contribution Toward a Bibliography*. San Marino, CA: The Huntington Library, 1957.

ABOUT THE EDITOR

Tony Tremblay is Professor Emeritus (retired) at St. Thomas University, where he held the Canada Research Chair in New Brunswick Studies. He has written extensively about the province's literature, his most recent book *The Fiddlehead Moment: Pioneering an Alternative Canadian Modernism in New Brunswick*.

www.ingramcontent.com/pod-product-compliance
Lightning Source LLC
Chambersburg PA
CBHW031523310726
48971CB00008B/2339